Red Fern Press

Red Fern Press books may be purchased for educational, business, or sales promotional use. For more information, please e-mail the marketing department at redfernpressquery@gmail.com.

First Edition

ISBN 978-1-967038-24-4 (Kindle)
ISBN 978-1-967038-25-1 (Paperback)
ISBN 978-1-967038-31-2 (Hardcover)

Get back up.

Acknowledgements

Thank you to Sean Pronger, R.J. Umberger, and Dan Hinote, who lent their time and expertise to *The Third Period* story. To Aaron "Porty" Portzline for his willingness to read my words, then use his musical expertise to send me songs that matched their meanings. To Jesse Boone, one of my favorite creative collaborators, you are a constant source of inspiration and support. To my kiddo, who is a continuous flow of good and light in this world. For my beta readers of both the script and the novel, you are invaluable to the process. To the Columbus community, and the individuals and businesses who are supporters of this story and its development. And to all the actors, creatives, athletes, friends, and family who believed in *The Third Period* from the start. As Sean says in the Foreword, "You only lose when you quit." Thank you for never quitting on me.

Content

Suggestions for Further Reading

Clean Break by Steph West (Red Fern Press, 2026)

Newcross by Steph West (Red Fern Press, 2024)

Videos on *The Third Period* Film

Stanley Cup Champion Dan Hinote talks *The Third Period* film, currently in development.

Author Steph West talks *The Third Period* film, currently in development.

Disclaimer

This is a work of fiction. Names, characters, businesses, places, and incidents either are the product of the author's imagination or are used fictitiously, and any resemblance to actual persons, living or dead, business establishments, events, or locales, is entirely coincidental.

Foreword

When Steph West asked me to write the foreword for *The Third Period*, I had two immediate thoughts:

1. I'm honored.

2. She must be out of people.

The Third Period isn't just a hockey story. Sure, it's steeped in the culture of the game—rink smells, bus rides, bad coffee, broken sticks, and bruised egos—but what makes this book special is that it's really about everything *around* the game. It's a story about family. About teammates. About cities that shape you, communities that rally around you, and the people who pick you up when life slashes you in the back of the knees.

It's about the team—not just the one in the locker room, but the one waiting at home, sitting in the stands, or cheering from halfway across the country.

This is a comeback story—the kind we all need. It's about second chances, redemption, and never giving up. About falling down hard and finding the guts to get back up when no one would blame you for staying down. Steph doesn't just tell the story—she opens it up and lets us feel the highs, the heartbreak, and the healing. And she does it with honesty, humility, and that sharp, dry wit that all the best hockey people seem to have.

If you've ever played a sport, had a dream, lost something you loved, or stood at a crossroads wondering what the hell comes next—this book is for you.

Because hockey, like life, is simple at its core: You only lose when you quit. As long as you keep skating, keep grinding, keep showing up—there's always a chance.

The Third Period is proof of that.

Steph, thank you for writing this book and reminding us that the best comebacks aren't always on the scoreboard. Sometimes, they're in finding your way back to yourself.

—Sean Pronger
Author of *Journeyman*
Professional Hockey Nomad
Grinder Extraordinaire
Comeback Believer

The Third Period

1

The Final Buzzer

Oh, Christ, I'm gonna die.

The headlights blinded John's eyes as they crossed into his side of the narrow two-lane highway just outside of Pittsburgh. He dropped the cell phone from his hand, and it tumbled and clanged to its final resting place between the driver and passenger seats of his little four-door Honda Civic. The slim, black glass bore the last thing he'd ever read in his fifty-one years of life: *luv u too dad.*

Teddy.

His son was celebrating in a Boston bar right now. His teammates and him were drinking it up after last week's huge win of the biggest trophy in pro sports: the Professional Hockey League Cup. John had memorialized the winning night in glossy, four-by-six photos that were now skidding across the slick tan surface of the passenger seat. They jumped ship into any crevice that would catch them. John was doing his best to avoid the bright white lights and save them all, but he was failing.

He gripped the steering wheel and tried to swerve away from the lights that were bearing down on him like a bull chasing a red cape. He was running out of time. Milliseconds. He had milliseconds to live.

"Oh, God!" The steel of the car—no, it was a truck—were almost to him now. "Please!"

He didn't want to feel it. He hoped to God he didn't feel it; that the shock kicked in before the pain. He tried to get out of the way, but he couldn't tell anymore if his foot was on the gas or the brake. It didn't matter. Death was here. The final buzzer.

Game over.

The freshly printed photos burst into the air on impact and hung there at his eyeline for a split-second. He was grateful for one last look of his son. Teddy was wearing a Boston Bears uniform and holding the Cup.

John threw his hands up in front of his face as he heard the steel rip and tear at his car. The explosion of sound in his ears was deafening.

His son.

John hoped he'd be Teddy's guardian angel and look out for him from heaven. At least that's where John thought he was going. He was certain his parents had made it to heaven and since they were standing in front of him now, welcoming him with open arms, he assumed he was there, too.

He hugged his mother, then turned to his father.

"They got hockey up here?" he asked his dad.

"Wouldn't be heaven if they didn't."

John laughed as his parents turned and disappeared into nothingness. He looked around him at the blank space and warm, white light emanating a peace he could feel deep in his bones. He looked down at his body, slightly transparent now.

Wait. I probably don't have bones anymore.

He felt a tingling where he presumed his shoulder used to be and turned to face his father.

"I grabbed ya before you could feel it."

"Thank you," John said. He grinned at his dad, who shoved his "hands" into those familiar overall pockets.

Ted Hendrix had been a farmer his whole life. John remembered with nostalgia how his father used to shove those dirty, calloused hands in his pockets and laugh, or do it and yell, or do it in protection of him.

"You been watchin' out for me?" John asked.

His dad's chest rumbled with a deep laugh. A pang of emotion struck John in the chest. God, he'd missed that sound.

"Wouldn't be much of a father if I didn't," Ted said. He tipped back on his heels and grinned at John.

John nodded. "I wanna watch out for my boy."

"I knew you would," Ted said. "That's why I waited. Let me show you how."

John nodded. *Thank God.* He was going to get to see his son one more time after all.

* * *

Carter heard shards of glass clink and fall from his hair as he shook himself awake. There were police sirens, too, somewhere in the distance. Someone was yelling. He didn't understand what they were saying.

"Ugh," he groaned. Words made no sense to him. His head pounded with a fury usually reserved for the mornings after he'd drank himself almost to death.

He'd held his shit together while Stacey battled breast cancer, but once it took her, he couldn't hold on to human decency anymore.

He tried to open his eyes, but they were stuck together. When he finally forced them open, he saw red. He tried touching his face, but his body was wrecked with pain. Lifting his arm was like pulling it through sludge. When he finally got the damn thing moving he touched his thick fingers to his eyebrows. *Sticky.* He pulled his fingers back. *Blood.* Blood on his fingers. His hands.

"What the fuck?" The crimson thickness gelling on his body forced him awake. He finally could see his cracked windshield. The hood of his Ford F-150 crumpled. "No. No, no."

Adrenaline surged through his veins forcing his heart and mind awake. It couldn't be. *Please, God, please. Don't let it be.*

He grappled with the door, finally shoving it open and falling out onto the ground.

"No, hey, stay put," some guy yelled. It sounded like he was one hundred miles away even though the man was right next to him. Carter felt rough hands trying to help him out of the truck, then laying him down on the black top. Carter's whole body seemed broken. He turned his head and saw what looked like a junk pile of steaming, smoking metal with a Honda logo.

"No," Carter whispered. A wave of agony crashed through his body. "Oh, Christ, no."

He saw another man in workout clothes reach inside the Honda.

"Please," Carter whispered.

A few seconds passed before the man pulled his hand out. "He's gone."

Carter heard someone crying and looked around for the source before he realized the howling was coming from his chest. The tears slid down his face as he glanced to his truck and saw the cans of beer lying around it. The shattered glass. The parts and pieces of metal from both of their vehicles.

"Oh God, oh Christ," he cried as he started to hyperventilate. "Please. No. Please."

Pain surged through his body as he shut his eyes to the horror of what he'd done.

"Forgive me."

2

Captain

Three years later
November

Columbus Thunder v. New York Liberty
Columbus, Ohio

Mike Olsky scratched his two-day scruff and wiped the sweat from his brow as he exhaled a deeply held breath. He'd been in rooms like this since he could remember. It had been almost forty years of listening to, and giving, speeches just like the one he was about to shove down their damn throats.

"This is bullshit," he hollered. He twisted his neck and shrugged his left shoulder—the one bearing the "C"—in annoyance. The third letter of the alphabet was sewn over his heart, exactly where it should be. This game had owned him since his father first put skates on him and glided him across the frozen pond on their family's property in rural Ohio.

Now he wanted his team to pay attention to it. To recognize its meaning. Get riled up. This group, of all the groups he'd led, needed to be pissed off to finish strong. Not all teams were like that, but these boys were the kind that needed a little spark. And if they needed to be pissed off at him for telling them they were playing like shit, fine. Either way, the anger would work in their favor.

"We're leading the league and you're fuckin' gonna let these last-place pussies shove us around? On our own goddamn ice?"

Yeah, adding that last line was good. He could see that got under their skin as they showed varying levels of annoyance from shifting in their sweat-soaked uniforms to giving him a nasty side-eye. They were bruised and tired. He knew they were drained. He didn't give a shit. No team can be number one at this level and let the losers come in and wipe the ice with their own blood in front of their own fans.

These fuckers knew that. He was going to make sure they understood the ramifications.

"And you, new fuckin' guy. Harvey. Mr. I don't want my ass sent down to the minors again. If you don't get Jonahs off my ass that's exactly where you're headed. Do your job."

Yeah, that worked, too. Harvey was pissed. So was everyone else. It didn't matter if they were twenty or forty, black or white, Canadian, American, or Russian. Getting called out that you're not doing your job, on a prideful team like this one, was a stake in the gut.

Olsky glanced at the door as a sudden rush of cold air filled the steamy locker room along with the team doctor. Traveling on the bitter breeze were the cantankerous notes of a Columbus fan base incensed at their team.

"Fuck!" Olsky shouted. He kicked over a bucket of pucks with his wet skate. Yeah, his team was prideful, but Olsky's ego bordered on arrogant. He'd been born with a competitive streak a mile wide, and he'd made it his job to be the best at everything to do with hockey. Always. Anything less than that from himself or his team drove him to depths of rage he didn't even know he had. Losing was insufferable. There was no such thing in his DNA.

Olsky watched the team doctor whisper something to the Coach. Probably about one of the healthy scratches. Maybe Maize. He'd been in earlier to workout, before the team got there. Exiled like most of the healthy scratches until he was back in the show. Didn't matter.

"Get your fuckin' shit together right now and get this win tonight, boys," Olsky ordered. "Get it fucking done!"

He roared that last line. Like a lion. Pulled it from deep inside the place where caveman instinct was King over carefully constructed communication. There was a time and place for both. Right now, they needed the King.

"Nice." Tuck was the first off his ass and led the team out as he slapped Olsky's uniform with his stick and shot him a wide grin. Olsky gave him the nod. His best friend was loyal beyond words and knew what he was trying to do. He appreciated the support.

But more than that, Olsky appreciated the eruptions of "hell yeah" and "let's go" that followed his rant as the boys poured out of the locker room into the hallway. The shouts meant they were on board. Bought in. Ready to kick ass. That's the mindset he needed them in. Fire and fury. It was the only way to compete at this level.

He slapped their shoulders as they walked past him. This was their year. They all knew it.

Olsky put his helmet on and grabbed his stick on the way to the hallway. He inhaled the energizing burst of icy air into his lungs. It was as familiar to him as the touch of his wife's hand. He loved them both.

"Mike Olsky! Mike Olsky!"

The tiny voice cut through his thoughts. He turned to see a little girl, bald, wearing pink high tops and an oversized Columbus Thunder sweater running toward him down the frosty, white hallway. Her smile was bright even though her body was pale and thin.

"Honey!" Behind her appeared a tall, thick man with a competition-ready beard. He came from the private event room and chased her down. "Casey, stop!"

Olsky grinned and waved him to slow down as the girl approached. The man was right on her heels carrying a small ball cap.

"Sorry," the man said. "We're, uh, new to town. Children's Hospital. In the event space. Name's Kirby. Kirby Clark."

"Mike. Olsky." He removed his glove and shook Kirby's hand. "Totally fine. Wife and I have three, two daughters, so, I get it." Olsky peered behind Kirby but saw no one else coming.

Kirby followed his gaze. "No wife. She, uh." Kirby scratched his beard and dropped his hand. "Well, divorce. A while ago. Just me and Casey. Right, kiddo? We do okay, huh?"

Casey nodded with a big smile at her father as he lightly touched her back, then put the hat he was carrying on her head. He glanced at Olsky.

"Too cold without it."

"Ah," Olsky said as she turned her large blue eyes back to him.

"Hockey is our thing, you know?" Kirby said. "Time away. To just…have…hope. Fun."

Olsky nodded. He understood what the game could mean to fans. Especially ones like this. He quickly bent down, laying his stick on the cold cement floor, followed by his gloves, and taking the team flyer from the girl's hand. He eyed her hat.

"You like bears?" he asked.

The girl nodded with a big smile.

"Me, too." He glanced at Kirby. "Got a pen?"

"Oh," Kirby uttered. He patted himself down and stopped on his jacket pocket, surprised. "Wow. I do."

Olsky took the pen then turned over the flyer to the blank back and balanced it against the thigh pads under his uniform. He quickly started to sketch on the program as Kirby and Casey watched.

"So, the Thunder. How come AC/DC's Thunderstruck hasn't played yet? Thought it'd be the theme song."

Olsky kept drawing as he glanced down the hall and saw the assistant coach nodding him down. He grimaced. Not just because the assistant looked irritated, but because his knees were already screaming at him. He used to be able to stay in a bent position like this for an hour. Now, it was minutes.

10

"Nah. Only way Thunderstruck plays in this arena is when I'm sure we're bringing home the hardware."

"Ah, well, keeps going the way it's going, it seems like the fans will definitely hear it this year."

Olsky hoped they would. But superstition ran rampant in this league. Speaking such a thing only brought trouble.

"One game at a time," Olsky corrected.

Olsky looked at the girl and handed her the flyer. Her face was priceless and worth the ass-chewing he was about to get from the coach as the assistant walked up to them.

"It'll be a shame when you retire at the end of the season, though. Change like that is tough. But you're probably ready for the golf course."

Kirby said it nonchalantly. Like it was common knowledge. Like it was just the next thing to do. Olsky shrugged his left shoulder and twisted his neck as he grabbed his stick, his gloves, and gingerly stood up, pushing himself off the floor with his fingers to make it easy on his knees.

It seemed like everyone in the damn world knew he was retiring.

Everyone but him. He slid his gloves on.

"No hockey player's ever ready for the golf course." Olsky tried unsuccessfully to hide the irritation in his voice.

"Oh, of course, I just meant—"

"Enjoy the game."

Olsky smiled and tousled the girl's hat with a wink as the assistant coach smirked at him and made sure his ass made it to the ice this time. He grinned as he walked away and heard Kirby ask his daughter for the flyer, followed by a "Wow."

It was only a drawing of a bear. But it was a damn good one. A hidden talent. Even with all the media coverage over the years, that was a story they'd never done.

It always surprised people when he could show he was more than hockey. Not that he ever wanted to be more than the game. His plan was to stay in it forever, in one form or another. Just like he'd trained for. Just like his father had helped him train for.

Mike would never betray the game. Never leave it in the hands of anyone who loved it less than he did. And he couldn't think of anything that was going to change that simple fact.

Not now. Not ever.

* * *

Tuck skated to the bench in time to hear Mike get his ass chewed out for hanging back. He grinned. Their captain gave a real fuck about people and always had.

Mike understood the game and its fans in ways that were almost supernatural. That was his blessing and curse. Hockey flowed in Mike's veins like a natural spring. When someone talked about bleeding the game, Tuck always knew they were talking about guys like Mike. And with guys like that, what happens when the game ends?

12

"Alright, close it the fuck out!" Coach Jackman's voice sliced through Tuck's thoughts as they all nodded. Coach was a fucking livewire. The man was in his sixties and grizzled to the bone. He was famous for his hot and cold personality that could kill you with kindness or rip your fucking heart out in one look.

It was hilarious to Tuck that the digital age had now made Coach's mustache more famous than the man himself. The bushy lip hood had its own fan-run Instagram account—@CoachStacheman—that was as off and on as Coach was. Mike's daughter, Ana, had told them about it. Her and her high school hockey team constantly reposted the AI-generated images.

"Something fuckin' funny?"

Tuck realized he was grinning at the "Stache," and had to recover quickly.

"Just thinkin' about laying Jonahs the fuck out, Coach."

"Good," the Stache said. "Then get the fuck out there and do it."

A quick smirk passed between him and Mike as they skated onto the ice.

"Stache?" Olsky asked.

"Of course."

"That fuckin' thing gets bigger every day, I swear to God."

They laughed as Tuck glanced at the scoreboard. *Fuck.* Tied at ones in the third. They should have won by now and had these New York assholes back on their heels. He gave a side-glance to Mike. He couldn't let his best friend down. Not now. Not when they were number one. And not after last year's sickening game seven loss. It had been the second time in Mike's career he'd come within seconds of finally winning the top prize in pro sports.

Tuck had let him down then with his hesitation and worrying about a penalty. Tuck should have jumped in and asked questions later. It was a bad look and one that had never left him.

"I'll get on Jonahs' ass."

"Fuck that guy. Dirty." Mike waved it off as they glided toward their net.

"Briggs, too." Tuck smirked as the restless crowd let the team know how vexed they were. "They're pissed."

"I would be, too," Mike said.

Tuck barely noticed the signs with his name and number anymore. He was probably jaded.

Fan support was a double-edged sword. He'd been stabbed with it a few times in his career. As a young man in the league, he would have bled on the ice for his fans, like Mike. And Tuck genuinely hadn't understood when the older guys in the room laughed at his blind devotion.

Two weeks after the wiry veterans fileted him for his naivety, he got booed off the ice by the same people who loved him only a day earlier after his game-winner clanged off the post. What followed was his first negative ink in the paper and a tap back to the minors.

Then he understood.

"Eye on Briggs. Slip'ry fucker," Mike said to their French-Canadian goalie, who was appropriately nicknamed "Frenchie." The All-Star met them at the top of his box.

Jean-Luc Paquet was his real name. Hell, Tuck couldn't think of anyone in the league who was called by the name listed on their birth certificate. Even the fucking fans got their names shortened. He looked to the upper deck. Yep, there was Bones. Real name: Kip Bonuras. Tuck's own name was Garrett Byron Tucker. But once he'd been christened in pee-wees with only the four letters, it stuck, and he never looked back.

Whatever you decided to call Frenchie, the mother fucker was a stoic force to be reckoned with.

"Fuck him. Cocksucker won't score on me again." Frenchie banged either side of the net with his stick, dropped his face shield, and got in position.

Mike gave him the nod and skated to the face-off circle. Tuck followed, glancing at the crowd who was antsy. There was Mike's family sitting ice level behind the team.

"Head in the game, son," Pops yelled.

Mike's dad, "Pops," never missed a home game.

Mike was a franchise player in his hometown. A rare feat. Mike and Tuck had become fast friends when they were traded to Columbus at the same time. They were inseparable. Magic on the ice. Once that happened, Tuck's passport had been stamped, too.

Mike's family had quickly become Tuck's, who had no siblings, and whose parents lived in Vancouver. Mike's wife, Bella, sitting next to Pops, was like an older sister to Tuck. She was a stunning woman with her long, golden hair and bright, blue eyes. People said Mike married her for her looks.

They were wrong about that.

"You got this, baby." Bella clapped enthusiastically.

Lots of guys teased Tuck that he had a thing for Bella. Jessie's girl syndrome and what-not.

They were wrong about that, too.

"Private fucking cheering section," Tuck quipped.

"Jealousy looks like shit on you, man."

They laughed as Mike leaned in for the puck drop where he was quickly joined by New York's other biggest asshole aside from Jack Jonahs—Zack Briggs.

Fuckin' twenty-three-year-old prick.

"Damn man, fuckin' retire already," Briggs spat.

Mike eyed the linesman, who laughed it off. And now Tuck was now itching to get at the kid.

"Remind me who you are again?" Mike asked.

"Check your wife's phone."

The linesman stepped in. "Alright, let's move this shit along, boys. C'mon."

They both took a quick step back, then leaned back in. This time Tuck followed.

"Briggs, you and me can finish this after the drop if you want."

"Fuck you, Tuck," Briggs said as the linesman laughed.

"What I thought." Tuck smirked as he leaned back. Asshole had all the bark and none of the bite.

16

Mike laughed as the puck dropped, then he snaked it up and out as Tuck skated right up to and past Briggs.

"Someday, son."

"Suck my dick, asshole," yelled Briggs.

Yeah, Tuck liked being an agitator. He enjoyed his job. Was good at it. He caught the puck on his stick as he raced down the ice.

Tuck expertly handled the frozen black rubber before passing it to his D-partner, twenty-five-year-old Russian comrade, "Glaz," real name Boris Glazkov. Canadian phenom Simon Bouchard, nickname "Chary," twenty-four, hollered at Glaz for the puck.

Mike skated past the bench as the players chirped at him.

"Let's go, let's go," they shouted.

Tuck glanced at the scoreboard. Getting on the board right away in the third would ease the haters and shift the momentum. "Come on, Mike," he said under his breath.

Chary passed to Mike for a one-on-one with Briggs.

Tuck glanced over in that single millisecond and saw Jonahs eyeing Olsky.

"Oh shit."

Tuck could see the moment happening like it was in slow motion. He knew he was too far away to stop the trainwreck about to fuck up his friend's life as Mike took his shot from the top of the circle.

"Mike!"

The captain didn't even have time to turn before Jonahs came in with a dirty hip check, low to the knee. Mike flipped up and over onto the ice as the puck slid in for a goal.

Tuck's gut twisted with rage as Thunder fans jumped up and the Columbus goal cannon sounded. Half of them were excited for the goal, the other half were indignant about the dirty check.

Tuck raced to Jonahs and laid into him, right in front of Mike's family. Lit from the inside out, Tuck grabbed Jonahs by the sweater and landed fist after fist into his helmet and face. If Tuck broke his fucking hand, so be it. He'd play broken.

He could hear the crowd bellowing with delight. Vengeance was a reason to stand up and roar. All he could think of was Maximus Aurelius. *Are you mother fuckers entertained?*

Jonahs' fist landed on Tuck's cheek then, but the fury inside Tuck was too much for this match-up. He dropped that mother fucker to the ice for Mike. His teammate.

His family.

"Beat his ass, Tuck!"

Tuck knew that was Pops. He could single that voice out anywhere. He could hear it in the old man's tenor that he was yelling at Tuck like a son defending his brother.

"Tuck, you're good!" That was Bella. Always concerned about him like he was her younger sibling getting into trouble on the playground.

In this case, she was right. Tuck had won this fight handily. It was Mike who needed him now.

Tuck stood and faced his brother as the crowd cheered.

Mike gripped his knee and tried to stand. Stumbled. Dropped. Laid still. The number one in the room would be pissed if anyone tried to help him before he was ready. A man needed to stand on his own. And it was only if he asked for help that you went and did so.

Tuck glanced at the trainer, Beau, who stayed firmly behind the bench as well. Tuck peered at Jonahs.

"Fuck you, Jonahs."

Jonahs headed to the box with a smirk.

Mike finally gave Tuck the nod. Tuck slowly skated out and helped his friend stand.

"Thanks," Mike said quietly.

"Yep."

The crowd gave an approving standing ovation for their captain as Tuck helped him off the ice.

Tuck flicked a look at Pops, who was popping buttons with his pride-filled chest as surrounding fans slapped his back for the son who "never laid on the ice a day in his life."

Tuck had heard the old man say it a million times. He wasn't sure what to think of it. He moved his stare to Bella instead. That's where he'd get what he needed.

Their eyes locked. Yep, Bella was concerned, as she should be. Tuck gave her the look. The one that said, "All is not well."

She immediately stood and he knew she was on her way.

Tuck had been in the game long enough, and knew his friend well enough, to know this was bad.

Bad in a way he wasn't sure Mike would be able to take.

3

Time on Ice

Three months later

Bella glanced at herself in the floor-length mirror and ensured everything was exactly as it should be.

"Good."

Her light blonde hair cascaded in beach waves down both sides of her shapely face with its dimples and icy blue eyes. The delicate strands landed on her generous bosom that was stretching the blue fabric of her thin, crew neck sweater. It was March and still cold in the Buckeye state, a fact she would never get used to after a life spent growing up in California.

She turned her hips away from the mirror and checked out her backside in the skin-tight blue jeans she'd picked up the day before. She flicked up her eyebrows.

"Not bad."

Mike had always been a butt man, so she did extra Pilates to keep it tight. If his hands were to be found anywhere besides gripping a stick, it would be gripping her ass.

"Sick." She gave a devilish twitch of her nose, then turned back to face herself. She admired the calf-high leather boots and her wedding ring. She glanced down at her left hand and twisted the nearly two-karat diamond with her left thumb. A soft smile touched the corners of her lips as she watched the morning sunbeams flick sparks of light from the stone around the ample master bedroom.

Mike had offered several times to upgrade her ring for her.

"Come on, let me at least get you the full two karats. Five, if you want," he had said. "I'm the captain, for Christ's sake, my wife should have a better diamond. You've earned it."

She'd laughed at him and agreed that was true, then told him that if he wanted to buy her a big diamond, he could.

"But it won't replace my ring," she had said.

The next week he had bought her an eight-karat, yellow diamond. On special occasions, she'd wear that sparkler on her right hand and people would fawn over it. Mike would swell up with pride because he'd done that for her.

But she would never love any of her jewelry more than she loved her engagement ring and wedding band. Mike had given them to her. Slid them on her finger and said, "I do." And from that moment on, she'd never taken them off.

"Perfect."

She put down her hand and glanced in the mirror with a critical eye worthy of the Queen. Bella wasn't just any wife. She was the captain's wife.

She picked at the lint on her sweater, then turned sideways and sucked in her already flat stomach. Back fat? None. Check. Thigh gap? Visible. Check. She smiled in the mirror. Teeth white? Yep. Check. She smiled bigger. Un-smiled.

"Stop it." She shook her head and pulled her phone out of her back pocket and scrolled through social media, checking. Always checking. Her name. Her husband's name. Her children's names. The Olsky name. The Thunder. Columbus. Last game. Next game. The standings. Last night's scores. Last night's stats. Tonight's games. Tomorrow's games. The PHL. Hockey. Sports. Sport's wives. WAGs. Puck bunnies. Hottest wives.

She exhaled with relief. She was still in the top five.

"Hmm," she murmured. She shoved the phone in her back pocket and took one more glance at herself in the mirror.

Everyone thought being a hockey wife was the easy life. The grass might be a different species, but the color was the same.

Their life was demanding and always shifting gears. One day it was an agonizing pressure cooker of loneliness and scrutiny and the next day it was opulent privilege marked by celebrity, money, and the finest of everything you could ever want.

The pressure to move the family mid-season if a trade happened was work. Fathers missed their children's births all the time. Money could be great one day, if your man was in the show. If he wasn't, it was macaroni and cheese with hot dogs. Status always mattered and she'd be lying if she said there wasn't pleasure in her voice at being able to say her husband was on the jet and not the bus.

Affairs ran rampant. Anxiety and depression were King and Queen. Disillusionment was the third party in the relationship if you and your other half didn't understand that hockey was a business.

Marriages were always sitting on the fine line of disintegration. Wives and girlfriends were responsible for the mental health and superstitious egos of their counterparts. And if you weren't, you had failed in doing the one thing you were supposed to do: keep them winning.

Bella lived her life keenly aware that her and Mike could easily be the couple just one day away from going up in flames.

She kept her own career. That made being Mike's wife infinitely more and less difficult. It had been hard early on in her career, when they first got married, for her to set up her gallery and make a name for herself, independent of Mike's. The digital age had helped with that and so did setting up a permanent home in Columbus once Mike became a franchise player.

Her art could go for tens of thousands of dollars now, hundreds of thousands just last month. A feat she earned all on her own.

She sighed at her mirror image, then glanced over to the framed sketch of her face hanging by their door. She passed it every morning on her way out. She, of course, had put it there strategically. Because Mike also had to look at it every morning when he left. A reminder of where they came from and who they were.

"My baby," she whispered.

Art itself could be credited with bringing her and Mike together. He'd had a day off in California

between games and had gone wandering. She had
been showing her work at a small gallery that was
friendly to UCLA students. He'd tried to hit on her,
and she had ignored him. Then he tried to play off his
hockey player status and she crinkled her nose at
him.

"I don't date hockey players."

"Wait!" he had yelled when she turned her back on
him. "Please. Here. Just sit."

There had been something in his eyes that she
couldn't resist. So, she sat on a hard stool, and waited
while he hustled around the gallery for a pen and
piece of paper. Then he had sat across from her on
another stool and sketched her face.

The resulting drawing had been damn near perfect.
She had been confused why he was playing hockey
and not in art school somewhere.

Mike hadn't been like anyone she had ever met in
her life.

She grinned at the framed sketch now. Mike was
proud of that drawing. He was proud of her and her
career as an artist. Proud of their children. He was a
prideful man. And sometimes it caused them trouble.
She'd be the first to admit that they weren't perfect.
They'd gone to counseling twice in their eighteen
years of marriage. Once, when she contemplated
divorce; the other when he contemplated cheating.

She glanced backed to the mirror and spotted the
crow's feet.

"Fuck," she whispered. She leaned in until her
nose almost touched the glass. Thirty-eight years of
life were showing their wear and tear.

When had they gotten older?

She shook her head and leaned back, did one final sweeping approval.

"Whatever," she uttered.

She turned to the door, then stopped. She turned back to the mirror and glanced at herself once more.

"Yeah, okay." She pushed a slow breath out of her lungs then headed for the door, pausing before she opened it. She could hear Ana plodding around, gathering her things. It was hard to believe that Bella had only been three years older than her daughter was now when she married Mike.

"Twenty," she whispered. Mike had been twenty-one. She was certain that most of their problems had come from the fact they married so young. They had grown up together. And sometimes, they'd taken space to grow apart and then come back together.

But always, together.

She knew, even at twenty, that Mike was her love. Forever. Always. No matter what. If they had gotten through all the shit they had and were still together, there wasn't anything that could tear them apart.

"Morning, honey," Bella said brightly as she swung open the bedroom door.

Ana crashed out of the bathroom that was situated across a carpeted area leading to the other side of the house where the kid's bedrooms were located. On one side of the space was a wall that made up the back of the bathroom and the kitchen below. On the other side, it was open railing overlooking the expansive kitchen and dining area below it.

26

This was the nerve center of the house, and everything piled in around it.

"Mom," Ana whined. She tucked her dark, curly hair behind her ear as her green eyes crinkled. "Where's my book report for art class I gave you to read?"

"Kitchen. On the island."

Ana grabbed the last of her things and headed for the staircase.

"Cool."

"It was good," Bella said. "You're an expert on the Impressionist era now."

"I don't know how you do that stuff, mom," Ana said. She gave Bella a quick kiss on the cheek. "So not my thing."

Bella chuckled. Ana was not creative like her or Mike. Ana was like Bella's father, Gus, who was a brilliant mathematician, analytical, and logical. He and Bella's mother, Lynne, were twin flames, burning bright. Married for more than forty years. Bella had hoped her parents would move to Ohio, but the winters were too hard on them. Maybe she and Mike would move to California instead.

"Ana, I've got a charity meeting this morning for the Thunder's spring fashion show fundraiser. Can you drop Johnny and Piper at school for me?"

Ana turned from her descent down the stairs.

"But Paige is walking over now. And I can't fit everything in my car. Why can't Dad do it? Or Pops?" Ana asked.

Bella raised her eyebrow at the mention of Pops.

"Unauthorized ice time this morning," Bella said as though she had just swallowed vinegar.

The old man was too hard on Mike; had taught him too many bad habits, one of which was hockey over everything else, including the pain it could cause. Today's practice time on Mike's private ice was a prime example of Pops' bad influence.

"Pops is just tryin' to help, Mom. You know how important it is to dad."

Ana never missed a thing that happened in their house, including Bella's concern about Pops' influence.

"I do know how important it is for your dad to heal properly, yes," Bella said as she took in their son, Johnny, running down the hallway. Late, as usual. She couldn't believe he was eleven and almost in middle school. "I'm the only one, apparently."

Ana sighed as she turned a dirty look toward Johnny.

"Where's Piper?" Ana asked with annoyance.

Bella smiled as she walked down the stairs past Ana giving her a tap on the shoulder.

"Thanks, honey."

"Yeah, whatever," Ana said with a sigh. "Hurry up, Johnny!"

"Stop rushing me you dictator," he yelled as he slammed the bathroom door.

"How do you even know that word?" Ana yelled back.

Their arguing got quieter as Bella turned the corner from the stairs into the kitchen. Bella ducked behind the fridge when she saw Piper sitting like a statue by the window.

"Dad, I have to go," Piper said. She barely moved her lips.

"Hang on," Mike said. He was sitting at the table, sketching their blonde-haired daughter on a plain, white piece of paper. Piper would be getting her driver's license in a year. *Unreal.* She grinned at the sweet scene before her. Moments like these were coming and going too fast these days.

"Dad!" Piper murmured from pursed lips.

Mike put the finishing touches on his drawing and turned it to her as she finally relaxed and admired his handiwork.

"You should have gone to art school," she said.

"I'm better at hockey."

She grinned, hopped up, and gave him a kiss on the cheek.

"Love you, daddy."

"Love you, too, sweetie." He looked his work over as she chowed down her breakfast of bacon and eggs.

"Son!" The booming voice jarred Bella back to reality as Pops crashed into their home and slammed the front door on the other side of the kitchen. "You're back to practice next week. Let's get that little extra time in, huh? Let's go. Piper, sweetie."

Pops gave Piper a hug as Mike shoved the drawing under the newspaper.

Bella tensed up. *Yeah, of course he did that.* Because Pops would never approve of Mike loving anything else more than hockey.

"Yeah, yeah," Mike said as he stood up gingerly, his knee brace on.

Bella plastered on her best smile and walked into the kitchen.

"Oh, hey baby," Mike said smoothly. She watched his gaze take note of her figure, so she turned and bent over the counter feigning to get something so he could see her ass. If she'd learned anything in eighteen years of marriage it was that sex was important.

Damn important.

His grin was wide as he walked over and gave her a kiss, then a little slap to her butt.

"Take care of that later," he whispered.

"I certainly hope so," she said quietly.

"Gross," Piper exclaimed as Mike pulled away with a grin and Bella greeted her father-in-law.

"Pops."

"Bella."

The coldness in each of their words carried equal weight as Ana and Johnny crashed into the kitchen.

"Bacon!" Ana yelled as she dropped her gear and piled her plate high with breakfast. "Pops. You see my name in the paper? Time on ice. Twenty-eight minutes."

Pops high-fived her and said, "I hope you're working on your—"

"She's good," Mike interrupted.

"Fine," Pops said, raising his hands in surrender fashion as the kids ate at a breakneck pace.

Bella grinned to herself. *Good job, baby.* Mike wouldn't say anything to Pops in defense of himself, but when it came to Ana, Mike rarely let Pops get a word in about Ana's performance on the ice.

"Hey, slow down," Bella said as she grabbed her coffee and took a sip. "Don't need anyone choking today."

Ana grinned at her then held up her phone to Mike.

"Dad. There's more stories about the Hendrix trade."

"I'll grab the paper," Pops said.

"On the table," Piper noted as she nodded to it.

"No wa—"

Pops grabbed it before Mike could say anything else. Bella watched her husband and father-in-law closely. Pops glanced at the sketch of Piper Mike had hidden, ignored it, then flipped the paper to Mike, showing him the headline: *Hendrix set to help Columbus in Thunder playoff race.*

Bella glanced at Piper who quietly said, "Sorry, Dad," to Mike. He gave her a wink then turned to Ana and said, "I saw it, kiddo."

"He sounds good, but maybe a head case," Ana said.

"What's a head case?" Johnny asked.

"It's…Ana, really? It's nothing, Johnny. And he's not a head case," Bella said. "Hendrix has just…he's had a lot to deal with, that's all."

Ana rolled her eyes and grabbed her gear as Pops eyed Mike. Bella watched as the elder Olsky waited for his son's eye contact, then not-so-nonchalantly dropped the paper over the drawing with a hard slap.

"Hey people," said Paige, Ana's friend. She strolled into the kitchen. Bella was grateful for the distraction.

"Hey Paige," Bella said. "Breakfast, kiddo?"

"No, she's good. Let's go." Ana grabbed her bags and art paper from the island then rushed Paige out of the house, while yelling at her siblings. "Come on Piper. Johnny. Move."

They did as they were told, grabbing their things in a hurry as Ana and Paige disappeared out the front door.

"Ana's bossy like you," Pops quipped.

Bella let out a huff. Pops was the kind of person who would say something snide with a smile so when you protested, he would say, "I was just kidding. Take a joke."

She hated that.

"If Ana was a boy you'd call her a leader."

"Okay, you two," Mike said. He glanced at Johnny as the kid rushed out the door.

"Hey, breakfast was good, right?" Mike yelled.

"Nailed it, dad," Johnny answered over his shoulder.

Johnny was gone as Piper hustled up to Mike.

"No worries, kiddo." Mike kissed her forehead, and she sighed a breath of relief as she hustled out.

"Family time's over. Let's go." Pops walked out the front door as Bella cast her stare on Mike. She tapped her fingers on the counter.

"What?" Mike asked.

Bella threw up her hands. "Really, Mike?"

"Son!" Pops yelled from the door.

She gave him the most annoyed wife look she could muster and whispered, "You are *not* supposed to be on the ice without a team trainer or doctor or someone. You know that. Why are you letting him talk you into this?"

"He's an old man. He's not gonna change," Mike said.

He walked over and grabbed her hips then gave her a light kiss. "And who said he had to talk me into anything? It's only a little bit of extra practice, okay? Team doesn't need to know. It's fine. Alright?"

She said hesitantly, "Mike, I don't—"

"I love you," he interrupted. He gave her his signature smile that no one could resist. She grinned as she shook her head at him, and he pulled her closer.

"Come on," he said. He grinned wider and pulled her even closer.

"Fine," she said quietly. "I love you, too. Please be careful."

"I will." Mike kissed her then gingerly walked out of the kitchen. Bella crinkled her forehead as she watched him go. She grabbed her bag and a coffee to go, then spied the newspaper on the table and eyed the headline.

Hendrix was an elite talent like Mike. The guy had the capability to be a franchise player and captain. Well, at least he did, until his dad died. No team had been able to reach Hendrix since then; his game lost to grief. Mike had said players were calling him "selfish" and "in it for his own reasons" as opposed to being a team-first guy, which he used to be.

There was an underlying dialogue in the PHL that if someone could just break Hendrix, like a wild stallion, they could get the old him back. It would be like hitting the jackpot. But no team had done it yet. Mike had said Columbus brass thought they could be the Hendrix-tamer.

"But that's not good for you, right?" she had asked Mike as her brow had furrowed into worry. "If they do break him, what would that mean for you?"

She hadn't said the word retirement, but worry had bloomed in her gut that day. If they brought in someone *like* Mike, then that could only mean one thing: they were preparing to replace Mike.

"Never happen," Mike had said with confidence. "Hendrix won't make it."

She sighed as she glanced at Mike's drawing of Piper, which was almost an exact replica of her face.

"Brilliant," she whispered.

She smiled at the drawing, walked over, grabbed it, and hung it on the fridge. She went back and picked up the newspaper and threw it in the trash.

She put on her sunglasses, let out a tightly held breath and plastered on her famous smile as she headed for the garage.

"It's gonna be a great day."

4

Crashed and Burned

Dani Ashton never thought the day would come when she'd be glad to *not* be heading into a bustling newsroom alive with reporters. A day when the musicality of fingers clicking keyboards was less appealing than the soothing sounds of her Spotify playlist through Bose speakers. Or a day that the yelling of her editor across a packed bull pen with "Where the fuck is your story, kid?" would be considered an H.R. issue instead of motivation.

COVID and millennials had changed all that, of course.

She leaned back in the desk chair of her home office as she waited for her post-heart attack editor to let her and her colleague into the Zoom room.

"Come on," she whispered as she double-checked that her video and audio were off. She never turned those on until she was certain who was in attendance.

"He's late, Mac." She peered at her golden retriever who lazily glanced up at her, yawned, and immediately went back to sleep. "My thoughts exactly."

A Slack channel notification popped up on her laptop with a ding: *Message from Bobbi Bromba.*

She leaned forward and clicked it, then laughed at the GIF Bobbi sent her from the classic show "The Office." He followed it up with: *Let's gooooooo!*

Dani Ashton: *You got a hot story or something?*

She grinned as she waited for his reply.

Bobbi Bromba: *Is lunch with the wife a hot story?*

Dani Ashton: *Depends on whose wife it is.*

Bobbi Bromba: *lol hilarious*

"Hello? You there?" Ed's voice cut through their hijinks as his five o'clock shadow and wire-rimmed glasses suddenly filled up the screen.

Dani clicked her audio on.

"We're here, Ed," she said.

Bobbi Bromba: *Is he trying to eat the screen??*

Dani let a chuckle slip.

"Are you laughing at me?" Ed asked annoyed.

Dani turned on her video.

"Can you see me?" she asked.

"Oh," he said. He pulled away from the camera. "There you are."

Bobbi's round, ruddy face popped on the screen alongside her narrow face with its angled jaw, brown eyes, and soft, long brown hair with gray flecks. Her and Bobbi were a pair. She was Jack Sprat in this work-marriage.

"I'm here, too, boss." Bobbi's chubby fingers saluted them both as Ed shoved a straw in his mouth and started gnawing on it like Mac on his dog bone.

"That straw helpin' at all?" Dani asked.

"Does it look like it's helpin'?" Ed barked. "Sorry. Apparently, a triple bypass post-heart attack means you have to eat nicotine gum like candy and chew on straws to keep cigarettes out o' your mouth."

Ed's voice rose in fury on that last line. Clearly, the straws, which were his newest attempt at keeping cigarettes out of his mouth, weren't helping.

She glanced at her screen when it dinged again.

Bobbi Bromba: *Also: maybe stop eating meatball subs loaded with cheese??*

Dani frowned as she examined the Zoom screen. Sure enough, there was a meatball sub wrapping sticking out of Ed's trash can.

Dani Ashton: *Can't believe you caught that.*

Bobbi Bromba: *He has to know we can see everything in his background.*

Dani Ashton: *We need to teach him how to use the virtual backgrounds.*

Bobbi Bromba: *Good luck with that.*

"Alright, the gist," Grober said as he tossed the straw in his mouth into the trash can, then grabbed another one.

"Team crashed and burned after Olsky got injured, you know that," Bobbi said. He leaned back in his office chair as his tabby cat, Piccolo, walked across his keyboard, disappearing in and out of the space-themed virtual background.

"They need fire power to make the playoffs," Dani added.

"Teddy Hendrix." Grober filled in the blanks as he tossed the new straw and grabbed another one.

"Yeah. Pure goal scorer, like Olsky," Dani said.

She grinned. Dani had been covering the Thunder and the PHL for fifteen years and there were always a handful of skilled, elite players that were an absolute pleasure to watch on the ice. But none of them had ever held a candle to Olsky.

The truth was, there had always been something special about the Midwestern lad whose dad put him in skates at the age of two and taught him the game over dinner every night. Mike Olsky had that thing. The intangible. The "it" factor. The thing scouts can't put into words but "they know it when they see it."

That was Mike Olsky.

The man didn't skate on the ice, he glided. He didn't bang pucks into the net, they went willingly. And he never started a fight; he just finished it.

Olsky had been breathing rarefied air since the day he was born. With or without Pops, hockey would have found the man. There was no doubt about that.

There wasn't anyone in the modern game like Mike Olsky.

Until Hendrix.

"Teddy's got a reputation, though," Dani noted.

Her lip twitched. Fucking terrible what happened to that kid. Dad died in that tragic car accident almost four years ago. Left the twenty-something hockey phenom with no family. Kid spiraled from fierce leader and player to near recluse and "go fuck yourself" behavior. She couldn't imagine the pain he was in.

"This is his third trade in three seasons," Dani continued. "He's won the Cup, though. Olsky hasn't. Olsky won't wanna retire without it."

"Olsky starts skatin' with the team next week," Bobbi added. He grabbed his cat and tossed it to the ground as he sneezed.

"Why don't you get rid of that damn thing since you're allergic to it?" Ed snapped.

"It's the wife's cat," Bobbi said. He sneezed, then grabbed a tissue and blew.

Dani grinned as Ed shook his head and looked back to her.

"There tension?" he asked.

"Not yet," Dani said.

"How's Olsky handlin' the pressure?"

Dani shrugged as she and Bobbi glanced at each other on their computer screens. Dani had heard rumors. Maybe some unmonitored practice time. Maybe a little extra "help." But they were, as of now, only rumors. Nothing she was ready to tell Ed about.

"Well, get me five hundred words for tomorrow and a cover for Sunday," Grober said. "And Dani?"

"Yeah?" she asked.

"I smell trouble," he said.

Dani grinned. It was like the guy could read her mind. If Ed had been an editor during the Watergate era, he would have busted Nixon's ass himself. The man had a nose for news. So, if Ed Grober said trouble was brewing, you could damn well make a Vegas bet that it was.

"Stay on it," he directed.

"You got it."

Ed and Bobbi dropped off the screen as she clicked herself out, too.

Her computer dinged again. Mac stood up and stretched at its beckoning, ready for his walk.

Bobbi Bromba: *No confirmations yet?*

Dani Ashton: *Not yet.*

Bobbi Bromba: *Think Hendrix will make it here?*

Dani glanced at Mac, wagging his tail. She turned back to the computer.

Dani Ashton: *He can't afford not to.*

She closed her computer, grabbed Mac's leash, and tousled the fur on the canine's head.

"You think Hendrix is gonna make it this time?"

The dog barked happily and twisted in a circle.

"Yeah," Dani said hesitantly. "For some reason, I think so, too."

5

Teddy Hendrix

Teddy Hendrix pulled into his designated parking spot at the Columbus Arena garage and immediately smirked. His rusted beauty, "Old Blue," stuck out like a sore thumb against the overblown sports cars of some of the other players.

He dropped the gear into neutral, pulled up the emergency brake, and shut off the engine. Teddy sat in the cab and listened quietly as the cooling engine clinked and moaned like an old man sitting down after a long day.

"Take a break," he whispered. He pulled out the keys and ran a finger across the restored dashboard. He had added the new Bluetooth technology and speaker system himself. Occasionally, he'd play Frank Sinatra through it as a nod to his grandfather.

Teddy easily remembered the senior Ted Hendrix, Old Blue's original owner. Gramps had navigated the potholes and rough trails around the family farm in Old Blue while Teddy had sat on the passenger side of the cab and bounced around wildly before car seats were a thing. They'd stop every once in a while to get out and check the animals. It always ended the same way.

"Teddy, stop chasing the damn chickens!" the elder statesman would yell. At first his grandfather would be angry at the dust up. But after a couple minutes of watching the littlest Hendrix race around like a tiny fool, he'd shove his hands in his overall pockets and a deep laugh would rumble out of his chest.

Teddy smiled now as his hand splayed across the refurbished blue leather seat. It was quickly followed by tears that threatened to spill out and down his face. He yanked his hand back like a snake bit it and sniffed the wet reminders back into his head.

It was hard to remember Gramps without remembering his father. The two were intricately intertwined into all of Teddy's childhood memories, and this truck specifically.

Teddy and his dad had been restoring it when his dad died. His father had pulled that little Honda from a junk yard and got it working, so he could drive it while they finished this truck. Teddy remembered how excited his father had been to repair "the old man's Chevy."

His grin had been a mile wide.

Teddy shook his head. He could shake it a million times. The image of that grin, of the accident scene— the tiny four-door no match for a Ford F-150—of his father's frozen face when he identified the body, were never going to leave him.

He swallowed it all down, straightened his tie, and grabbed his gear.

Another team.

An ironic huff escaped his lips. The only thing he knew to be true about this team, the same as all the others, was that his father wasn't here, and that small fact would never change.

Teddy sighed and stepped out of the truck, threw the bag over his shoulder, slammed down the lock on the driver's side, and closed the door.

As he walked to the arena, his dress shoes made a rhythmic clicking sound that echoed in the near-empty garage. It didn't matter how many times he made this walk, it always felt like the first day of school. Would he have to eat alone at the lunch table? Would anyone ask him to join up in kickball on the playground?

He stopped at the door and sighed. *Fuck 'em if they didn't.* That was how to survive.

He pulled out his cell phone and twitched his lips. He glanced down to it and entered his code, opened his photos, scrolled to the one he needed.

Luv u.

The last text message his dad had ever sent him.

"Shit."

The tears were back. Persistent little fuckers. He pulled his black aviators out of his bag and slid them on. Took a deep breath and exhaled slowly, mindful of pushing the air out with purpose. He wasn't Teddy anymore. He was Hendrix.

Game face.

He cracked an arrogant smile and opened the door.

"Welcome to the Thunder, Hendrix." It was one of the team trainers. The guy had probably been waiting at that door for who knows how long for Hendrix to arrive. For all the bullshit people said about him—and most of it was true—no one could question that Hendrix was always at the rink when he said he'd be. He was drawn to it. Like a siren luring him in.

In this case, Columbus brass told Hendrix to be there at one o'clock. He arrived fifteen minutes early, which his father would have had said was fifteen minutes late. And this poor fuckin' guy had probably been standing there since eleven.

"Let me get that for you." The trainer grabbed his bag and Hendrix winced at the swarm of people who surrounded him as he walked to the locker room. Communications people, teammates coming and going, coaches, more trainers, team doctor, a couple folks from the media. He could see in their faces they were excited but uncertain. He'd lost his game. And his anger flowed out and over like a tragic oil spill to everyone around him.

He was Columbus' head case now. His last shot. He'd been a basement bargain. Ninety percent off the clearance rack. A fire sale. Someone at the top thought they could break him. He'd be the next Olsky. Save them all. And if he wasn't the miracle they expected, he'd be on to team number four. Or, more likely, off to a golf course somewhere in no man's land. Out of sight, out of mind.

Hockey was a business. Not a grief counseling session. If you didn't understand that you were a game piece, then you were setting yourself up for fucking heartbreak.

"Thank you," Hendrix said politely as one of his teammates welcomed him in passing.

Finally, the locker room. His second home. He exhaled. He hadn't even realized he was holding his breath.

"What the fuck?"

44

Hendrix glanced to the sarcastic voice and immediately recognized Tuck. Whatever you thought a grizzly, long-haired Canadian defenseman looked like, well, that was Tuck. Guy wore an "A." Olsky's right-hand man. There were rumors about him. Hendrix gave no fucks about all that.

"Take those off, pretty boy," Tuck cracked as he finished getting dressed.

A smile tugged at the corners of Hendrix's lips. He removed his sunglasses and glanced around the room for his bag. It was next to Olsky's stall and caddy-corner from Tuck. He moved toward it as guys came and went after morning skate. Some shook his hand. Others nodded. He glanced at Tuck as he took his place.

"Let me guess," Tuck said. "Hendrix."

Hendrix let out a laugh as he relaxed a little. The best greeting a player could get was the no-bullshit one.

"Savior's here, I guess." Tuck stood up and grabbed his shit from his stall.

He liked Tuck already. "I wouldn't go that far," Hendrix said quietly. "Tuck, right?"

Tuck gave Hendrix a nod as he extended his hand.

Hendrix warmly reciprocated.

"Good to meet ya, man," Hendrix said. "Happy to be here."

"Happy for Columbus over Tampa? Or just happy to still be in the show?"

Hendrix grinned. Yeah, he'd much rather have that shit thrown right in his face than behind his back. It was a sign of respect. The ballsy thing to do.

"Good flight?" Tuck asked.

Hendrix smirked.

"Same ol', you know."

"Jesus, Chary, let's gooooo, I'm fucking starvin' you asshole."

Hendrix glanced over at the booming bass voice to see Frederic Cote. Kid was only twenty-three-years-old and already an elite player. Team was lucky to have him. What'd they call him? *Cots.*

"Oh, hey." Cots immediately noticed Hendrix and walked over and shook his hand. "Nice to meet ya, man, welcome."

"Thanks," Hendrix replied as Chary appeared from the showers and walked up. That guy was a badass, too. The two were, apparently, like twins. Brothers from different mothers was the story. They were, as Hendrix had already experienced, tough to play against.

"Yeah, man, welcome," Chary said.

Chary shook his hand.

"Yeah, thanks."

Cots groaned, "Plannin' on eatin' if Chary gets his fuckin' shit together in this lifetime."

"Fuck yoooouuu," Chary retaliated as he jumped up and down then moved to his stall and finished up.

"You in?" Cots pointed his finger at Hendrix.

"I would, but—"

"He's got shit to do, eh?" Tuck interrupted. "Go fuckin' eat, already. Tired o' hearin' you assholes."

"Alright, alright. Damn man," Cots said as he walked to his stall and got his keys and sunglasses. "Beers soon, man."

"Sure." Hendrix eyed Tuck as the two Canadians bickered back and forth on their way out.

"Do I wanna get a beer with them?" Hendrix asked.

Tuck laughed. "Not your first one. Get settled in. I'll take you. After that you'll be ready for that comedy fuckin' duo."

Tuck hollered after the two as they continued squabbling outside the locker room. "Shut the fuck up already."

Hendrix laughed as Tuck headed out.

"See ya tomorrow," Tuck said on his way out. He hollered over his shoulder, "Try not to get traded before then."

"Ha, fuckin' hilarious, thanks."

Hendrix smiled as Tuck disappeared out the locker room door and argued with Cots and Chary outside it. He glanced around the room, empty and quiet now.

His chest lost its tightness as he exhaled.

Maybe there was hope for him after all.

6

If He Wants to Win

The sweat poured down Mike's stoic face as he raced through drill after drill in his private rink. The cold building was situated just behind their house and separated from their living space by a short, stone walking path. It was his home away from home and today he was skating at an intensity he hadn't hit since his injury.

He gulped for air as he tried to ignore his body. His thighs were like two burning logs and the pain in his knee was skewing him like a kabob as he raced across the ice.

Where's Bella?

He glanced at the rink door. He'd texted her for a snack, but she hadn't come home from the charity meeting yet. If she were here, he'd stop. He'd take a break and check his knee. She'd kiss him, even though he smelled like ass, and tell him it was time to go in and take an ibuprofen.

"Tapering," she'd remind him. "Get you off those pills."

"Right, baby," he'd say and then he'd distract her with sex or a grin or art. That's how he'd distracted her this morning. And when she'd asked him about not returning some of his hockey equipment from previous seasons, he'd distracted her then, too. She knew he wasn't supposed to be practicing beyond the prying eyes of the team, and the equipment helped him do it. She'd protest, again. And he'd have to distract her, again.

"Ahh," he groaned as he skated harder.

He guzzled more air as his knee screamed at him. His body was suddenly foreign to him. Traitorous, even. The pain in his knee should be better by now. His body shouldn't ache the way it had been. He shouldn't need the extra pills. His surgeon and the team doctor had said pain pill dependence was likely, and it could cause withdrawal symptoms, but "Tapering will work, Mike," and "It'll prevent addiction."

He shook his head as sweat raced down his back at the same clip he was moving.

Time was up.

He had to go back to the team if he wanted a shot at the Cup. Plus, he sure as fuck wasn't going to let Hendrix show him up. So, whatever this pain and aching was, he'd manage it now and deal with the repercussions later.

Mike's left shoulder twitched. He could feel the weight of his father's stare without even looking.

"C'mon, let's go!" Pops yelled. The old man clapped a few times, then crossed his arms against his chest. The stance was a familiar one to Mike; Bella couldn't stand it.

She thought his father was too hard on him. Mike agreed. But where he and the love of his life disagreed was on whether it helped or hurt him.

"Fuck," Mike yelled as he finally finished the drills and skated toward the bench, away from his father's stare. He winced.

"You look ready to go back." Pops' tone was laced with pride.

Mike tapped the wall with his stick as he turned to face the man who had taught him everything about the game. Mike's wince was gone; a smile was plastered there instead. "Yeah?"

Pops nodded. "A little tired, though. How's the pain?"

"What pain?" Mike quipped.

"Good man." Pops coughed as he rubbed his chest.

"You okay?" Mike asked. *Weird.* Mike couldn't think of a time he'd ever seen his father sick.

"Chest cold. So says your mother."

They both glanced toward the rink door as it opened, and Bella strode in.

Finally.

"I'm not your concierge service, Mike."

She held up protein bars as Mike smiled. Goddamn, he loved that woman. They had been through a lot of shit. *A lot.* She was still his favorite teammate. He wasn't sure he'd ever told her that. He probably fucking should.

"You're hotter than concierge, baby."

She started to hand him the bars, then yanked them back with a teasing smile.

"Get over here." He lunged for her, grabbed the loophole of her jeans, and pulled her to him.

"You stink, baby," she joked.

He kissed her as she laughed.

"I love you," he said quietly.

"Love you, too," she whispered.

"Thank you," he said as he grabbed the bars and started mowing them down. Fuck, he was hungry. For food. For the game. For her.

He glanced over to Pops, who was ignoring them.

"Pops, you want one?" He held up a bar.

"No."

Mike glanced at Bella, who rolled her eyes. Mike hated being the referee in their heavyweight match-up. His baby versus his father. For eighteen years. *Brutal.*

He tried to open his bag one-handed for his sports drink when Bella intervened. Panic whipped through his body.

"No, wait, I—"

As she pulled out the drink, his tiny plastic bag of pain pills slipped out.

"What the?" she asked quietly. She looked at it, then Mike.

Mike swallowed hard under her questioning stare. Clear, orange medicine bottles meant a doctor prescribed them. Baggies meant something else entirely.

"Everything okay?" Pops asked. He started to move toward them. Bella quickly grabbed them and shoved them in her jeans' pocket.

"Fine," she said quickly.

Mike caught her stare. *Fuck. That's a discussion later.* What could he tell her? Wait, he could tell her he moved them from the bottle to the baggy so he could take them to the rink. Convenience. *Easy.*

Bella swung her look toward Pops.

"He doesn't have to go back this soon," she said.

"If he wants to win, he does," Pops countered.

"If *he* wants to, right?" she asked.

Mike was stuck firmly between them. He shifted uncomfortably.

"Come on, son, another half hour."

Bella's stare was on him, so he turned to meet it.

"It's temporary," he said quietly. "I'll be okay."

"But—"

"Mike! Let's go!" Pops yelled.

Mike knew she was worried. She probably had good reason to be, given where he'd gotten those pain pills; given that he was supposed to be reducing the amount he was taking. But it was short-lived; an interim solution for a few months to get him what he needed. And he had no intention of telling her anything other than they were prescribed anyway. So, it didn't matter.

He skated away from her troubled gaze and pushed harder than he knew he should. He just needed a little bit more to help him through. That was all. No big deal.

He grimaced against the pain as he thought about the Cup—and Teddy fucking Hendrix.

He emptied the air in his lungs through a concentrated stream of air as he glided skillfully across the ice.

7

The Weight of Pain

Tuck walked out into the cold Columbus arena from talking with the trainers and felt his stomach growl. He needed some food STAT as well as some time to think through how to handle the team once Mike came back.

Mike and Teddy in the same room. *Fuck.* Two alphas, both with something to prove, cut from the same cloth, battling for the Cup, and more importantly, the team. It was like that time in Toronto eight years ago when one of the "A's" made Tuck drink whiskey mixed with gin all night.

"Ugh," he grimaced. Those were two fucking spirits that should never share the same glass. Tuck had held his puke and proved his worth, but he'd never wish that combination on anyone—he felt the same way about the Mike/Teddy situation.

As he started toward the parking garage his worried frown swung into a thoughtful grin. His lunch date would be a good sounding board for all this shit.

He shifted the bag on his shoulder with a lightness in his body he wasn't used to yet. For the first time in a long time, Tuck was in a relationship that had some potential. Most of his liaisons hadn't made it past a month or two. Not being able to go public was usually the straw that broke everything apart. But this new love understood why it had to be that way. At least for now.

The two had met just after Mike's injury, at the hospital. Jaime was an N.P. in the emergency room. Tuck had gone back to say thank you for his excellent work. Two months later, the Olsky clan invited the new couple for dinner, and everyone gave the thumbs up. Bella was a fan and Tuck trusted her more than anyone in the world, except for Mike. So, he was feeling pretty good about it.

Tuck was not, however, feeling very good about Mike and Teddy.

If Hendrix was even a shadow of the player he was before his father's death, he'd be first in line for the "C" if Mike retired. Hell, even if Mike didn't retire, Hendrix—with a return to form—would be in the captain conversation, period.

That was the business and culture of hockey. Only one man could lead the room. And usually—not always—but usually, it was the guy with the game. And if it wasn't him, it was the guy with the passion.

Mike and Hendrix had both. Hendrix was younger, though. Fresh blood. Something different. And hockey brass liked shiny objects.

"Fuck!"

At the sound of the male voice, Tuck turned his head toward the practice ice where he could hear hard skating, grunting, and pucks clanging.

Who's on the ice?

He moved toward the sounds as Glaz walked past him in his famous red suit, followed by Frenchie.

"Jesus, man, with that thing." Tuck shook his head as Glaz cockily modeled his red threads and black tie.

Tuck quipped, "You look like a tampon."

"On day one," Frenchie added.

"I get more pussy than either of you," Glaz chirped. He stood like a cover model and grinned. "Meetin' Cots and Chary for food. Join?"

"Nah, I'm good." Tuck waved them off. "Your suit makes me fuckin' gag."

Frenchie laughed as Glaz flipped him off.

"I look fucking gorgeous," Glaz purred as he turned for the door, followed by Frenchie.

Tuck grinned as he headed toward the practice ice. He walked into the darkened icehouse and spied Hendrix, alone, with a pile of pucks.

"Fuck," he whispered. He folded himself into the shadows and watched as Hendrix skated with an intensity Tuck had only seen in one other player— Mike.

Most hockey players could skate well, of course. Some were better than others. Some guys tore up the ice with their shitty stops and starts, others were like CIA ghosts barely leaving a mark.

But Mike had always been on a level that looked like he was walking on water. It's like his skates didn't even touch the ice. It sounded fucking ridiculous, but it was like Mike was in tune with the ice. A part of it. When you saw him on the ice, you knew how inadequate you truly were.

That's how Tuck felt now watching Hendrix.

Even in this darkened space, Tuck could see the fluidity of the phenom's movements as he glided across the slick surface. The sound of sharpened blade against solid water was like hearing your favorite song suddenly come on the radio. Surprising, exciting, and joyful. It made you want to move.

"Shit."

Hendrix was the real deal. Tuck could see that. An uneasiness gathered in his gut as Hendrix buzzed around the pucks, grabbed one, flicked it up on his stick, and bounced it around with clear expertise.

"Wow," Tuck said quietly.

Hendrix dropped it to the ice and swung hard with a warrior's yell as the slap shot hit the back of the net and threw it backwards toward the glass. Hendrix fell to his knees.

Tuck felt that shot in his bones. Pain was the only thing, other than love, that could drive a shot with that much force. He understood it. He understood the weight of pain and how powerful it could be.

I shouldn't be here.

This wasn't hockey. This was grief. Hendrix wasn't trying to improve his shot; he was trying to erase his pain.

Tuck knew the private hell of grappling with personal demons. It wasn't something you showed anyone. Not until you were ready, anyway.

He silently slipped out the door and stepped outside the practice rink into the arena.

He waited until the door shut quietly and let out a slow breath.

Hendrix was broken, no doubt.

The question was: could he be fixed? And if he could, what would that mean for Mike?

* * *

Teddy loved practice ice when it was dark and quiet. He could lose himself in the shadows. Dip in and out of them as needed. Let the blackness spill out of his body.

He circled around the pucks and flicked one up on his stick, making it dance like a puppet on the strings of the master.

His mind wandered to the Boston bar he was in the night his dad had died. Celebrating with his teammates. His dad had just picked up the photos from the night they won the Cup. The two had been setting up his dad's next visit.

Luv u.

Luv u too dad.

Teddy hadn't even noticed the two cops who walked in a couple hours later. The tap on the shoulder. Hendrix knew from experience that the tap always meant you were going back. Back to something you didn't want. And then they told him.

"We're sorry…dad…dead…" and then Teddy had zoned out. His teammates had to help him walk to his car.

Sometimes Teddy woke up from his nightmares feeling that tap.

He shook the memory from his head, dropped the puck, and wristed it at the net, tipping it back.

"Ah!"

He skated around the pucks again, flicked another one on the tip, made it dance. His mind floated back again.

He had been wearing a suit and tie. His father's casket lowered into the ground. The most expensive one money could buy. It would never be enough for the man who worked double-shifts as a mechanic to send Teddy to hockey camps, hire elite coaches, put him in club, pay for anything Teddy needed to bring his game to life.

His father was the reason he was here. And now he was gone.

The pain seared through him as he dropped the puck and swung from the depths of his gut, breaking the stick, and ripping the puck so hard into the net it slid almost back to the glass.

Teddy dropped to his knees as a sob break through his steely exterior. As the next one rose, he heard a quiet creak and glanced to the door. Someone had been standing there but was gone now. Teddy let out one more pained howl and slowly stood.

Who had it been?

Doesn't matter. He was a head case, right? Acting as he should.

He wiped his nose with his sleeve and skated to his things as he pulled off his right glove. He grabbed his water and took a long pull then glanced to his bag where a familiar envelope, worn and frayed, peeked out from its darkened depths. Teddy yanked on it, pulled it out, and studied it for a moment.

The unopened envelope was addressed to him. The return address was the state correction facility in Pennsylvania.

Carter. Carter Jenkins. DUI. Vehicular Manslaughter. John Hendrix, a human being. Guilty as charged.

He rubbed his thumb over the worn ink and sighed.

He buried it in his bag, took one final drink, and returned to the ice.

8

The Goods

Playoff Clincher
March

Columbus Thunder v. Chicago Mantis
Columbus, Ohio

The Columbus crowd chanted loudly as the Thunder fought for two points against the Chicago Mantis. Hendrix eyed the jumbotron during the TV timeout.

That must be Bones.

Hendrix swallowed his grin as he sat forward and leaned his arms on the wall. Bare-chested mother fucker was wearing a blue wig and had the "T" of "Thunder" on his chest. His idiot friends had all the other letters on their bare chests, some double-fisted, giving the "number one" symbol to the camera.

He loved it.

As the game came back on, Teddy felt the moment of happiness drain out of him. Back to reality: they were in a wild playoff race that saw them teetering on the edge of getting to play for the ultimate trophy.

Tonight was their shot.

Focus.

Hendrix glanced to the scoreboard: They were tied at twos in the third with less than three minutes left.

His performance so far had been relatively muted. He wasn't playing like shit, but his old self hadn't made an appearance yet, either. He'd done enough to keep their playoff hopes alive; lots of assists, meaningful plays, but no goals. The fans had been supportive, for the most part. There were signs on the glass and a couple jerseys bearing his name. Of course, a few fucking trolls showed up on social media and made their presence known. *Fucking assholes.*

Hendrix kept to himself on the bench as the other players chirped around him. He hadn't found his groove in the locker room yet, either. Everyone was waiting on him to do *something*.

Tonight was the night. If they won, they were in the playoffs. He had to make his move and do what he came here to do. Now was his chance to prove himself.

Power play.

Tuck whacked Hendrix's knee with his stick.

"Alright, kid, time's up. Let's see if you've got the fuckin' goods or not."

Hendrix exhaled a sigh of relief like steam from a kettle. Tuck, it seemed, was the only one who was going to force his hand and give him a real challenge.

"Try and keep up," Hendrix said with a grin.

They hopped on the ice and Hendrix and Cots cycled in the corner before Hendrix passed to Tuck at the point.

Hendrix had read Chicago from the start. He knew they'd forget about him when he tucked behind the net. Just like he was doing now.

Quietly. Stealthily.

Tuck wasn't looking at him.

Doesn't matter.

Hendrix had watched game tape. Tuck had vision. *Ice vision. Spidey senses.*

Everyone thought that was only with Mike.

Hendrix knew better.

I'm ready.

Tapped the ice.

Come on, Tuck.

There. The puck was coming at him.

He met it for dinner. Tapped it toward the net.

Fuck!

Saved by the goalie glove-side. Kicked it out like a bad habit.

You're mine.

Magnet mode. Puck to stick.

Bang!

Red light.

Goal!

"Fuck yes!" Hendrix swiped the ice with his hand as he slid across the frozen tundra on one knee.

Boom!

Columbus goal cannon.

Teammates. *Tuck.*

"You got the goods, asshole," Tuck yelled as he banged Hendrix's helmet.

Thanks for believin'.

"Hell yeah," Hendrix said as he gave Tuck a nod.

He looked around him as he skated for the bench.

Wild crowd. Gloved hands waiting for his. He banged them as he strolled the line.

"Helluva move there," Coach Jackman yelled.

I'm not a head case.

"Thanks, Coach," Hendrix said. *Coach Stacheman.*

He laughed.

Camera on him. *Smile.*

Jumbotron. Cheers.

Relief.

"In his first Columbus goal, Teddyyyyy Heeendriiiiix!"

Helmet smacked. Shoulder punched. Glass banged.

Warmth.

Face-off circle. Puck dropped.

Final buzzer.

Game winner. Two points. In the playoffs. Deal sealed.

My team.

He filed off the ice.

"You're first star!" Howie yelled at him in the tunnel.

He grinned.

Fuck yeah.

He skated back on the ice to the roar of the crowd.

This could be home.

And if it was, he'd fight with everything he had to stay.

* * *

Mike shrugged his left shoulder and twisted his neck as the final buzzer sounded. It seemed louder in the suite above the ice.

We're in the playoffs.

Mike tugged on his tie as he glanced at the coaches and teammates surrounding him. The rag-tag group included the same guy whose ass he'd chewed only four months ago: Harvey. The kid was now a healthy scratch, as he should be.

We shouldn't be breathing the same air.

"Holy shit with that shot right there," Harvey exclaimed.

"Kid's talented," Mike said. *Yeah, that's what I should say.* "Good we got him."

Yeah, I should say that, too.

"No shit, right?" Harvey said. "Took us straight to the playoffs. Maybe the Cup. Hopefully me too if I stick around."

Mike forced a terse smile. *Doubtful.*

The room cleared as Harvey stood. "You comin'?" he asked.

"Nah, go ahead," Mike said. He took a slow sip of his water. "I'll be down in a second."

"Alright, man." Harvey slapped Mike's shoulder and it sent a shudder of annoyance through his veins.

Goddammit.

Mike sighed as he waited for the suite to empty. He should be happy they were in the playoffs. Why wasn't he?

Fuckin' Hendrix.

Mike attempted to stand, favoring his injured knee, but he didn't quite make it. He stretched it out and inhaled a deep breath as he tried again. One attempt...two attempts...finally, he was up. He limped to the glass, wincing as he went.

He studied the ice and the crowd as they herded out of the arena. The fans were happy tonight; the Thunder had delivered. The team's sweat and ire had gotten them all free chili with that third goal and punched their ticket to the playoffs.

Mike huffed a laugh.

Hendrix was supposed to be a head case. What the fuck had happened? Had management made the right call after all?

His face scrunched with worry.

Who the fuck was he kidding? Mike knew they had. The team now had a shot at the Cup and Hendrix was responsible for that. The selfish asshole had delivered.

Mike pushed air out of his lungs, pulled it back in, then out again. He knew greatness when he saw it.

Mike could go downstairs, pull up his game tape from the 2018 game versus Detroit, fast forward to the third period, and hold his game winner up against Hendrix's third period heroics tonight and they would look almost the same.

"Fuck," he hissed. He reached into his pocket, glanced around him, pulled out a plastic baggy with tiny, white pills he'd gotten from one of Maize's guys, and tossed a few back as the remnants of a game gone right dissipated under the Zamboni.

The team had won.

Without him.

Not exactly.

They had gotten into the playoffs with a younger version of him.

The future.

He glanced over to where Pops and Bella normally sat.

No one had been there tonight.

He swallowed the pills down with the rest of his water, then headed out of the suite to the locker room.

9

Camera Loves Me

Mike breezed into the locker room like he'd done a million times before, opening the door to his team with confidence. He prepared himself for the chorus of "welcomes" they'd offer. He needed it right now.

"Mike." The trainer gave him a slap to the shoulder and breezed by. Mike glanced at him with confusion. Maybe the guy was sick or something. Mike shrugged and stepped further into the room where he found Tuck and the boys in a lovefest with Hendrix.

Disappointment rifled through his system. He shrugged it off. Hendrix had earned the post-game salute.

"What a win, boys!" Mike said as he walked up to the guys. *Yeah, that's the right thing to say.* "Playoffs!"

"Holy shit!" Cots said. He hopped up and greeted Mike with a handshake, followed quickly by Chary.

"Ah, yes! Captain!"

Mike's mood rose as Tuck and the team followed suit. He glanced to Hendrix, who stood still.

"Nice game," Mike said. *Be a leader. Stay in command.* He walked halfway to Hendrix and extended his right hand. "I'm Mike."

Hendrix reluctantly met him in the middle and took his hand in a firm shake.

"Teddy Hendrix. Good to meet ya, man."

Hendrix firmed up his grip.

"Impressive shot in the third. How we get to the Cup," Mike said. He equaled Hendrix's strength.

"That's what I'm here for."

They eyed each other for a second, hands in a tight grip. The team's eyes were on them as their pissing match came to a standstill.

Challenging me in my own fucking locker room?

"Hendrix. Media's waiting," Howie interrupted. The team's communications manager gave Hendrix a nod.

"Have fun with that, kid," Mike said as he tightened up on Hendrix's hand. *Fuckin' punk.*

"Please. You thought that shot was good?" Hendrix returned the favor, then leaned into Mike. "Camera loves me."

Hendrix let go of Mike's hand and slapped him on the arm as he winked at the boys, drawing a laugh.

They like him.

Hendrix walked out then, and Mike eyed the team as they went about their business and cleared out to go celebrate.

They saw what I saw.

He balled his fists, uncertain what to do next.

"I'm out," Tuck said as he walked up to Mike. "You okay?"

Mike grinned with relief. He could always count on Tuck to have his back.

"Uh, yeah. Yeah. Next week."

"You sure?" Tuck said. His stare was piercing.

"It's been a minute. I can swing by later."

"Nah, man, I'm good." Mike slapped Tuck's shoulder. "Go. Celebrate."

Tuck hung back for a second. *He knows something's up.*

"Seriously, I'm okay," Mike said.

"It's just…the last month or so, you've been…," Tuck said with hesitation. "Are we in a pissing match I don't know about?"

"Never, no, all good," Mike said. *Be more convincing.*

"Go have a good date, huh?" Mike said quietly. "Jaime's a good one. The whole family thinks so. Celebrate the playoffs."

Tuck grinned. "You're sure?"

"Go," Mike ordered. He nodded Tuck out.

"Alright."

Tuck slapped Mike's arm then headed out. The guy's loyalty was also his downfall. He'd be like Bella. He'd question too many things. Mike had to keep him at arm's length for the moment.

Mike peered around the mostly empty room as he started to fidget. *Where's Doc?*

Relief flooded his veins as the team doctor walked in. *Say exactly what you practiced.*

"Doc. Wait up." Mike limped to him as the Doc turned around and smiled.

"Mike. Good to see ya," Doc said. He held out his hand and Mike shook it quickly then let go. "Ready for next week?"

"Uh, yeah, good. Ready."

"Good."

"Uh…listen, can I get a replacement round?"

There's the suspicious look. Say what you practiced.

"Johnny," Mike said with confidence. "He was cooking. Knocked the bottle over. All the pills…right down the disposal."

Now grin. The confidence.

Doc took a step back and looked hard at Mike. "Uh...yeah, sure, Mike. Just, don't forget. We're tapering. So, if you lose a few down the drain, it shouldn't be a big deal. Right?"

Act like it doesn't matter.

"Oh, absolutely. I'm not one hundred percent I even need these, but a little insurance never hurt, you know? In case the transition is a little tough."

Doc nodded his head slowly as Mike gave him a friendly slap on the arm.

Almost there. Keep it up.

"Uh, sure, yeah. I get it. No problem."

"Thanks, Doc."

"Sure thing."

Doc patted Mike's arm as he walked out.

Mike shrugged his left shoulder and turned to look at the near-empty room. He cracked his neck and walked out.

Easier Questions

Mike limped into his and Bella's six-bedroom home from their four-car garage and heard Ana and Bella chatting in the kitchen. That sound was one of his favorites and normally a comfort to him. Tonight, though, it hit different. He balled his fists again.

That mother fucking Hendrix. Challenging me like that. And no one said anything, Not even Tuck.

Mike turned the corner and found Johnny in his usual spot, in front of the oven, baking some kind of concoction. Mike swore that kid was the next Gordon Ramsey.

"Dad, you made the playoffs, congrats," Ana said as Mike wobbled in. She jumped up and ran over to him, giving him a hug.

"Hey, babe, congratulations," Bella said as she stood to greet him. Her face crinkled in concern at his shoddy movement as Ana stepped away and went back to her seat.

"Congrats, Dad," Johnny and Piper said at the same time. Piper had her books sprawled across the kitchen table doing homework. They hustled over for a hug, then went right back to it.

Mike's arrival made five of them. They were an All-American, picture-perfect family. He smirked.

Wife wasn't even at the fucking game to see us make the playoffs.

Bella moved to give him a kiss, and he turned his cheek into her lips instead. She flinched at his rejection. *Good.*

"Good practice?" Mike asked Ana.

"Yeah. Coach practiced me on the PK tonight."

He nodded.

I mean, Christ, I'm still the captain. This is still my fucking team. And none of my fucking family there.

"You don't think I'd be good on it?" Ana asked.

"What?" He glanced at Ana and shook his head. "Sorry. I think you'd be great on the PK. Just tired."

Bella added, "Honey, Coach said you did great at practice." She nodded at Ana with encouragement as Mike gave Ana a quick smile.

And where the fuck was Pops tonight, anyway? He knew this was my first game back. Playoffs on the line.

"Dad. Cookies. Want one?" Johnny asked. He held up the cookies he'd shaped like the PHL Cup.

"Huh?" Mike gave Johnny a blank stare. "What?"

Johnny flicked him a questioning stare.

"It's a cookie, Dad. Should I start with easier questions?" Johnny smarted.

Mike shook his head as they all got quiet. Johnny was the first to move, putting the cookies away and heading out.

"Call o' Duty. Out."

"Only an hour of that," Bella said.

"I saw Hendrix tonight. He was good on the power play," Ana said.

Mike let out a low growl.

That fuckin' kid has been here a hot second. Give him another few weeks and his true claws are gonna come out.

Mike walked to the cabinet and grabbed his pain meds. His knee was throbbing more than usual, and it was more pain than he could take tonight.

They were probably all celebrating. Without him.

"What's going on with you?" Bella asked.

"What?" Mike turned and noticed the kids were gone. "Where'd the kids go?"

"I sent them to their rooms."

"Why?" he asked. He tossed two pills back, turned on the faucet, cupped the water and slurped it down from his hand. He shut off the water and wiped his face with his suit. He glanced at Bella.

"Why do you need those now?" she asked. "You were in the suite tonight. And why are you limping so much? It's like you can barely walk. I told you Pops was push—"

"Bella, stop. I'm fine." *Put on the smile.*

She glared at him. "Don't you try to give me that bullshit P.R. smile you use on everyone else," she snapped.

"Fuck, fine," he said exasperated. He should have known he couldn't get that past her.

"Aren't you supposed to be taking less of those pills? Doc said—"

"It's fine, Bella, fuck, I promise. It's nothing."

He sighed at her penetrating stare and leaned against the counter. He could either tell her about his night or she was going to keep pressing about the pills. *Pick your poison.*

"You weren't at the game," he said accusingly. "You knew how important it was."

"I had the kids. Piper's science fair, I told you that," she said matter of fact. "We talked about this, Mike."

"Well, Pops wasn't there, either," he said. "I called. Mom said he hasn't been feeling well."

He crossed his arms over his chest and shrugged. "The guys were assholes. Hendrix was fuckin' great."

He uncrossed his arms and banged his fist against the counter. She walked over then and ran her hands up his arms. He looked down into her blue eyes and his body stirred.

"You made the playoffs, baby," she said quietly. "Why aren't you happy?"

He glanced away from her stare. *I don't know.*

"Hey." She turned his face back to her.

"I'm sorry you had a rough night," she whispered. She rubbed her body against his and squeezed his arms. "I know this transition is hard on you. And Hendrix is a bullshit asshole."

He grinned at her playful expression as his empty hand found her ass and dug in. "Don't make me feel better," he whispered.

"Oh, come on, let me try." She nonchalantly slid her hand down one of his arms and took the pills out of that hand. She set them aside as she kissed down his neck and ran her hands up and down his body. "We should be celebrating."

The woman knew how to get him out of his head, that was for sure. She'd figured out all his buttons and knew how and when to press them. He slid his

74

hands into her hair and kissed her deeply as passion took over.

"Mmm, baby," she murmured as he slid his hands under her shirt and unhooked her bra. Fuck, he needed her right now.

"Come on," she whispered as she grabbed his hands and led him out of the kitchen.

"Mmm, yes," he said silkily. He let go of her hands and when she turned to him, he said, "Shit, I think I left my phone in the car."

She took her shirt and bra off as she moved up the stairs. "Don't take too long."

"Fuck," he whispered. She tiptoed into their bedroom and closed the door with a wink. For a second, he thought an hour with his wife might be all he needed. But something slithered awake inside him.

He moved stealthily down the stairs and into the kitchen. He turned the water on its quietest setting and glanced behind him. No one was coming.

He quickly grabbed the pain meds Bella had set aside, shook two out, tossed them back with water from his cupped hand, and carefully put the pills back where Bella had left them. She wouldn't understand that this was temporary.

He just needed to get to the playoffs and then he'd be done.

"Mike?" Bella yelled from their room.

"Got the phone. Coming!"

He pulled his phone out of his jacket pocket, shut off the water, and switched off the kitchen light as he shuffled up the stairs.

11

That's the Tap

Tuck was moving as fast as he could.

This day was important for Mike. It was his first practice with the team in four months and yet, Tuck had taken too much time with his new love this morning. Now, he was fucking late getting to the ice and had left Mike hanging.

"Hurry the fuck up, Tuck," the assistant coach hollered as he headed out of the room.

"Comin'," Tuck yelled over his shoulder. He grabbed for his phone to shut it off during practice. Didn't need anyone fucking with it when he wasn't around.

"Fuck."

He'd left it in the bathroom. *Stupid.* He ran to the sink and saw a text from Jaime. He glanced around. No one was here. No one saw. He relaxed.

Jaime: *Fun morning. See you later?*

Tuck stood there texting and grinning.

Tuck: *Absolutely. Make you dinner?*

Jaime: *I'll be there. Love you.*

Tuck took a deep breath.

He wanted to say it back, but he hadn't been able to. Not yet. And not by text. *Maybe tonight.*

He grinned.

Tuck: *Can't wait.*

"Shit." He rushed back to his stall and tossed his phone inside his bag, then froze in place. His heart ticked up. He quickly looked around. The room was empty. He looked back at the paper taped to the back of his stall. The handwriting was nondescript. It could have been anyone's. He sighed as he shifted uncomfortably.

It wasn't like these things never happened. They did, worse than this, even. He remembered vividly the beating he got in Juniors. It's why he just shut the fuck up about it. He just didn't expect it here. After all this time. After months, years, of nothing. It was shocking to see it now.

He snatched the note from his locker and ran his thumb over the word, "Faggot."

It couldn't be his teammates. There were rumors, but none of them knew for sure. Only Mike and his family knew. And Dani.

It had scared him when she saw him with his date at a restaurant outside of town a few years ago. She had found him the next day in the rink and privately said she'd never say anything. And she never had. He respected her for that.

Goddammit.

Maybe it *was* a teammate. Maybe someone saw him and Jaime. *Maybe Jaime said something, and it got around?* Things change fast when innuendo becomes reality. And Jaime was real. A real person. A real relationship.

"Fuck," he whispered.

"Dude, the Stache is losing his shit you're not—"

Tuck couldn't hide it in time as Hendrix stopped mid-sentence at his stall.

"What the fuck?"

Anger rose in Tuck's chest. "You know what, you fucker, you can—"

"Stop," Hendrix ordered as he put his hand up. He reached over and grabbed the note, crumpled it up, and handed it back to him. "I give no fucks about that."

Tuck couldn't hide the surprised expression he knew was plastered on his face.

"If anybody's got a fucking problem with you over that, then their fucking priorities aren't straight."

Fuck. He really misjudged that situation. Tuck shoved the note deeper in his bag and zipped it shut.

"Thanks," Tuck said. He turned back to Hendrix. "Just let it slide."

"Sure." Hendrix nodded as he reached in his stall and grabbed his ibuprofen bottle while Tuck eyed him.

"Hungover?" Tuck asked.

Hendrix threw back two of the orange pills, grabbed his water bottle, chugged them back, and threw the bottle back in his stall as Tuck finished up. Hendrix grinned. "You could say that."

"Oh yeah?" Tuck grabbed his helmet and stick.

"Jennifer and Christine wanted to give me a proper welcome to Columbus," Hendrix said with a Cheshire smile.

"I'm sure they did." Tuck laughed as he put his helmet on.

"Look, not to be a dick," Hendrix said, "But I don't feel like a bag skate, so move your ass, huh?"

Hendrix grabbed his stick and walked out as Tuck followed.

"Yep." They headed down the tunnel and onto the ice.

"Glad you assholes could join us this morning," the Stache hollered as they glided into practice. Tuck gave the Coach a nod as Hendrix fucked with him.

"Wouldn't miss it, Stache," Hendrix joked as the team laughed.

"What the fuck did you call me?" the Stache shouted.

"I called you Coach," Hendrix said innocently.

"Don't dick with me this morning, Hendrix."

"Never, sir."

Tuck cracked a smile at Hendrix, who gave him a nod.

"Alright, bring it in. Cap is back," the Stache said as stick taps to the ice made their own soundtrack.

Tuck noticed the tense smile and tired eyes as Mike glanced at him and then Hendrix. *Fuck.* He should have been here for Mike. He could tell his friend wasn't doing well and favoring that knee, which was supposed to be better.

"Alright, one-on-ones. Line up either side," the Stache hollered.

"Later, man, thanks," Tuck said as he whacked Hendrix's pads with his stick.

"Yeah, man, anytime," Hendrix said with a nod.

Tuck slid in by Mike and whacked his friend's pads. "You good, man?"

"Yeah," Mike said tensely.

"You don't look so good."

Mike shrugged his left shoulder as Coach blew the whistle to start. Hendrix was first up and easily broke by his defender to slide one in five-hole.

"Yeah, man." Chary bumped gloves with Hendrix as he skated by, while Cots tapped the ice.

"Nasty," Cots said.

Tuck peered at Mike, who cracked his neck and glared at the ice. Tuck knew that look. It couldn't be easy for Mike with Hendrix looking like that. And the locker room antics the other night…Hendrix had challenged Mike right there in front of everyone. No one had known what to say, not even Tuck.

Everyone could see the writing on the wall. And now Mike could, too. He didn't know how to help his friend navigate that.

"Glaz!" Hendrix yelled.

Glaz defended as one of the forwards drove to the net. He made a sweet move and stole the puck easily. The boys hollered appropriately for his efforts.

"Killin' it today," Tuck added.

"That's right. Thank you, thank you." Glaz bowed like the hilarious asshole he was. Tuck couldn't help but grin.

"Come on, Chary," Cots yelled as Chary lost his breakaway to a rolled puck.

"Fuck!" Chary slammed his stick on the ice and skated to the end of the line.

Cots joked, "That looked like somethin' you'd do in the Q. Jesus."

"Fuckin' ice is chippy," Chary defended.

They both glanced at Mike, waiting for a patented Cap'n reaction. Nothing. They switched to Hendrix.

"Stick handling's dick handling, boys," Hendrix quipped.

"No wonder Chary's not gettin' any," Cots finished.

"Fuck you, assholes," Chary said as they laughed.

Tuck peered at Mike. No reaction.

"Alright, fuckin' focus, you assholes," Tuck rumbled with a grin.

"Harvey!"

Everyone turned to see the assistant coach standing at the edge of the tunnel. They all looked at Harvey.

"Shit," Harvey said quietly. His shoulders slumped at least an inch as he skated slowly to the assistant. "That's the tap, boys."

"Enjoy the bus, baby," Cots said.

"We'll keep the jet warm for ya," Chary chided.

"I'll be back, fuckers," Harvey said as he waved them off and headed down the tunnel.

"God, I hated those days," Tuck said. He nudged Mike.

"Yeah. Brutal."

Tuck noticed Mike's nervous eyes and his fists clenching and opening as he started his turn.

Mike was trying to keep the weight off his injured knee and his movements were stiff as his shot rang off the post.

"Welcome back, Cap'n," Chary said with a laugh.

"Yeah, Cap," Cots added.

Mike smirked as he got back in line, his breaths were hard and heavy. Tuck saw him glance over to the press area and search the seats.

"Tuck, get your ass moving," the Stache yelled. "Jesus, what's your problem, today?"

Tuck quickly moved through his turn then filed in behind Mike.

"No Pops?" Tuck asked.

Mike shrugged. "I guess he's sick."

Mike skated to the bench alone and Tuck caught Dani watching his friend closely.

"What the fuck?" he said quietly.

Something more than just retirement worry was going on with Mike. Tuck wasn't sure what it was, but it had started just before the captain's return. Mike had been more agitated, probably skating more than he should have been. *Did the team know?*

Mike had been shutting him out. Tuck had been at the Olsky's house almost every day up until a month ago. And then, it was like Mike pulled the curtain on him.

Tuck's brow furrowed as Mike grabbed a bottle of water and caught Dani looking at him. He gave her a nod, then turned away and slipped something from his hand into his mouth and chugged it down with water.

"Oh shit," Tuck said under his breath. He looked over to Dani and saw her make a note.

Tuck had been in this league long enough to know what that probably was. He knew the lengths players would go to stay in the game. The shots, the "remedies," the "just stitch it up and I'll play through."

The pills. *Fuckin' Maize and his hook-ups.*

All athletes played through pain.

Hockey players, though, were a different breed all together.

Tuck asked under his breath, "What are you doing, Mike?" as his friend returned to the line-up and waited for his turn.

12

Should Have Said So

Mike had only a vague recollection of the time that had passed between when he left morning skate and when he ended up here, pulling into his parent's farmhouse at dusk. He was certain he had gone home. Bella hollering at him was a stark reminder of that.

"How long have you been out here?" she had yelled. "You're lucky your hat tipped onto your face. You're right in the sun. Mike?"

He had looked around then and realized he'd fallen asleep on the patio, a drained martini glass beside him.

"Hey," he had said groggily, trying to wake himself up.

"Mike, what is wrong with you? Why were you drinking in the middle of the afternoon? Didn't you have morning skate?"

"It's one drink, Bella, calm down."

A fight had ensued then, and he had walked away in the middle of it claiming he needed to shower, even though he'd already taken two that day.

Was it two?

He had gone to their walk-in closet instead and found his stash of pills buried in his hockey bag. He'd quickly swallowed down two then sat against the wall in the closet. He had waited there for a few minutes in the quiet before remembering what caused him to drink in the afternoon in the first place.

Pops hadn't been at practice.

Something was going on with his father that his father wasn't telling him.

And I sucked.

Hendrix was great. Again.

Mike reached into the baggy and swallowed down one more pill. And Tuck had come onto the ice with Hendrix. What was that about? *Are they fucking best friends now?*

Mike had gotten up then and grabbed his keys, moving stealthily through the house, avoiding Bella's detection. He had gotten out of the garage just in time to see her run out and throw her hands up in exasperation as he left.

Now he was at his parent's house and feeling much better. His gait was even half-normal. There was hardly any pain.

"Hi, honey," his mother, Marie, said as he walked in. She was finishing the dishes.

"Mom. Where is he?" Mike asked.

He gave her a kiss on the cheek.

"Diggin' through old boxes downstairs. I don't know what he's looking for. He's upset he hasn't been to see you. You know he lives by it," she said.

She turned and faced him then with a big smile that quickly faded as she searched his face.

"You okay? Your eyes look a little glassy."

She reached to touch his face and he backed away.

"Uh, yeah. Fine."

Pops walked in.

"Where have you been?" Mike asked. It came out like an accusation. An attack. And, in some way, it was. This man had been on Mike's ass since day one and all of sudden he decided to just not show up to anything for a week?

"He's sick," Marie said.

"I'm fine. For the nine-thousandth time." Pops swatted at her and walked to the sink, where he grabbed a glass and poured himself a water.

"You need to go to the doctor," Marie pressed. "I think it's the flu."

She nodded at Mike as she pulled out a chair and sat down at the table with the newspaper. She was ready to do her crossword puzzle like she did every night.

"I'm not gonna see the damn doctor, Marie, and that's final," Pops said. He drained the remaining water in his glass, put the glass in the sink, and turned back to Mike. "Let's talk about this Hendrix."

"Not now." The last fucking thing Mike wanted to talk about was Hendrix. He squeezed his arms and shifted uncomfortably. He couldn't tell exactly where the pain was coming from this time.

As if on cue, Pops asked, "How's the pain?"

"What pain?" Mike said tiredly.

He glanced at Pops. His father looked initially concerned, then extremely tired. Pops sat down quickly, almost too quickly, and nearly missed the chair.

"Honey!" Marie exclaimed, reaching for him. Mike beat her there.

"Whoa, Pops," Mike said as he steadied the man.

Pops waved him off, but not before Mike noted the beads of water around the elder man's brow.

"You sweating?" Mike asked.

"What?" Pops touched his forehead and looked at his fingers. Rubbed them together.

"No. No, of course not."

"Mom?" Mike asked.

Marie got up and tried to examine Pops, but he waved her off, too.

"I'm fine. It's too damn hot in here, Marie," he said in agitation.

"I'll turn on the A.C.," she said. She rolled her eyes at Mike then checked the thermostat.

"Go. Go home, Mike," Pops said. "Get ready for the playoffs."

"I don't—"

"Mike, go," Pops ordered.

"Okay," Mike said. He glanced to his mother, who smiled at him. "I'll go."

Mike started to leave.

"Hey."

Mike turned at his father's voice.

"The Cup. Can't ya taste it?" Pops asked.

"Yeah. Yeah," Mike said, nodding. "G'night, Pops."

Mike wasn't sure why, but he walked back to his father and leaned down to give him a hug. After a moment, he attempted to let go, but when he did, Pops gripped him tighter.

"That drawing of Piper," Pops said quietly. "It was good. I should have said so."

Mike pulled back and eyed his father as Pops slapped his shoulder.

"Go. I'm good. Work on your speed."

"Okay," Mike said. He pulled out of his father's grip and walked over and hugged his mom. Then he left the house into the cool night air.

Mike glanced back to the white-washed wood and all the warm light coming from the windows. His brow creased as he shook his head. *What the hell?*

He shifted uncomfortably on his knee, then reached into his pocket and pulled out his baggy. Two more white tablets would help. In a few minutes, he'd feel better. He could sleep tonight. And tomorrow would be a fresh start. He could stop with the pills and get back on track.

He climbed pensively into his SUV and headed home.

13

Drinking Wine is a Crime

As Mike pulled into his garage and the door closed behind him, he glanced at his dashboard, put the SUV in park, and shut off the car.

How did I get here?

He pulled his keys out of the ignition and crinkled his face as he strained his memories. His father. Right, Pops. The old man had been tired, and maybe sick.

Did we hug?

Yeah, they had hugged. And Pops had said Mike's drawing of Piper was good. *Weird.* Pops would never, ever say something like that. *Had he actually said it?*

Mike shook his head and tumbled out of his car into the garage. He reached out and balanced himself against the black metal. "Whoa."

He smacked his tongue against the roof of his mouth. Why did it taste so strange? *The pills.* That's right.

Mike stumbled into the house from the garage and saw Johnny doing dishes while Ana and Piper worked on their homework.

Was Pops trying to tell him something tonight?

"Hey," said a chorus of voices. The kids all turned to him and greeted him, he knew that. He heard it. He glanced at them.

"How's Pops?" Piper asked.

Why isn't Bella here?

"Where's your mom?" Mike asked.

"Wine night," Ana said.

The kitchen was suddenly quiet. He wasn't sure why. Normally, the kids were chattering about one thing or another. He glanced to them again and found they were looking at him. He stepped back in surprise.

"Where's Bella?" Mike asked again.

The kids looked at each other and back to him.

"I just said she was out with the girls for wine night," Ana said.

"Don't be a smart ass, Ana," Mike spat.

"Whoa," Johnny said.

"Dad," Piper said with concern.

"Wait, what?" Ana snapped.

"You have hockey practice?" Mike asked. He stepped toward them, and Ana reached out her hand to his arm.

"What?" he asked.

"You were swaying, dad," she said with concern.

"Oh." He turned to them. *Why are they looking at me like that?* "Where's the food?"

"Plate in the fridge." Ana stood and slammed her chair into the table. She grabbed her books then headed out of the kitchen.

"Stop slammin' shit," Mike hollered as he opened the fridge and grabbed his plate. "Mmm."

He started eating the chicken and potatoes with his fingers.

"This is good," he murmured. He could suddenly smell Bella's perfume.

90

"What's going on?" she asked. He heard her drop her purse on the island. His baby was home.

Mike popped his head out of the fridge and eyed her. She was beautiful, put-together, standing there with a bottle of wine and the newspaper.

"Need a fork?" she asked sarcastically. "Mike, you have shit all over your face."

Fuck her. Mike slammed the fridge shut with his foot, dropped the plate on the island, and used her jacket to wipe his face. She jerked away and yanked her coat from him.

"Mike!"

He wrenched the wine bottle from her hand and pulled the baggy from his pocket.

"Johnny. Piper." Bella nodded them both out of the kitchen as Mike pulled two pills out of the baggy. He tossed them in his mouth and cracked open the wine bottle as he stared right at her. She threw the sports section on the island. *Teddy fucking Hendrix.*

He took a long pull of the Cabernet and slammed it on the island as rage crossed his face.

"What fucking now, Bella?" Mike yelled.

"Really? You're supposed to be taking less of those pills, goddammit," she said. "And now with alcohol?"

"What, drinking wine is a crime all of a sudden? You brought this shit home."

She quickly reached for it, but he grabbed it first. She crossed the distance to him and grabbed hold of the bottle.

"Gimme it."

"No."

He yanked back on it harder.

"Mike!" she yelled.

"Stop it!"

They pulled back and forth until the bottle slipped from both their grips and broke all over the floor, the red wine staining the white tile.

"Nice." Bella said as she tiptoed around the broken glass.

"I'mma take a shower."

Mike limped out of the room, the pain now clearly coming from his knee. She was right on his heels as she followed him into the bedroom. He ripped his shirt off his body and threw it behind him at her. Anything to stop her from getting too close.

"Mike, what the actual fuck?" she yelled as she slammed the door. "Are you actually getting better or not? I want the truth. Pills in baggies? I don't believe your bullshit those are from the prescription bottle. And now drinking during the day and with the medication? This shitty behavior. Are you still in pain?"

"What pain?" Mike asked as he stripped off his jeans. When she didn't say anything for a second, he turned to face her and saw what she was looking at.

A bottle of pain pills on the bathroom sink. The extra prescription from Doc. They locked eyes and before he could process it, she was in the bathroom with the bottle in her hand.

"Find another way to win," she said.

She started out of the room.

"Bella, you don't understand." Mike grabbed her by the wrist before she could open the door and squeezed. Hard. Harder. Hardest.

She dropped the bottle from her hand.

"Ow!" She jerked away and rubbed her wrist, now red and lightly bruised.

Her blue eyes on his were more than he could take. He flicked his stare away and to her reddened wrist.

What the fuck am I doing?

"I'm sorry."

He bent down to pick up the bottle and nearly fell over. He felt her hands on him as he stood up.

"Fuck, Bella," he said quietly. He faced her questioning gaze as he handed her the bottle. "I'm sorry."

She took the bottle from him, and he saw something in her eyes he had never seen before: fear.

"You're scaring me," she whispered. "I don't know who you are right now, Mike."

He shifted uncomfortably under her stare. He didn't know what to say. He didn't know how to answer.

"How many more bottles?" she asked.

"The one downstairs. That's it."

"There's ibuprofen in the cabinet." She stormed out as he winced.

What had he done? He started to wear out the carpet between the bathroom and closet as the pain in his knee reverberated through his body.

* * *

Ana glanced at Piper and Johnny as they listened
to the screaming behind their parent's bedroom door
from the hallway. It wouldn't be the first time.
Parents fought, and so did theirs. No big deal. They'd
heard worse from their mom and dad. Like that time
their mom packed them up and they left for a week.
Or that time she kicked their dad out of their house
for a month.

"Find another way to win," her mom yelled.

"Bella, you don't understand," her father hollered.

Her mother had never understood what it was like
to be a hockey player. An athlete. It wasn't her thing.

But even Ana had to admit that it had also never
been like this before. Ana couldn't remember, ever,
when her father had yelled at her the way he had
earlier. And now her mom? It just wasn't him.

She glanced at Piper and Johnny with a
questioning stare as silence fell over the house.

Footsteps.

"Get in your rooms," Ana whispered quickly.
They all ducked inside their bedrooms as Bella
charged out.

Ana peered around her door frame and saw her dad
pacing and her mom going down the stairs. She
waited until he walked out of view then quickly ran
to the stairs and peered over the railing.

Her mom was going to the downstairs bathroom.

Ana quietly snuck down the stairs behind her and
hid behind the kitchen island. There was wine and
broken glass everywhere. She was careful as she

peered around the edge. It was a straight view into the cream and dark gray bathroom.

"What?" Ana whispered as she saw her mother examine her wrist. Then she opened the pill bottle in her hand and dumped it into the toilet.

Aren't those dad's pills?

Bella was coming toward the kitchen.

Shoot.

Ana hustled around to the other side of the island, carefully avoiding the glass. Bella maneuvered the sharp shards then grabbed a different medication bottle and headed back to the bathroom.

Two bottles?

Ana scurried back to her spot. Bella dumped the second bottle into the toilet.

"Mom?" Johnny yelled from the staircase.

"Yeah?"

"You okay?" he asked.

"Yeah, honey," Bella said. She walked out of the bathroom and stood in the kitchen. "You need something?"

"I need my meds," he said.

Johnny and his A.D.D. It caused him massive learning issues, but the meds helped.

"Okay," Bella said. She pulled her dirty coat off and threw it on the kitchen chair, then pulled her long-sleeve shirt down over her wrist and headed upstairs. "Coming."

Ana waited until she heard her mother walk in Johnny's room, then into the upstairs bathroom. Ana started to head upstairs, too, when she heard another

set of footsteps. She scurried back to her spot and
watched the bathroom.

"Dad?" she whispered.

Her dad looked around quickly, then grabbed toilet
paper from the roll and laid it on the counter. He bent
over the toilet and quietly slid his fist into the water,
stayed there for a second, then pulled it out. He
dropped a handful of pills onto the toilet paper, then
went back for another fistful and did the same thing.
He pulled more toilet paper and dried the pills. Then
he pulled a baggy out of his pocket and scraped the
pills into it.

He closed the baggy, put it in his pocket, crumpled
up the toilet paper, wiped the counter and toilet, and
tossed it in the trash can.

He pulled out a different baggy with white pills in
it and dumped those quietly into the toilet, then
shoved the empty baggy back into his pocket. He
wiped his hands on the towel and turned, listening
carefully at the door.

He quickly tried to walk, winced in pain, and then
proceeded gingerly to the stairs and up them.

Ana stood from her hiding place, peeked around
the island, and saw her dad stumble into the bedroom.
She moved to the bathroom and glanced in the toilet;
a pile of white pills gathered in the bottom. She
pulled up her sleeve and quietly reached in, grabbing
a few of them. She pulled them out of the toilet and
fingered them with their big "A's" stamped on them.

"Aspirin," she whispered. She heard Bella coming
down the hallway, so she quickly dumped the pills,
and went back to her hiding place as her mother came

96

down the stairs and went back to the bathroom. The toilet flushed and the light clicked off.

Ana glanced down at the mess. She was probably coming to clean the kitchen. Ana quickly moved to the other side of the island as Bella started cleaning. Ana snuck quietly up the stairs and into her room. She clicked her door shut and grabbed her phone. She Googled "what does it mean if someone is hiding pills?"

She glanced at the long list of results.

"No way," she said quietly as she read them. "Addiction? It can't be."

14

A-ha

Pops had been in this damn, frigid basement for the last five days looking for that damn letter and he still hadn't found it.

"Where are you at?" he said to the pile of papers on his desk and the overstuffed boxes. "Show yourself."

He sighed as the sweat gathered on his brow. He touched it lightly then pulled his fingers down in front of his face and rubbed them together. The sweat was slippery as he slid his thumb and middle finger together.

That can't be good.

He wiped his brow and glanced back to the mess. He wasn't sure why finding this admission letter was so important to him suddenly, except that he just didn't feel well. It was bad enough that he'd missed Mike's practices, but to miss his first game back? The playoff clincher? Pops knew something wasn't right.

At first, he thought it was the flu, too, like Marie did. But as it wore on and anxiety built in his chest, he could tell something was off. And then Mike showed up tonight, worried and tired. That had done it. Pops was glad they had that online booking thing. Marie just hopped on and made an appointment for next week.

I hope it's not cancer.

Whatever it was, he hoped it was fixable. But if it wasn't, well…at his age, when you started worrying, you started thinking. And once you started thinking, you looked back. And sometimes, you didn't always love what you saw.

"A-ha." He grabbed the letter from its hiding place in a box by his leg. He glanced at it, then dropped it to the ground as a searing pain ripped through his chest. He couldn't breathe anymore.

"Ma…rie…".

He lurched for the phone on the desk and grabbed it before falling to the ground and pulling everything to the floor as he collapsed.

* * *

Bella thought a baby was crying as she shook herself awake. She quickly realized it was Mike's cell phone ringing.

"Mike," she said sleepily. She tried to shake him awake but he wasn't moving. "Mike!"

She tried again. Nothing.

"Fuck." She rolled across him and grabbed the phone from his nightstand. She glanced at the screen.

"Oh no."

She sat straight up and answered.

"Marie? Is everything okay?"

She could hardly believe the words as Marie choked them out. *Pops? Dead?* It just couldn't be.

"We're on our way."

Bella peered down at Mike.

"Fuck."

15

Stubborn Mule

Mike limped into the hospital room that contained his father's body.

"Christ," he said in shock.

He wasn't prepared to see his ashen father like that. The color was drained from him in a dramatic fashion, with the sheet up to his chin. It was a far cry from the solid, healthy man who had raised him, taught him, trained him.

The pain seared through his knee at levels he hadn't felt since he first injured it.

He fidgeted as he peered at his mother, still in her pajamas and a robe, no make-up, her eyes were red and swollen. She was clinging to a tissue in one hand, and Pops' hand in the other.

"The doctor said he went fast," she said quietly. "A widowmaker."

Mike nodded and hobbled toward her. He leaned down and kissed her forehead as she whimpered. His body felt weak as he took it all in. His parents had been so strong his whole life. This wasn't them. It couldn't be them.

He stood up and pulsed his hands into fists, then out again, the pain in his knee was like one hundred hot pokers driving into the joint.

"Oh my God. What am I gonna do?" she asked tearfully. She dabbed at her eyes. "I don't even know where the checkbook is. Or his favorite suit. We didn't even say goodbye. Just good night. He was supposed to see the doctor next week. I made the appointment. I made the damn appointment."

She shook her hands in the air and then covered her face with them.

"Mom, it's okay."

"I should have taken him. I knew. I should have taken him sooner." She laid her head on his hand.

"I can help, Mom. I can—"

"He didn't even cry out, you know," she said, lifting her head and getting angry again. "Just like him. Damn stubborn mule. Never asked for help. And he needed it. He really needed it this time."

And now she was crying again. Mike took a deep breath to control the unmanageable pain, then balled his fists and squeezed.

"I know where the checkbook is," he said. He exhaled and unclenched his hands. "And, uh, the gray suit, dark gray one...with the, uh, blue tie. It's in the back of his closet."

"Gray? Maybe the black tie?" Marie asked. Her eyes were dry now as she dabbed at them.

"Blue."

She nodded. "He loved you so much."

Mike nodded as the most intense pain he'd ever felt exploded in his knee. He winced at its sudden appearance.

"I'll give you a minute with him," his mother said. She stood and he embraced her. She held onto him tightly. He wasn't sure how his mother was going to go on without Pops. They'd been together since high school. High school sweethearts. That was a long time to share a life with someone.

"Thank you," she whimpered.

He nodded as she let go and stepped out of the room.

He stared at his father. He didn't even know what to think. He couldn't seem to feel anything except the pain from his knee as it radiated through his body with its own pulsing beat.

He limped to the hospital bed, the smell of antiseptic leeching onto the insides of his nose and setting up camp. He touched his father's hand. Stiff. Cold. He yanked his fingers away.

A corpse.

Mike stumbled away from the bed and into the wall. He struggled to catch his breath as he shoved himself away from the cool surface and headed for the door.

* * *

Bella got the kids their sodas and snacks from the vending machine and handed it to them as Marie walked out.

"Oh, Marie," Bella said tenderly. She rushed to her mother-in-law and grabbed hold as Marie gripped her back. "Stay with us tonight."

Marie pulled away and nodded as she wiped tears from her eyes with her hankie.

"Grams," Ana said. She got up and hugged Marie as the other two followed.

"Thank you," Marie choked out as she squeezed the kids.

"It'll be okay, Grams," Piper said.

"Yeah," Johnny said. "I'll make you pancakes in the morning."

"Oh, that would be lovely," Marie said. She smiled as Bella tucked Marie's hair behind her ear. She couldn't imagine what Marie was feeling right now, but she had an inkling. Even as mad as she was at Mike right now, and concerned and fearful about what was happening to him, she loved him, for better, for worse. If anything happened to him…she shook her head.

Don't.

"Mike?" Marie asked.

Bella looked up as Mike walked out of Pops' room. She shook her head. *Why didn't he stay longer?*

"Mom, stay at the house tonight," Mike said quickly. He touched her back as she looked at him, surprised.

"Oh," she said. "Yes, that would be good."

Marie touched his arm. "Are you sure you don't need more—"

"I'm fine," he said. "Let's go. Do they need anything else from us?"

Marie shook her head. "We can go."

Bella reached for him, but he shook her off. When he did, her sleeve fell back and exposed her reddened, bruised wrist. Marie saw it and glanced at Bella. Bella quickly pulled her sleeve back in place.

"Good, let's just go then," Mike said. He quickly left the ER as the family glanced at Bella, then followed him out. As she pulled up the rear, she glanced over to Pops' room and saw his ashen body.

"Jesus," she choked out as tears hit her eyes. No wonder Mike couldn't stay in that room.

"Mrs. Olsky?"

Bella turned to see a concerned nurse. "Yes?"

"Your father-in-law's watch and wallet," she said as she handed them to her.

"Thank you," Bella said as she took them. She thumbed the leather of his wallet as the nurse walked into the room with Pops. Bella swallowed back the tears and walked out the door.

* * *

Mike tried to move quickly from the car to the house, but the pain was unbearable now. He sucked air through his lips as he squeezed his arms. He winced with every move. There wasn't anything in his body that didn't ache.

As soon as they were in the house, Mike peeled off from the group and headed up the stairs. He heard Ana question Bella.

"It's fine," Bella said. She must have turned her attention to his mom, then. "Marie, I'll make us some tea, okay?"

Bella would handle them. He hobbled into the bedroom, shut the door, and slid down its cold frame, gripping his knee in pain.

"Fuck," he moaned quietly.

He army crawled to the closet, every stretch feeling like someone was jamming a knife through his cartlidge.

He finally slid inside the spacious walk-in and grabbed a belt that was hanging on the wall. He put it in his mouth and bit down as he let out a primal moan. He crawled to his hockey bag and dug out the baggy. The sweat poured from his face as he dumped the pills out and grabbed four. He shoved them in his mouth and swallowed them dry.

His breaths came hard and fast as he waited for their effect. Instead, a tide of emotions swelled in his chest. He shook his head.

"No," he said quietly.

The tide rushed higher and higher, from his chest to his throat, squeezing in pain. He shook his head.

"No."

The tide made its way to his eyes and spilled out down his face.

"Oh no," he sobbed.

The pain ripped through him repeatedly until the pills mercifully took hold, and a wave of calm brought him a moment of peace.

How in God's name was he going to exist in a world without his father?

16

Over the Edge

Dani sat in the cold, blue seat of the Columbus arena during morning skate along with twenty or so other folks. They were an eclectic group sitting quietly in the stands as practice was set to begin. There were the media people in casual attire, team marketing and communication people in snazzy business wear, and then the upper echelon of the Columbus brass with varying shades of blue ties squeezing their necks. They sat above them all like Kings on high.

She peered up at them and nodded, then turned back to the ice as players started to arrive.

"PHL Cup Playoffs" was now visible in the ice. There was a whole process for adding that language. First, the ice had to be removed, then the words and accompanying logos were added layer by layer. All of that was followed by the final shiny gloss of the Zamboni.

Dani had posted a photo of it on her social media. She glanced at it now: Almost two thousand retweets; twenty thousand likes. Just a typical day, except for the palpable weight of expectations now sitting heavily on the shoulders of the Columbus franchise.

There was excitement, of course, and the team was bought in, as were the fans. And Dani could practically feel management's collective breath of relief that their gamble on Hendrix had paid off. They had been number one when Mike went down, then they had quickly skidded out of first and had become the tragic story of the league. Hendrix had been a wild card at the trade deadline. A dangerous one. Had he failed, their blue ties would have hung them all. As it stood, they looked like hockey savants. They were the brass with the balls who knew something no one else did.

But nothing was guaranteed in this league until a team brought home the Cup. And sometimes, not even then. After last season's messy game seven loss, everyone in the stands watching today's morning skate knew the pressure cooker had only gotten hotter when they punched their playoff ticket.

"Let's go," Coach yelled as the team gathered around him.

At the center of all these compounding concerns was Mike. Not only had rumors been slowly gathering steam that he, allegedly, hadn't totally healed but also that he was taking more pain meds than he should. And now, his dad was dead, too.

Dani winced as she took a deep breath.

Pops had been like a member of the team and the organization itself. A part of its story, legend, and legacy. Everyone knew Pops and respected him for what he'd done to help Mike to this point. He was revered.

Pops was the gritty hockey dad you told tall tales about around a campfire. The most famous story was the time he took Mike out onto the ice of their pond after a middle school loss and made him shoot the puck one thousand times before the kid could go to bed. Mike had been twelve years old. He didn't take his uniform off that night until two-thirty in the morning.

No one questioned it. Not even Mike.

Dani was on the fence about it. Tough dads were a dime a dozen in sports. Golf. Tennis. Football. Soccer. The list was long. Especially in hockey. It was part of the vernacular and formed the fabric of the game's culture.

In hockey, you couldn't say "mom" or "dad" without the word tough. They were like peanut butter and jelly. They had to be. There was the traveling, the equipment, the cost, extra jobs, extra time, extreme competition—it all went together. Hockey players were a different kind of animal, and the parents who raised them had to be that, too.

Dani leaned back in her seat and tapped her voice recorder on the arm rest as the coach talked the first round.

On the other hand, how far should a parent go for a kid? Dani wasn't sure that question could be answered collectively. It seemed that was up to the individual family and the individual kid. Was it borderline abuse? Or was it the extreme parenting necessary to elevate a kid to the highest levels of competition? The kind of parenting kids thanked them for later.

Dani stared at the players on the ice. They were the one percent of hockey players in the world who got to stand on it.

Could they have gotten there any other way?

Dani shook her head. The only thing she knew for sure was that Mike was a grown man. The guy made his own choices. If he didn't want to push himself, he wouldn't. Bottom line: Mike Olsky was going to do whatever it took to play for the Cup. Period.

"Olsky is with his family," Coach said.

Dani's ears perked up at Mike's name. *Finally.*

"Not sure if he'll play," Coach lamented. "In the meantime, stay focused. Alright, first drill."

A look passed between Hendrix and Tuck. *What's that about?*

"Hope this doesn't push him over the edge," Bobbi said as he hurriedly sat down next to Dani like the rabbit from *Alice in Wonderland.* His squishy body lopped over into her seat, so she scooted over to make room for him. He made a motion like he just tossed back pills. Dani smirked.

"Gary," Bobbi said to the play-by-play man sitting behind them as he shook his hand.

"Bobbi," Gary replied. "Great piece on Buckeye State Sunday."

"Oh, thanks, thank you," Bobbi said.

Dani rolled her eyes. She knew Bobbi got a thrill when the guys complimented his work. She gave him a side-eye and he sneered at her.

"Rick," Bobbi said as he extended his hand to the color commentator and Gary's sidekick. "Good to see you boys."

"Bobbi," Rick said.

Bobbi pulled his arms in and glanced at Dani.

"Campaigning done?" she asked quietly.

"Job security," he ribbed.

She laughed. "No such thing."

She glanced at Bobbi as he gave her a questioning stare. "I hope it's not true," she said. "The pills."

She shouldn't be defending Mike. That wasn't her job. She was a reporter, and she had to be objective. And when the day came, she would be. She always had been. She had the battle scars to prove it, too, from air let out of her tires to getting "accidentally" checked into a stall in the locker room for a story she did on a player's courtroom drama.

It was never a good day when she had to report the news that made players close rank on her, and P.R. people squirm. But she had a job to do, too. She had to get close to them, but not too close.

Mike, though, had always been different. She liked the guy. His core was solid. If he was in a skid, it would be surprising and unprecedented. Mike just wasn't that guy.

And it was hard to print bad ink about good people.

"They need him. His leadership," she quipped. She shrugged her shoulders and tapped her voice recorder on the arm rest again.

An uncomfortable silence settled between them. It was laced with an unspoken truth her and Bobbi both understood: The team was in the playoffs. And they'd done it without Mike.

Dani flicked a side-look to Bobbi, then back to the ice.

No, it was more specific than that. The team had done it with Mike Olsky's replacement, AKA: Teddy

Hendrix. And if you've got the newest version of the iPhone, why would you ever go back?

"Do they need him?" Bobbi finally asked, acknowledging what she was already working through.

She let out a sigh and banged her voice recorder against the armrest as they watched the team run through one of the best practices she'd seen in a while.

17

Art School

Ana stood near her father as they combed through the boxes, drawers, and shelves in Pops' office. She did it with a deep respect and love for her grandfather.

Pops had gone to almost every single one of her home games and was one of her most fervent fans. She grinned as she touched a photo on his desk of her and him. That was when her team had won the high school hockey championship. Ana had been a freshman playing Varsity. The refs had threatened to toss him if he kept yelling about bad penalties.

She chuckled. That was Pops. When he believed in you, he made it known. And when you messed up, he made that known, too. She flicked an eyebrow up as she moved to a box on the floor he must have been going through the night he died.

Pops was always honest with her about her performance. A lot of people who heard him yell at her after a game thought he was being mean, including her own father, who would stop him almost immediately. But she didn't think that. Her grandpa had watched the greats, played the game; he knew what he was talking about, and she wanted to be better. Just because Pops had never been good at delivering the message didn't mean he wasn't worth listening to. Ana was the player she was today because he gave her the real talk.

She glanced over at her dad, pounding through the various piles of paperwork stacked neatly on Pops' desk. Her grandfather had never pushed her as hard as he had her dad. Maybe that was because she was his grandchild?

She hoped it wasn't because she was a girl.

"Oh wow, Dad, look what I found," Ana said as her fingers stumbled upon a framed photo of Pops with one of hockey's greatest. "I didn't know Pops met Bobby Orr."

Her dad leaned over the desk to look at the picture, and she was glad to see a smile touched the corners of his mouth. Her heart clenched as warmth spread through her. She hadn't seen her dad smile much in the last couple months.

"That's when Orr was inducted into the Hall of Fame," he said. "Pops loved this picture."

She grinned at the lightness in his voice as he reached over and ran a finger across the smooth glass. Ana's grin slowly disappeared as the look on his face changed. As quickly as his smile had appeared, it was gone, replaced by something else. Her heart ticked up a notch.

She was having a hard time these days reading her father. It used to be so easy. They were so much alike. Before his injury, before Hendrix became such a dominant part of every conversation, people used to compare *her* to her father. They would say she had the goods to be just like him…for a girl.

Then her dad went down on that bullshit hit from Jonahs, and Hendrix came along. Now they compared *Hendrix* to her father. She stopped mattering as much, except to her father who had helped with college scouts, and the women's pro league. He'd talk her up and tout her brilliance.

But the last couple of months, he'd barely been reachable, even when he was standing right in front of her. She hadn't realized, until now, how much hockey had been the center of their world.

She searched his face as a rush of emotions threatened to escape from her eyes. She felt lost to her father.

"Dad? You okay?" she asked quietly as his troubled expression stared at the photo.

"I wish everyone would quit fuckin' askin' me that," he cursed. And then, like something snapped inside him, he became someone else entirely right in front of her. She sucked in a breath at the change in his eyes.

"I'm fine!" He ripped the photo from her hand and slammed it onto Pops' desk, shattering the glass into the air and all around.

Ana ducked and lurched away from him. She slowly lowered her arms from in front of her face and peered at her father.

Holy fuck.

"Daddy?" she whispered. Her body had as much tension as a high wire rope.

"Clean it up."

He didn't even look at her as he shot out from behind the desk and roughly passed by her, leaving the room.

The tears came hard and fast to her eyes as a single sob shook the tension out of her body. She stopped the next round with a held breath as she covered her face. As fast as it had started, the sniveling stopped. She relaxed her body, sniffed back the pain, and cleaned up the glass.

Girls cried, sure.

But hockey players didn't.

And especially not a captain like she was.

She scraped some of the broken glass fragments from the desk into her hand and walked it to the trash as she pulled herself together. As the shards clinked down into the can, a colorful letterhead off to the side caught her eye.

What the...?

She walked over and yanked on the slip of heavy paper and quickly saw the logo was for the New York Art School. It was addressed to her father. She read through the letter and a flood of emotions seared through her.

"What...?" she whispered.

She walked to the door and listened for her dad, then looked back into the office at the broken glass.

I'll ask him about it later.

She folded the paper into a rectangle, grabbed her phone, took off the case and put the paper against the glass. She put the cover back on and slid the bulkier phone into her back pocket. She went back to the glass and finished cleaning up the mess.

She didn't know what was happening to her father, but she was confident her mother would know what to do. Between her mom and Uncle Tuck, they'd figure out how to get the father she knew back to them all.

* * *

Mike limped into his parent's kitchen and went straight for the sink. He quickly turned on the cold water and cupped it in his hands, splashing it onto his face as his breaths came fast.

He'd never in his life yelled at any of his children like that. *Never.*

And him and Ana, they had a tight relationship. She was the first-born, the oldest, the most responsible, the most like him, and, of course, there was the hockey. She had his sensibilities. Ana was responsible with the puck, took chances when she needed to, and captain of her high school squad.

He dipped his neck under the bitter stream and caught his breath.

"Fuck."

He shouldn't have done that. *What's wrong with me?*

He pulled his head up and shut off the faucet as the excess water ran down his neck and under his shirt to his back and chest. It cooled the heated mess inside of him.

He grabbed his mother's kitchen towel, with its apple pie and gingham design, and wiped his face and head. He threw the towel down on the sink and glanced in the mirror above the stainless steel.

He'd seen better days. He understood now why Bella had bitched at him to shave this morning. He touched the unkempt playoff scrub on his face. That combined with his glassy, tired eyes, unbrushed teeth, and uncombed hair made him look less than stellar.

"I didn't marry this," she had said as she flicked her hand in an up and down motion at his body and face.

"Then fuckin' leave," he had yelled, slamming the bedroom door on his way out.

He studied his worn face in the mirror now. He looked like he did when him and Tuck went to Vegas with their buddy, Vance, for his bachelor party. There had been eight of them and they hadn't slept the entire weekend, foregoing shut eye for gambling, drinking, and the strip club.

That was the weekend he'd met Kira. She had been ten years younger than him, with long, dark hair and brown eyes. Her smile had been open and bright and had drawn him in.

"Hey," she had said smoothly. They'd spent the day together walking around, doing stupid shit, laughing. She had been there for a conference and skipped the whole day for him.

"You're a bad influence," she had said. And she'd run her finger down his chest. Mike had come close to going to her hotel room that night, but he had stopped himself.

"I'm not gonna tell you to do it or not do it," Tuck had said later that night. "But I know you love your wife. So, what's goin' on?"

When Mike had gotten back from Vegas, he had looked exactly like this. Like he was sick. Him and

Bella, they had to fight their way through that tough time, and others, to get to this point. Just grinding and working the angles until they would find the net and get back to good.

He was always glad he had said no that night.

He leaned against the sink and stared hard at himself in the mirror.

But what was happening now was different. This wasn't between him and Bella. This was between him and something that had latched itself to his insides. Something that didn't have a name yet. It was like black tar stuck to his bones and he couldn't scrape it away, tear it out, or fight with it.

From the corner of his eye, he saw one of his favorite photos on the kitchen wall. He turned to it and his gut lurched. The thing inside him was on the move.

Mike stared at the photo of him and Pops when Mike was fifteen. It was on the farm pond in winter. They'd gone ice fishing that day and they were laughing because they'd caught nothing. What could there possibly be in a frozen Ohio pond in January?

A guttural sound escaped Mike's lips. He wasn't even sure what that sound was, but he knew it was some form of pain trying to break through. He rerouted it from his eyes to his fist, slamming the photo as hard as he could, breaking it into a rainstorm of delicate glass.

The thing inside him settled.

He glanced at his bloody hand with pieces of glass sticking to it. He turned back to the sink and switched the faucet on, rinsing off the blood and glass, then shutting it off. He looked around and spied the bar. He hobbled over to it and grabbed the whiskey, then hobbled back to the sink. He held his bloody hand over the drain and winced as he poured the whiskey over it.

He twisted the glass bottle toward him and admired the black label. This had always been his father's favorite. He put it to his lips and drank it like a thirsty man. The heat of it going down his throat was comforting. Mike pulled it away from his lips and reached in his back pocket and grabbed the baggy, now a familiar staple of his wardrobe.

He put down the whiskey and counted out four pills, putting the baggy back in his jean's pocket. He tossed them into his mouth, grabbed the whiskey, and drank a deep pull of the brown liquid that his father used to sip every night before bed.

He glanced at the broken photo as he put the bottle down.

Mike had to be ready for the game later. He was feeling better already.

18

He's Here

PHL Cup Playoffs
Round One, Game One

Columbus Thunder v. St. Louis Warriors
Columbus, Ohio

Dani walked through the parking garage of the arena passing players and team personnel alike. The atmosphere crackled with energy as the team was set to begin their playoff journey with game one of the first round against St. Louis.

"Hey," she said to one of the communications interns. A touch of excitement tingled in her gut. The feeling of the first playoff game never got old. She was certain Bones, and the upper deck fans, would be lit up tonight. There was so much hope and promise in game one. It could go in either direction. You could dream about the Cup without it feeling like a longshot. No one knew the truth of what the series would be yet. So, they were all free to dream.

"Dani," Grines said as he passed her on his way in.

"Have a good game," she quipped to the announcer.

"You, too."

By now, everyone had left the special event the team had hosted outside the arena earlier. The four-hour lovefest featured a special red-carpet walk-in for the players and fans alike. A banner bigger than twenty people was strung across the front of the arena and there were special places where fans could take Instagram photos. The first five hundred people through the door got special T-shirts and the mayor had issued a special congratulations. Bandwagon fans suddenly knew what the blue line was, and everyone was all-in.

Dani grinned as she walked into the arena. She had gotten used to the playoff run every year over the last ten years. For the decade before she started covering the team, they'd had no playoff appearances. Then the team had gotten Mike and hadn't missed an appearance since.

Mike hadn't missed playoff ice time during that span, either. But with his dad's death, this might be the first time Mike would miss the most important minutes of any hockey player's life.

She winced. It would be devastating for the guy to miss it. Not just from the ice, but even from the suite. Guys like Mike needed to be with their teams during games like this.

"Dani," Howie said as he passed her in the arena's underbelly.

"Howie." She nodded as she headed to the media dining area. Bobbi was already there.

"Over here." He waved at her. She acknowledged him then grabbed a plate and went through the line.

"Roast beef," she said to the server. He nodded and cut a nice, juicy slice, then put it on her plate. She grabbed some potatoes, carrots, and a roll, then headed for her seat.

"You turn in the Party on the Square story?" she asked Bobbi as she sat down.

"Hour ago," he said with his mouth full of cheesecake."

"Shit," Danie quipped. "They got cheesecake, tonight?"

"And chocolate-covered strawberries."

"Playoff dining." Dani laughed as she stabbed at her cut roast beef and took a bite.

"Definitely not the ballpark." Bobbi grinned as he shoved the last bite of cheesecake into his mouth.

"Anybody heard yet whether Olsky's gonna be here or not?" asked the color commentator, Rick, as he sat down. "I haven't gotten a straight answer."

"I don't think they know," Bobbi said as he cleaned himself up and sat back in his chair, his robust belly full of dinner and dessert.

Dani kept quiet. She'd gotten a tip from team personnel that Mike was planning to be there, but no one would confirm.

"I think—"

"He's here." Howie appeared from nowhere, interrupting her with the news. "He's not playing."

Dani dropped her fork and grabbed her phone from the table. She immediately tweeted the information to her followers, then headed straight for the press box to start her story.

19

Blessings Before Slaughter

The locker room was quiet but energized, like standing next to a power line on a quiet day.

Hendrix anxiously peered around the room. This was the atmosphere he played best in. The one where everything was on the line, every night. He was born for moments like these. There was no other way to play the game.

He grabbed the tape and started in on his stick as others launched into their pre-game rituals. He'd done that, too, of course. He had his usual home game routine.

He went to bed the night before by ten, up at five, a light workout, six eggs, a quart of strawberries, and four packets of oatmeal. Then he played video games for an hour, team stuff, and a nap. After that, shower, come to the arena in his suit and tie, and before anyone could see him, go to the ice, stand in the middle of it, and breathe deep as the smell of it permeated the deepest part of his lungs. He swore it made him feel the pulse of the ice in his body as he played.

There were variances for away games and start times, and, of course, a single variance for playoff games: the stick tap.

Him and his father had come up with it at the start of his career.

"Tapping the ice, it's a sign of respect not just to the crowd, but to the game, son," John had said to him.

"Like when you tap the table with a shot before you take it?" Teddy had laughed.

"I don't know about all that," the elder Hendrix had laughed. "But it's a nod, for sure."

Teddy had interpreted it as a nod to the game itself, win or lose. It was a moment he shared with the slick surface to pay tribute to such sacred ground. That single tap at center ice before anyone touched it was like a prayer of thanks before dinner, cheers before drinking, blessings before slaughter.

Teddy had won his first Cup after that.

He glanced up from taping his stick to a flutter of activity at the locker room door.

"What the fuck?" he said under his breath.

Mike stumbled through the void, completely dazed, without saying a word, and ran straight into one of the call-ups.

"Whoa, man," the rookie said as he steadied the captain.

Mike patted the kid on the shoulder, and then his head, before continuing past him to the bathroom.

The rookie glanced over to Hendrix and shrugged, then went about his business. Hendrix glanced over to Cots and Chary and found them staring at him, before switching to Tuck. Tuck quickly turned away and looked at Hendrix.

Hendrix raised an eyebrow. Surely, of everyone who witnessed that nonsense, Tuck would be the one to do something about Mike and whatever the fuck that shitshow was that just made an appearance in their locker room on day one of the playoffs.

Tuck turned away from Hendrix's stare and stood up.

"Need to hit up the trainers, boys." He gave Chary a slap on the shoulder and left the room.

Cots and Chary eyed each other and then turned to Hendrix. It felt good to have them recognize his leadership already. He wasn't trying to bury Olsky; but he wasn't going to run from a spot in the room, either. Not now. Not when he was starting to care about this place and this team.

He grinned.

"We're battling for the Cup boys. Stay focused."

Hendrix put his stick down and grabbed his towel, tossing it in the bin. He waited until the two went back to their normal bickering to peer into the shower room.

Where is he?

Olsky was still fully dressed, leaning his head against one of the mirrors, eyes shut. He bent down to rub his knee, then quickly and quietly slid pills from his pocket and put them in his mouth, chewing them like candy before swallowing.

What the fuck?

Abusing pain pills was an entirely different problem then just coming back from injury and trying to get back in the game. It was a dangerous path that ended nowhere good. Teddy knew that better than anyone.

Does Tuck know?

And if he did, why wasn't he doing anything about it? Didn't matter. Even if Tuck didn't do anything, Hendrix would.

He didn't give a shit who it was or what it took. Teddy would never let happen to anyone what had happened to his father.

* * *

Mike sat above the ice and stared at the game from the Thunder suite. It was the worst seat in the house.

His eyelids were heavy as he tried to track the plays. His concentration was waning. A yank on his tie helped bring him to life for a second.

"Fuckin' Hendrix," he whispered as Hendrix hopped the boards for a shift, picking up the puck and taking it down the ice with Tuck to his flank.

Mike sneered at the pair as his eyes closed. When he opened them again, Hendrix ripped it from the top of the house. Mike chuckled as it clanged off the goal post.

"Weak." His eyelids drew closed then yanked open at the sound of the goal cannon. He crinkled his forehead as he glanced to the ice. The team banged Tuck's helmet.

"Good," he said under his breath.

His eyes fluttered shut once more. Then a slap to his shoulder and he opened them again.

"Hey man," Maize said.

Mike tried to focus on the healthy scratch and his confused look. "Yeah?"

"We won."

Mike nodded. "Cool."

He glanced over to the door as the Doc walked in and waived Maize out. Mike thought a look passed between them, but he couldn't be sure.

"Got a sec?" Doc asked as the room cleared.

Mike glanced at him. *God, I'm relaxed tonight.*

"Sure, Doc. Doc. What's up Doc?"

Mike chuckled a little, then stopped when he saw Doc's face. Where was the guy's sense of humor?

"Huh. That funny?" Doc asked.

Mike eyed him for a second. His look was familiar. Like Bella's. Mike straightened up.

"No. Sorry."

Mike tried to keep his eyes open as Doc observed him.

"So. How are things at home?" Doc asked.

"Fine." *Overstatement.*

"You're dealin' with a lot. I can make a recommendation—"

"I'm not crazy," Mike interrupted.

"Didn't say you were crazy. But talking to someone might—"

"I'm fine." Mike cut him off again. "What else you got?"

Mike smiled at the doctor. He thought he was smiling. He didn't have anything to smile about. Why was everyone pushing him to see a therapist? He didn't need a shrink. He needed to get in the game.

"Trainers said you were lookin' for another round. I thought you weren't hurting as much. That we were tapering."

"Yeah. Exactly," Mike said.

God, words were hard to form tonight for some reason.

"Just every now and then it flares up," Mike said. "It's, uh, insurance through the playoffs, right?"

Mike tried to focus on the Doc and that concerned look on his face.

"More insurance than what I already gave you?"

"Come on, Doc. You know me." Mike shrugged. *Did I shrug?* He tried again. He hoped he did that time.

"I do know you, yeah," Doc said. "Why don't you stand up and walk. Let me look at it."

Mike half-laughed. His eyes focused on the Doc. *He's serious.*

"Oh. Okay. Fine."

Game face.

Mike situated himself on the chair. It would be difficult to stand, so he needed to nail it in one shot. Performance mode. *Concentrate.* Mike stood and quickly turned from the Doc, gritting his teeth in pain as he forced himself to walk with a normal gait.

Get control.

Mike exhaled and turned around with a smile as he walked toward the Doc.

"Ta-da."

He met the Doc's stare with his own. He was pretty sure that's what he was doing, anyway. It was hard to stay steady with the pain raging through his body.

"Come here," the Doc said.

Mike smiled as he walked to the Doc, who began manipulating his knee. Immediately Mike started grinding his back teeth together against the searing pain to keep his face straight. A deep nausea started swirling in his gut.

"Any pain?" Doc asked, keeping a careful eye on Mike's face.

"What pain?" Mike asked. He'd said it one hundred times before. It was so rehearsed, such a permanent part of his vocabulary, that it just fell out of his mouth without any effort.

"Well, Mike, if there's no pain, there's no need for pain meds," Doc said. "Other than ibuprofen. You're done with the prescription."

Mike's grin dropped. "But—"

"You're done."

Fuck, that backfired. He'd have to go back to Maize's guy. Shit. Wasn't Maize just here?

The Doc stood to leave as Mike tried to hang back.

"You comin'?" Doc asked.

Mike put on his sincere face.

"Of course." Mike tried to walk a straight line as he followed the Doc out of the suite, stopping in the hallway.

The Doc glanced at him.

"Gotta piss," Mike said.

Doc nodded and peeled off in the other direction as Mike headed into the bathroom, a mannequin's expression plastered on his face.

As soon as Mike shut and locked the door, he grabbed a towel, shoved it in his mouth, and growled with pain as he collapsed on the floor and gripped his knee.

Everything in his body felt fucking broken. He couldn't tell anymore which part.

He pulled out the towel from his mouth and grabbed the baggy from his pocket. He emptied the pills out onto the floor. Mike didn't even count, he just grabbed what he could and shoved them in his mouth, chewing them like candy and swallowing the powdery elixir down his throat.

He yanked a flask from inside his jacket and gulped the whiskey as fast as he could.

He watched the ceiling spin in circles and waited patiently for the pain to disappear.

20

Figure it Out

Tuck glanced around the local watering hole and let out a long, relaxed sigh. They had won the first playoff game and they needed to let off some steam.

The boys had claimed Thirsty's as their own years ago. It had every beer you could imagine on tap and the walls were plastered with celebrity Chatzky's and signed memorabilia, from the framed Shania Twain guitar pick to Mike's signed stick from the playoffs. The wait staff was young and cute, and the guys could let loose without fear of the press; the owner, Tabby, a hulking wall of muscle, made sure of it.

Tuck sipped his tequila as his lip twitched with frustration.

He had waited around the locker room after the win for Mike to come down from the suite, but he never showed. Winning the first playoff game was an early marker he thought for sure the captain would want to celebrate, maybe even come out with them for a bit if he was feeling up to it. Especially since Tuck had the game winner, and even more so since the funeral was tomorrow. Mike needed his team right now.

But when Tuck had grabbed a trainer to ask where Mike was, the trainer had been vague and elusive.

"Go celebrate," he had said to Tuck.

It had struck Tuck funny that he was being dissuaded from even looking for Mike, so he sent his friend a text where he would be and left it at that.

Now he was with this fucking group of characters wondering where the hell their captain was.

He scanned their faces with a questioning glance. He couldn't help but remember the sign in his locker. It couldn't have been one of them. Could it?

Tuck's phone vibrated and he grabbed it from his pocket.

Jaime: *Headed to bed. So proud of you. Celebratory dinner tomorrow. Love you.*

Tuck smiled. Jaime was something else. Life with a hockey player wasn't an easy one. In fact, it was the most grueling schedule on the sports docket, and it never got easier. Not until you left the game. And sometimes, that was worse. There were perks, of course, but those things didn't matter at the inflection point of the pain it could cause.

Tuck: *Sounds perfect. Can't wait.*

He pressed send, then peered around at Cots, Chary, Glaz, Hendrix, and Frenchie. He trusted these boys in battle. He had to trust them here, too. The two were intertwined.

Tuck: *Love you, too.*

"Hot date later?" Hendrix asked as he walked up and handed Tuck a fresh drink.

Tuck eyed him as he put down his near-empty glass and took the cold, clear-colored beverage and sipped it slowly. He liked the kid and wanted to trust him.

"Not tonight," Tuck said. "Team first. We'll celebrate tomorrow."

"Good man." Hendrix nodded and took a sip of his drink.

Tuck eyed it.

"That got vodka in it?" Tuck asked. He nodded at the tall glass of dark brown liquid and half-laughed; surely there wasn't only soda in that thing?

"I don't drink," Hendrix said.

Tuck caught a slight frown on Hendrix's face. *Shit.* Tuck should have realized. Hendrix's dad was killed by a drunk driver.

"Oh, yeah, man, I'm—"

"Alright, assholes, who's payin' tonight?" Cots interrupted as he chewed an edible.

"Credit cards in the hats, bitches," Chary drunkenly ordered as he walked up to everyone and waited patiently for each of them to drop their credit card in the playoff hat. He stopped briefly in front of Tuck.

"Get the fuck outta here," Tuck said flatly. Chary had already had one or two gummies of his own based on those lazy eyes. Glaz, too. Frenchie was a beer man only. And Tuck couldn't get into weed edibles. Not his style.

"Yep," Chary said, moving along, and standing in front of Hendrix.

"Put your fucking card in there, new guy," Glaz ordered.

"Gettin' us in the playoffs doesn't get your ass off the hook, pretty boy," Frenchie yelled. He was

134

quickly distracted by two blondes who walked by. "Oh, hello."

Frenchie followed the giggling pair as Chary and Cots proceeded to collect cards by haranguing every member of the team in attendance. Tuck caught a glance of a familiar face out of the corner of his eye.

"Mike!" Tuck turned to his friend and immediately he was sick to his gut. He put his tequila down and moved quickly to his stumbling friend so no one else on the team could get too close a look at him. "Jesus, Mike."

Tuck could smell the whiskey on Mike's breath, saw the bloodshot eyes, the dazed look. Mike was high off his ass. *That's got to be the pain pills.* He remembered the trainer from earlier.

They know.

"Shit. You should be home, man."

"Huh?" Mike replied, dazed.

"Everything okay?" Hendrix asked as he walked up.

"Fine," Tuck said as he moved between Hendrix and Mike.

"Fuck off." Mike turned his attention to Hendrix. "I—"

"Leave me alone, you fuckin' little prick," Mike interrupted as he tried to lunge for Hendrix.

"Whoa," Tuck said. He pulled Mike in close, turned him away from the team, who briefly looked in their direction, then went back to their game of credit card roulette. Well, maybe not a game since it was rigged. He saw Cots and Chary picking through the credit cards and giving everyone their card back. Everyone but Hendrix. *Classic move.*

"Hey, look at me," Tuck said quietly. Mike turned his glassy, red eyes to Tuck. "Fuck, Mike."

Tuck touched Mike's jacket pocket, and Mike immediately swatted at his hand. Well, swatted was a leap. Mike was moving like he was deep in the Pacific Ocean.

"You like this guy?" Mike asked, turning his gaze to Hendrix, who had come in close, blocking Mike from everyone's view. "He's trying to steal my team. *My* team."

Mike lunged again toward Hendrix.

"Whoa," Tuck said, holding Mike back. It was an effort to keep Mike back and standing. He was on the verge of collapsing so Tuck was basically holding his body up. "Let's take a beat here."

Tuck saw the boys look over briefly, then go back to their game. He pulled Mike in closer.

"Fuckin' look at me," Tuck said quietly, capturing Mike's stare. "If you're in pain, we'll figure it out. We'll talk to the trainers, to Doc—"

"Don't you get it? I'm not...that's crazy, you know? It's not even...like, what pain? Right? What pain?" Mike said as he laughed.

Mike stumbled backward then and tried to hang on to Tuck, but Tuck couldn't hold the wet fucking noodle as he fell. Tuck glanced to the team who saw the captain fall. Thankfully, they just laughed. They were too distracted to realize what was happening; they thought Mike was just part of the fun.

"Captain got started early," Tuck added to the story they were writing in their inebriated heads.

Hendrix tried to help Mike up.

"Get away from me," Mike sneered, slapping him away. "Fuck you."

Mike stumbled to his feet as his keys fell out of his pocket. Hendrix quickly grabbed them and handed them to Tuck.

Mike drunk-leaned against a bar stool and looked straight at Tuck. "Fuck you, too, man."

Mike stumbled away, toward the door.

Tuck looked back at the guys, who heard the chorus of fuck yous from their captain and were now giving Tuck a questioning stare.

"We tried to get his credit card for the game," Tuck joked. "Fucker wouldn't play."

"Cap can get the next round!" Frenchie yelled as he wrapped an arm around a redhead in a tight skirt, the blondes now flanking Glaz.

"Fuck yeah he can," Chary laughed, as he returned the last credit card to Cots.

Tuck plastered on a grin as he turned to Hendrix and dropped the facade. He glanced toward the door. Mike was gone. He glanced back to Hendrix.

"He needs help," Hendrix said quietly.

"He'll be fine," Tuck whispered back.

"You're honestly gonna say that with a straight face?" Hendrix asked.

Tuck ignored him and turned back to the team.

"I'mma make sure Cap makes it home, boys. Make it an early night of it, eh," Tuck said.

"Yeah, for sure," Glaz said. Tuck didn't believe him, of course, since Glaz wasn't even fucking looking at him, instead focusing his attention on the redhead.

"You got it, Tuck," Chary said, giving him a bullshit grin. Tuck shook his head. He knew those assholes weren't gonna listen. But it had to be said anyway.

He turned back to Hendrix, who watched him with frustration. He understood where it was coming from, but Tuck was going to take care of this situation his way. Period.

"Don't worry about it," Tuck said. He slapped Hendrix's arm.

"Hendrix, you lose, man!" Cots yelled as Chary laughed and pulled Hendrix's card from the hat and raised it in the air. "Drinks on you, asshole!"

They handed him the tab.

"Ah, you cheatin' dicks," Hendrix said.

Tuck slowly backed out as Hendrix was engulfed by the team.

* * *

Mike stumbled out of the bar into the cool night air and leaned against the door as it closed. He stood there for a second trying to make the world stop spinning before the door banged his head and back as someone tried to open it.

"Oh," he grumbled. He stepped away and looked back. Two young girls wearing low-cut shirts and short shorts said something to him. He wasn't sure what. Maybe good luck? He mumbled something back and waved them off as he walked toward where he thought his SUV was in the lot. He slid his hand in his pants' pocket. No keys.

He patted his jacket down. No keys.

"Oh, fuck you."

Mike turned around and flipped off the bar as a chorus of laughs from people in the parking lot rippled around him. He dropped his fingers and when he did, he saw Tuck come out of the bar.

"Fuck." Mike turned and started walking toward the road. He'd fucking walk home.

"Can't wait to get you back," some guy said.

"Yeah sure," Mike mumbled. He flicked his hand in the general direction of the voice.

A girl said something to him.

"Whatever," Mike said back. He shrugged his left shoulder.

He stopped as a large, familiar fan climbed out of a tiny, used car. The guy slammed the door shut and turned. He recognized Mike immediately and stopped. A strange look crossed the man's face.

Damn. The guy didn't look much better than Mike did.

"Kirby," the man said. "I'm Kirby Clark. My daughter—"

"Yeah," Mike grunted. He tried to form the right words, but his mind was cloudy. "Casey, right? How is she?"

Kirby glanced down at his keys, shook them, then looked back to Mike. "She's uh…well."

Kirby searched the gravel for an answer, but there wasn't one to be found. "You think miracles are real, Mike?" Kirby asked with an embarrassed laugh.

Mike huffed a laugh and looked away, then back to Kirby. He shrugged. "Yeah, man. Sure."

Kirby nodded. Blinked away tears. Flicked a smile back at Mike.

"I hope you get back in the game," Kirby said. "If Casey can't get a miracle, I hope this team can. She'd love…," he cleared his throat, "she would love to see that before, uh...". He stopped as his eyes glistened.

The weight of Kirby's words sat like dumbbells on Mike's shoulders; the same way he always carried the weight of expectations from all his fans. They all wanted miracles. Whether it was as simple as a win to cheer up their day or a championship ring to fill the city's coffers, there was no end to the asks the team fielded on and off the ice.

Mike winced. Normally, he handled them all in stride. Mike was nothing without his fans; he treated them as such.

But when he looked in Kirby's eyes, somehow, this time felt different. Heavier. Like mercury in his blood. Kirby needed a miracle Mike couldn't deliver; in fact, Mike seemed to be coming up short of all kinds of miracles these days.

"I gotta go," Mike mumbled as he staggered away toward the road. He squeezed his arms; his whole body ached. Mike glanced over his other shoulder. Tuck was nowhere to be found.

Did I hallucinate him?

Mike looked down at the road and tried to stay on the yellow line, but his feet weren't cooperating.

"Get in."

Mike knew that was Tuck. He turned to see Tuck's black Escalade, the passenger window rolled down, and his friend sitting patiently in the driver's seat, creeping slowly along next to him.

Mike stopped and so did the Escalade.

"Mike, get in," Tuck ordered.

Mike exhaled a long breath and got in the car.

21

In the Dirt

Ana startled awake at the sound of her father yelling.

"What?" She shook herself conscious and listened carefully, her tired eyes drooping and begging for sleep. She hoped it wasn't another night like the last few since Pops died. Screaming. Yelling. Drunken fits. What would it be about it this time? Hendrix? Tuck? Pops? Bella? Coach?

She sat up and strained to hear the familiar notes of his anger ratcheting up as her heart fluttered with anxiety. Something had been going wrong with her dad for a while.

But now, it was much, much worse.

Who's that?

She heard another male voice in her house, whispering, and then Bella rushing down the stairs.

Tuck!

"Oh, thank God," she whispered. Relief flooded every cell in her body. *Was Jaime with him?*

She jumped out of bed and quietly opened her door, checking first on her siblings. Johnny's door was open; Piper's was closed. She tip-toed down to Johnny's room and glanced in. He was sound asleep. *Good.* She quietly pulled his door shut. She cracked open Piper's door and peered in. *Asleep.*

She quietly closed Piper's door and went back down the hallway. She got low by the open railing. Tuck half-carried her dad into the kitchen. No Jaime.

"Oh my God," Bella said as she helped. Her look was panicked. Her mother looked like how Ana felt the other day with her father. She winced at the sight. *Maybe mom doesn't know what to do, either.*

Tuck sat her dad down in a chair as he slumped backward, his head over the top of the padded back.

"Tuck, what happened?" Bella asked quietly. She touched Mike's face and her robe sleeves pulled back. Tuck gasped.

Ana had seen the bruising on her mom's wrist, but Tuck and Jaime hadn't.

"Bella, what the fuck?" he asked.

Good, now Tuck knew, too. And if Tuck knew, maybe he could help. And Jaime could help.

Tuck tried to take her arm and look at it as her dad lifted his head to see what was going on.

"It's nothing," her mom said, quickly pulling her hands back and stepping away from Tuck to the fridge and opening it.

"She's fine, Tuck," her dad bemoaned. "I'm fine. We're all fine. Christ!"

Tuck sighed as Bella closed the fridge and handed Tuck a sports drink. Tuck looked between them.

Come on, Tuck. Say something. Do something.

"He's gettin' worse."

Her mom nodded. "I know," she whispered.

Keep going, keep going.

"I think the trainers know somethin's up," Tuck said.

People know? Why aren't they doing anything?

"Oh shit," her mom said.

"Stop talkin' about me like I'm not in the room, you assholes," Mike yelled as he came in and out of consciousness. "Are you having an affair with him?"

Her dad leaned to the side making a vomiting noise but spit instead. Tuck grabbed one side of him, while her mom grabbed the other. They put him back into place.

Call Jaime! He's an N.P. He'll know what to do.

Her dad tried to settle down but then he glanced to her mom, then to Tuck, and took a swing at Tuck, falling off the chair onto the floor with a thud.

"Fuck," Ana whispered as tears hit her eyes. She gripped the railings. *Someone help him!*

"Jesus, Mike," her mom said as she tried to help him up.

"Christ," Tuck said as he pulled her mom away. "I've got him, Bella."

Tuck glanced at her dad and then her mom.

"I'll stay, okay?" Tuck said.

Oh, thank God. Ana exhaled a sigh of relief as she wiped the tears from her eyes. Tuck in the house meant they'd be safe for the night. Tuck wouldn't allow her dad to lose his shit with them. He'd rather die.

She could see the relief on her mom's face, too. Maybe her and her mom would be able to sleep tonight.

"Thank you," her mom said quietly.

"Of course," Tuck said.

"It'll be okay with Jaime?" she asked.

"Yeah," Tuck said. "He had to work earlier. He's in bed now. All good."

She nodded. "He have any advice?"

Tuck shrugged. "I haven't told him anything about this. Not yet."

Her mom nodded. Ana didn't get that. Why wouldn't he ask Jaime for help? Jaime would know what to do.

"Hey, baby," her dad slurred as he woke up again and saw her mom.

Bella shook her head with exhaustion. Ana felt that in her bones. Her and her mom were like walking Zombies.

"Get some sleep, Bella," Tuck said. "I got him, okay?"

She nodded, rubbed her wrist, and headed up the stairs. Ana quickly moved from the rails to her bedroom and slid into bed. Her emotions were running wild, but she couldn't pay attention to them right now.

Tuck was staying the night. She was gonna take advantage of that. She quieted her mind and curled into her blankets.

At least for tonight, they could rest without worry.

* * *

Tuck couldn't believe what he'd seen. Bella's wrist, bruised and red. She looked tired; scared. Something he'd never seen on her before. This was why Mike had kept him away. Why he hadn't had Tuck or Jaime over in the last couple months.

"Tuck! Are you faking gay so you can bang my wife?" Mike yelled.

"Jesus, man, no," Tuck said. He moved to his friend. He needed to get him out of the kitchen and to the couch to pass out. The last fucking thing this family needed right now was to see Mike like this.

This wasn't Mike. This wasn't even a fucking shadow of the friend he knew.

"Come on, man." Tuck got under his friend's arm and lifted him off the chair, helping him toward the living room.

"Tuck me in, Tuck," Mike said as he laughed. "Tuck, tuck, tuck, tuck, tuck, tuck."

Mike laughed at the clucking he was making as he lunged for the fridge, almost ripping Tuck's arm off. "I need water," Mike yelled.

"Fuck, Mike," Tuck yelped.

"No, wait, sports drink," Mike said as he tried to open the fridge, but couldn't get hold of the door.

"Stop!" Tuck got a hold of him and drug his ass to the living room.

"Christ. Couch!" Tuck ordered as he dropped his friend like a stone on the warm, brown leather.

"Where's Bella? Bella!" Mike yelled, trying to get up.

"Shut the fuck up, Mike," Tuck threatened. "You'll wake up your kids, you asshole."

Tuck wrestled Mike back down on the couch and gave him a hard shove to the chest as Mike looked at him surprised. Mike was skilled, but Tuck was a

146

tank. Mike wouldn't fuck with him for real. Not without getting his ass kicked, and he knew that.

There was a line Mike could cross with Tuck. And it started and ended with Mike's wife and children.

A hard look passed between them as Mike settled down at Tuck's warning stare. He started to drunk talk.

Tuck stepped away then and caught his breath for a second. He wished Jaime was here. For him. And for Mike. He'd know what to do medically.

But this wasn't just medical. There was a whole slew of bullshit intertwined with this. Mike's reputation. The family's reputation. The team's reputation. People would think Mike was an asshole. Mike wasn't an asshole. The pills had gotten one over on his friend. And what was it even? Temporary? Addiction? Christ, it couldn't be addiction, could it?

There had to be a way to help him without everyone fucking knowing Mike's business.

I need to tell Jaime.

Tuck wanted to. He just wasn't sure Jaime would understand. Or even that Jaime could keep it under the table. He had that whole oath thing. And Tuck didn't want to put his boyfriend in a precarious position like that.

"Tuck, tuck, tuck, tuck, tuck," Mike clicked as he zoned in and out.

"Right here, man. Relax," Tuck said. He gathered pillows and blankets, along with a trash can that he put next to Mike's head.

He stepped back and stared at Mike. He'd never seen him like this. Never. He honestly wasn't sure what to do.

Mike opened his eyes then and looked right at Tuck. "You know Pops is dead, right?"

Tuck's stare softened. "Yeah, man, I do. We all know."

"Does Pops know Pops is dead?" Mike laughed at himself.

"Jesus, man, you need to sleep. Seriously."

Tuck put one of the pillows under Mike's head, and the other between Mike's back and the couch. He needed to be propped up, so he didn't aspirate on his own vomit. Tuck laid the blanket over Mike and walked away.

"Tuck," Mike called out. Tuck turned back to his friend.

"Yeah, man, I'm here."

"I have to put him in the dirt tomorrow," Mike said quietly. "Everything my father did for me. And I'm gonna put him in a pile of fuckin' dirt."

Tuck couldn't stop his eyes from watering as tears formed in Mike's eyes. Not for long, though. The man who never laid a day on the ice would never permit that kind of weakness from showing through. Even to Tuck.

"Sleep, man," Tuck said.

"Sleep," Mike murmured. "In the dirt."

Tuck started to walk away but Mike called to him again.

"Should I cry, Tuck?" Mike asked. He stared at the ceiling. "Pops wouldn't like that. I don't think."

Tuck turned back to him again. "I don't know, man. I just know you're in pain. And we're gonna get you through it."

Mike looked straight at Tuck.

"What pain?" Mike asked as he closed his eyes and passed out.

Tuck sighed as he walked to the matching recliner across from his friend. He set himself up with a pillow and blanket and stared at Mike.

He glanced back to the kitchen, remembering Bella's wrist. Did the kids hear that? If they didn't hear it happen, they'd at least seen the bruising, he was certain. Ana didn't miss a fucking thing. What else had they seen?

He sighed. They couldn't have memories of their father like this. It wasn't their father. It wasn't Mike. This wasn't his friend.

Tuck shook his head, tossed the blanket, and stood up. He grabbed his phone from his pocket and scrolled through the contacts, found the right one, clicked the "call" button, and waited patiently for him to answer.

"Hey man. You got a second?"

He stared at Mike and started to talk.

22

Take it Back

The blurriness in Mike's mind made the memory of watching his father's casket go down in the rich, brown earth bearable. He stood in his parent's living room and watched as the people came and went, eating funeral food and giving their condolences.

His mother was wearing a black wrap dress with a tie at the waist; it was one of Pops' favorites. He had always complimented her when she had worn it for various events over the last few years. She had been furious this morning when she'd put it on. She came storming downstairs and almost broke the coffee pot as she shoved the grounds in it.

"Now I'm gonna have to burn it," she'd raged. And then she'd cried, and Bella had hugged her.

That was more affection than Mike had seen Bella show at any point today toward him. When he'd woken up, he'd been confused about why he was on the couch, his head pounding, his knee throbbing. He'd yelled for Bella, but she had been gone by then. The kids were gone. Tuck had appeared in the living room with a cup of coffee, dressed in his suit for the funeral.

"Get your ass up," he had said. And as Mike had struggled to stand, Tuck explained what happened the night before and what he knew. He had asked what Mike intended to do about it.

"I'm not addicted," Mike had defended. "I don't *need* the pills. It's just to help with the transition."

"But maybe you're not fully healed, Mike," Tuck had argued.

"I'm fine," Mike had fought back.

And then Tuck had said, in no uncertain terms, that he would be on his ass from then on out. Mike had limped away, shuffled to his room, struggled to shower, forced himself to get dressed, and for a moment, considered what he had said to Tuck—that he didn't need the pills. Then he had whispered to himself, "I can get through the day."

Mike had stood in front of his bedroom door for a solid ten minutes after that before he went to his closet, rustled around in his hockey bag, pulled a new baggy from it, chewed up about four pills, and shoved the rest in his pocket.

He had told himself that he just needed them for today, for the funeral. Then he'd quit.

He looked around his parent's house at the people milling about in various states of melancholy. He was stuck at this reception in a loop of sadness he couldn't get the fuck out of.

Pops would hate this shit.

He felt a stare on him and turned to glance at Tuck. Jaime had been at the funeral. He'd waited around until everyone had left, then walked over and shook Mike's hand. Mike caught the way Jaime had looked at him, like something was wrong with him. Tuck had walked Jaime to his car and gave him a quick kiss goodbye. Then Jaime had whispered something to Tuck, and Tuck had given him a look. It was the same look he was giving him now.

Mike jerked on his tie and shrugged his shoulder. What had Jaime said? That Mike was sick? Crazy? What?

And now, Hendrix was saying something to Tuck. Cots and Chary were listening, while Glaz mowed down meatballs. Were they fucking talking about him now, too?

"Sorry about Pops, Mike."

Mike turned his attention to the voice. Dani mother fucking Ashton. *Fuck.* The funeral was one thing. This was his father's home. He glanced to his mom, who smiled at him. His mother had invited her. *Christ.* He should have known. His parents loved Dani. They thought she'd been more than fair to him and the team over the years.

"Yeah. Thanks, Dani," he said half-heartedly. He needed a drink. His hands twitched and fidgeted.

"You doin' okay?" Dani asked. She searched his face. He reached up and straightened his tie, smoothed his hair, scratched his scruff.

"Thanks for comin'."

He limped away from her prying eyes and headed for the bathroom. He caught Bella's stare as he went. She barely looked at him, then turned away, adjusting the carefully placed cuff bracelet over her bruised wrist.

Where the fuck is the whiskey?

He secretly grabbed the bottle on the bar cart and put it inside his jacket as he hobbled away from the crowd and stumbled into the bathroom that was in his parent's bedroom.

Mike shut the door quietly, put the whiskey on the sink counter, and stared in the mirror. Now he understood why Jaime had looked him the way he had. Why Dani had asked if he was okay. His eyes were swollen and bloodshot, glassy. The scruff on his chin was wild and random. His hair still needed cut since the last time he looked at himself in the mirror. His suit was a mess. He looked disheveled at best.

"Shit." Bella had been right.

He turned on the faucet and splashed cold water on his face. Shut it off and moaned as his knee spasmed in pain. He leaned on the counter and his eyes glanced down at the toothbrush holder.

Two toothbrushes. One for his mother. One for…

He reached down and rubbed his knee as a groundswell of pain flooded his gut and threatened to work its way up his chest. He grabbed the baggy from his pocket, shook out a few of the pills, tossed them in his mouth, chewed them up, and washed them down with the whiskey.

He put the bottle down and the baggy back in his pants' pocket. He controlled the tidal wave rising in his chest and shoved it back down his own throat as he picked up the bottle again and took another long pull. He sat it back down and when he did, he glanced to the bottom of the bathroom door where he saw the shadow of feet.

He put the whiskey in the shower, then opened the door.

"What the fuck?" Mike spat.

"You're asking that of me?" Hendrix spat back.

"Stay out of it, you prick," Mike said, annoyed, as he tried to walk out. Hendrix prevented it, stepping in front of him.

"I care about this team and what you're doin' to it. To yourself."

"You've been here a minute. What do you know?" Mike hissed. "You destroy every team you're part of. Why do you think they traded you here? No one wanted you. Look at you right now. Approaching me here? Without my busted knee you're just a bullshit contract waitin' on a buyout."

"Fuck you." Hendrix gave Mike a small shove. "Without me your team's playin' golf at some wanna be club and your ass is camped on your couch without a career."

Mike shoved him back.

"Take it back."

"Take it back? We're not fucking five, take it back."

Hendrix shoved him again.

"Fuck off."

Mike tried to shove past him, but Hendrix wasn't budging.

"How many pills you takin' now? Four, five at a time?" Hendrix sniffed the air around Mike. "With whiskey now, too? Just like the asshole that killed my dad."

They gave each other little shoves as Mike stumbled backwards.

"I'll do whatever I have to do, to stop you," Hendrix threatened. "Know that."

Hendrix started to pat Mike down.

"Get the fuck off me," Mike hollered, grabbing Hendrix's wrist and shoving him backwards into the wall, knocking down a painting Bella had given his parents. "It's none of your business."

"Get the fuck off me," Hendrix yelled. He laid into Mike, who fought back mightily.

* * *

Bella knew the sound before she turned the corner to see Mike and Hendrix embroiled in a fight. Mike's fury knew no bounds these days and when he yelled, it came from a place inside him she didn't know anymore. It was like a howling animal.

"Bella, move," Tuck said, as he pushed her aside and ran in the bedroom, followed by Chary, Cots, and Glaz.

"Mike, fuckin' stop it," Tuck said as he grabbed his friend, and the others grabbed Teddy.

"Mike, stop!" Bella yelled frantically. This was just one more thing to push him over the edge, that could damage his knee even more, prevent him from playing, even.

"Lem'me go, Tuck!" Mike yelled.

Bella looked around her at the small crowd that had gathered. Their children. Marie. Dani Ashton among them. *Fuck.*

"Mike, please!" Bella yelled.

Mike glanced her way and quit struggling as Tuck released him. Mike pushed past Tuck and Bella, through the small crowd, and out the front door. Bella followed at a quick clip as she heard Teddy say, "His keys."

"Shit," Bella said as she quickened her pace. "Mike!"

She burst through the front door and saw Mike headed for the car.

"Mike, please," she yelled. "Please, stop!"

"Mike, stop!" Tuck yelled from right behind her.

"Mike!" Bella's voice must have been tinged with an urgency that got to him because he whipped around and faced her.

"Are you on their side now?" Mike screamed.

"I'm on your side. I'm always on your side. Just let me take you home."

She tried to take his keys as Marie ran outside and up to them.

"Michael Christopher Olsky! Stop this right now," Marie screamed. "Give Bella the keys and go home."

Bella had never heard her mother-in-law speak that way to Mike, but Bella could see that Marie now knew something was terribly wrong with her son.

"Your father would not want this," Marie said as the tears broke through and she began to sob. "Go home, Mike. Now!"

Mike stepped back from his mother's words like a wounded animal and threw the keys at Bella, barely missing her. Bella ducked, then quickly picked them up and glanced to Marie as Mike stumbled to the SUV and climbed in.

"Can the kids stay with you tonight?" Bella asked.

Marie nodded as she wiped her tears away then held her hand to her chest and nervously plucked at the black cloth.

"Ana," Bella said. She glanced to her daughter, already doing too much to hold them all together right now.

"I've got it, Mom," Ana said, stepping to her grandma and putting her arm around her waist to comfort her.

"I'll make sure they're okay," Tuck said.

Bella nodded to him as she turned and walked to the SUV, climbing in. She sat still for a moment in the cocoon of silence until her hands stopped shaking and the crowd outside had dissipated.

She looked over to Mike, who was drunk mumbling, unaware of her or anyone else.

She blinked back angry tears as she rubbed her cuff bracelet. She didn't know who this man was. Mike felt like a stranger to her.

She shook her head. No. Mike was still there. She just had to find a way to bring him back to her. She glanced to the porch and saw Dani standing there. She swallowed hard, started the car, and headed home.

* * *

Tuck glanced around at the mess that was now public knowledge to everyone still in attendance at Pops' wake.

"Ana, can you take Marie back in and get everyone settled?" Tuck asked.

"Yeah, Uncle Tuck," Ana said. She helped her grandma and her siblings back into the house as the crowd cleared.

"We're headed out," Chary said.

"Yeah, later," Tuck said. "Hey."

The boys turned back to him.

"No one needs to know about this, huh?"

"Yeah, no problem," Cots said, as Chary and Glaz nodded.

Dani walked off the porch. She glanced at Tuck, then got in her car and drove off.

"Fuck," he said quietly.

He turned his ire where it belonged.

"Jesus, man. What the fuck?" Tuck yelled at Hendrix.

"He's eatin' pain pills like fuckin' candy and you're jumpin' my ass?" Hendrix yelled back.

"You took it too far," Tuck hollered. "It's his father's funeral. Not your private counseling session to settle old ghosts. We're handling it."

"Is that what you call what happened today?" Hendrix asked sarcastically. "This is handling it?"

Tuck stepped back and took a deep breath. "You've been here two fucking seconds. You have no right to interfere with how I handle this."

The two challenged each other quietly with fierce stares. *Who the fuck does he think he is?*

"Fuck this." Hendrix flicked a hand at Tuck and walked to his truck, got in, and pulled out erratically.

Tuck watched him fly out of the driveway as his truck kicked dust in the air.

"This what you were talkin' about last night?"

Tuck glanced to the trainer, Beau, as he walked up and crossed his arms over his chest. Tuck nodded.

"Coach left, right?" Tuck asked.

"Hour ago," Beau answered.

"He know?"

"He suspects. Trainers know," Beau said. "And Doc. He won't give anymore scripts."

"Good. You give Coach the heads up about this? Dani was here. And too many people saw for her to stay quiet anymore."

Beau nodded. "Grief makes people act up. That'll be the official word."

Tuck nodded.

"What do we do?" Tuck asked.

"Doc's gonna get an MRI to see if the knee is actually healing," Beau said. "If it's the knee and there really is a new injury or it's overworked, we'll make a plan to address that."

"And if the knee is fine and this is…something else?"

"I'm on it," Beau said. "We'll cross that bridge when we get there."

23

Careful

PHL Cup Playoffs
Round One, Game Five

Columbus Thunder v. St. Louis Warriors
Series: Three-One
Columbus, Ohio

Mike's first game back after his dad's funeral was proving more difficult than he'd anticipated. He sat on the bench and tried to swallow air as fast as he could as the sweat poured like an open faucet down his face and neck. He was squirming in his own filth. How had his body forgotten the pace and effort required at this level?

He glanced at the scoreboard. They were tied at zeroes with thirty seconds left in the third. His performance was fucking lacking, and the team was waiting for the old Mike to return to form. Mike wasn't even sure if that guy existed anymore, not in its previous iteration, anyway.

Mike felt his heart start to slow a little and he was finally able to at least take a deep breath. Truth was, he had been concerned he'd even get the chance to play tonight. Doc had ordered that surprise MRI to check his knee and Mike thought for sure there would be damage.

What else could be causing this much pain?

But the results had shown that the knee had healed properly. So, any pain was a result of overworking the muscles and bands around it. It reaffirmed what Doc had said: No more pills. Injury healed. Switch to ibuprofen.

Mike fidgeted inside his gloves as he watched Tuck and Hendrix on the ice. He couldn't see Hendrix's face, but he knew the beating he'd given that asshole at his father's house left a black eye that was now turning a light green. Mike squeezed his hands. He hadn't had any alcohol in seventy-two hours. The pills on the other hand. Well, Bella and Tuck could only watch him like a hawk for so long.

The goal cannon booming cut through Mike's thoughts as he tuned back in. The team circled around Hendrix and banged his helmet.

"Fuck," Mike said under his breath. Of course it was Hendrix.

The crowd jumped up as the final buzzer sounded. Mike followed the team as they jumped the bench and circled around center ice, raising their sticks to the crowd. They were through round one, winning the series four games to one, and now they were on to round two to take on the Pittsburgh Scorpions. *Hate those fuckers.*

As Mike raised his stick, he glanced to Hendrix, who returned the same dislike. Mike shook his head, then skated to the glass and tossed his stick to a fan. Probably get some nice coin on eBay for that.

He skated off the ice and walked gingerly down the tunnel and into the locker room as the team filed

in. He had become an outsider to a team that was
supposed to be his.

Mike yanked his helmet off as he sat down at his
stall. He needed to get the weight off his knee. It was
healed, but it was overworked, and it still got sore
after games and practices. Mike quickly chewed two
pain pills as the Stache and his assistants breezed in.
He started pulling off his uniform and pads as
everyone else came in celebrating.

"Helluva win tonight, boys," the Stache yelled.
"You earned it. Round two!"

The room erupted into cheers as Mike quietly
rubbed his knee. A hand slapped his shoulder, and he
glanced over to Tuck who gave him a nod. Mike
nodded back.

"Tuck, do the honors."

Tuck pulled out the team's heavyweight champ
belt from his stall and grinned.

This was always Mike's favorite tradition, when
the players awarded other players for heroics. They
were all in the hunt, all in the battle, and there wasn't
anyone who knew what really went down on the ice
except for the guys in the room.

The belt meant something to all of them.

"Tough call," Tuck said. "Hendrix had the only
goal of the night."

The room cheered as Glaz slapped Hendrix's
shoulder. Mike dipped his head and stared at the floor
as he rubbed his knee. *Fuck that guy.*

"But Frenchie saved our asses on that PK in the
second. Protected the house," Tuck said. "Congrats,
man."

162

Mike nodded and clapped generously as he glanced to Frenchie with a grin. Frenchie gave him the nod as Tuck handed him the belt. The room cheered as Hendrix wiped the sweat from his face. Mike took pride in that asshole's shiner, visible to everyone. Hendrix glanced at Mike, and they shared a smirk.

"Speech, man, speech," Chary cheered.

Frenchie put the belt on and took center stage. Fuckin' guy was a character with that shoulder-length hair worthy of a Pantene commercial and tattoos on every inch of his flesh. Mike grinned.

Christ, he missed this.

"I suck at speeches," Frenchie said. "So, yeah, you're fuckin' welcome, alright. Bon wie!"

Mike laughed as the room cheered.

"Truly fuckin' terrible speech," Cots joked.

"Total bullshit," Chary agreed.

"Fuck you, guys," Frenchie said as he sat back down and gulped water.

"You earned it, Frenchie. Way to stand tall," the Stache said as he clapped. "And Hendrix, you didn't get the belt, but you've earned an 'A.'"

The room erupted into cheers as Mike's grin faded into rage. He swore to God his heart stopped beating for a second.

"You wear it next game," Coach said.

The world got quiet as Mike quickly put his things away and the team celebrated with Hendrix. Mike grabbed his shit, tucked his baggy into his towel, and headed to the showers with a slight limp as he heard the Coach tell the assistant, "Finish up with these guys."

Mike turned to see Coach right behind him as they walked into the shower area. Mike squeezed the towel closer to him, so the baggy stayed put. He didn't want to explain that to the Stache.

"Leadership in the room was a little lacking tonight," Coach quipped.

"I don't know what you're talkin' about," Mike said. Mike was trying to feign ignorance with the Stache, but it didn't work. The guy knew putting an "A" on Hendrix would light a fire under Mike's ass. Probably why he fucking did it.

"You haven't been the guy I bet this team's future on since you came back," the Coach said, shoving his hands in his pockets and shrugging.

"You mean your future."

"Careful." The Coach whipped his hand out of his pocket and pointed it at Mike as he leveled a stare at him.

Mike turned away from the warning shot and looked around the shower as the Coach reset himself, putting his hand back in his pocket.

"You still hurtin'?" Coach asked.

"Nope. Good," Mike said. *Toe the line and I can get out of this bullshit conversation.*

Beau walked in and set about putting towels in the shower area. Coach glanced at him, then back to Mike.

"That bullshit?" Coach asked.

"I'm fine," Mike said. "I'm your guy. I'm everybody's guy."

"I'll have Doc check you out."

"He already did. The other night."

"Maybe I'll just have him do it again. And then again. And then again."

Mike clenched his jaw as he played hide-the-lying-bullshit with his Coach. *All eyes on me. Got it.*

"Like I said, I'm fine," Mike said quietly. "You made the right bet. Just an off night. I'm still the captain."

Mike wasn't sure why, but something in the Stache's face made him ask, "I am still the captain, right?"

Coach nodded.

"It's not easy losin' a father," Coach said. "The boys are here for you. You know, when you don't beat the shit out of 'em."

Beau handed Coach the paper. *What the fuck?* Beau and Coach were Abbott and fucking Costello now? Trainers were in on this, too?

Coach shook the paper open to the front of the sports section and turned it to Mike. Mike had seen the story. It had been below the line, but it was still three hundred words of ink about Mike losing his shit. It was all over the fucking Internet and social media, too. Bella had told him Ana was already hearing it at school. Piper, too, and Johnny.

"Take a week," Coach said. He handed the paper back to Beau.

"I don't need—"

"I'm not askin'," Coach said smoothly. "Clean yourself up. We can wait to have you for the next round. We'll tell the media it's…I don't know, Beau?"

Coach glanced at Beau, who finished folding the paper back to its original form. Beau shrugged.

"Grief, maybe? Flare up?" Beau suggested.

"What the fuck ever. I don't care," Coach said. He shrugged, then turned to Mike. "Hendrix might be your doppelganger on the ice, Mike. But he's not you."

Mike looked at the Stache then.

"I need your ass on the ice and in the room if we're gonna pull this off. You fuckin' hear me?"

Mike nodded.

"Tell me you fuckin' hear me," Coach ordered.

Mike shifted his weight under the Stache's glare.

"I hear you," Mike said quietly.

"Good."

Coach grinned as he slapped Mike's arm and walked out. Mike eyed Beau.

"What the fuck, Beau?" he asked.

Beau walked up to him and slid something into the newspaper, then handed it to Mike.

"A little extra reading for later," Beau said. He slapped Mike's arm and walked out.

Mike opened the paper and pulled out a pamphlet. His heart ticked up a notch as he read it. He swallowed hard, put it back in the paper, and put the paper aside on the sink. He shook the baggy from the towel, picked it up, went to the shower and turned it on. He dumped the pills onto the drain and crushed them down with his heel as they broke apart and

166

dissipated down the drain. He threw the baggy away and looked in the mirror.

Fuck.

He swallowed hard, limped to the shower, and got in.

24

We Can Fix This

Ana stopped typing her homework as she heard her dad pull into the garage. Piper was at a friend's house for a party and Johnny was at a sleepover, so it was just her and her mom. She quietly got up and glanced out her door. Her mom must have been downstairs. She tiptoed to the railing and glanced over.

Yep, mom's drinking wine. Ana ducked down into her position at the railing and waited as her dad came in. *Oh no.* He didn't look dazed tonight, but he did look like he was in a lot of pain as he limped in.

"Oh, fuck. What? What now?" he said as soon as he saw her mom.

"Nothing, I...," Bella stuttered, exasperated.

Don't yell at him, mom. Don't get him started.

"Mike?" Bella put down her wine and walked quickly to her dad, helping him sit down at the kitchen island. She looked at him for a few seconds.

"Are you off them?" she asked.

Off what? The pain meds? Was that the problem?

She saw her dad pull a newspaper out from his bag, lay it on the island, and open it. There was another piece of paper inside of it, but Ana couldn't tell what it was. Her mom picked it up, then shook her head.

"Wait...this is for addiction," she said quietly.

Addiction? There was no way.

"Where did you get this?" her mom asked.

"What does it matter where I got it. It's what everybody thinks."

Her mom shook her head.

"No. No, Mike."

"Coach told me to take a week."

She shook her head harder and tore up the pamphlet, then threw it away.

"What are you doing?" her dad asked. "This is what you wanted."

He rubbed his knee as he eyed her. Ana didn't understand the look that passed between them.

Why wouldn't her mother want her dad to get help?

"You don't think I need help?" he asked.

"I mean, this isn't addiction, right? I mean, *addiction*? Are we going that far with this, Mike?" her mother asked. "No one has said it's addiction. Maybe it's just, like, a bit of reliance. A dependency. And we can fix that. You and me. Like dieting. Or cutting back on alcohol."

Ana furrowed her brow as she watched them. Her mom had a point. Ana had a hard timing believing this had gone as far as saying her dad was addicted.

"We have our kids to think about, Mike," her mom said. She walked over and took his face in her hands. "Rehab would be in the papers. Ana is already hearin' it at school about the funeral fight. Piper, too. Johnny."

Ana smirked. Jerks at school. If her dad was winning, nobody said anything. But now, Ana heard about it every day, from dumb guys saying, "Don't

come at me like your dad, Ana," to teammates
saying, "Tempers run in the family, Ana?" Stupid.

She'd take it if her dad needed the help. But
maybe it hadn't gone that far?

He's better tonight.

"Mike, we can do this, right? You and me. We're a
team. We'll be okay," her mom said, almost begging.
"And you can go back in a few days or so like Coach
said, take some ibuprofen and…"

Her mom drifted off as she looked at her dad and
her eyes teared up.

"Am I wrong?" she asked.

"No," her dad said quietly. "We can fix it. You
and me."

Ana sighed a breath of relief as her parents
hugged. It was the first time they'd touched each
other like that in weeks. When her mom pulled away,
she tossed the newspaper, too.

"Let's go to bed," she said.

Ana quietly moved to her room and hid behind the
door until she heard her parents go into their bedroom
and shut the door. She peered out and waited until the
TV switched on in their room, then she quietly
moved down the stairs to the kitchen and opened the
trash.

She pulled out the paper and put it on the island,
then she carefully picked out all the torn pieces and
laid them on it. She folded it up and went quickly
back to her bedroom, shutting the door.

She dumped the pieces onto her bed and carefully
put them back together.

"What the hell," she whispered as she read the cover: "Pathway to Hope Treatment Center."

No. Her mother was right. It hadn't gotten this far. It was dependency, not addiction.

She was sure of it.

25

Secret Stash

Two weeks later

PHL Cup Playoffs
Round Two, Game Four

Columbus Thunder v. Pittsburgh Scorpions
Series: Three-Zero
Pittsburgh, Pa.

Bella sat with Johnny on their plush leather living room couch as the air conditioner cooled the house and the television showed Mike in the face-off circle.

"Come on, Dad," Johnny cheered. He was sitting on the edge of the couch, a "PHL Playoffs" ball cap relaxing backwards on his head.

"They're gonna lose," Piper said from the recliner across from them. Her blonde hair was in a bun on top of her head, and she was wrapped in one of the gray chunky knit blankets from the bin. "They're not even showing the upper deck anymore."

"Yeah, Bones took off his wig."

The kids sighed in disappointment as Mike lost the face-off and drew a bad penalty.

"It's four to one, mom," Piper said.

"I know, sweetie," Bella said. Her brow wrinkled up as she rubbed her temples and listened to the play-by-play announcer.

"They had a chance to close this series out, but they just couldn't get it done, Gar," Color Commentator Rick Cotter said over the action as they watched.

"The Scorpions will go on the power play with three minutes remaining in the third," play-by-play announcer Gary Grines said.

Bella knew both men. They'd been to Mike and Bella's home for dinner several times, and for holiday parties. She hated hearing those words come out of their mouths as the camera panned to Mike in the penalty box, leaning his head back, sweating, and tired.

"Looks like Pittsburgh will go home with the win tonight," Grines said as Ana walked into the living room from her workout. She was dripping with sweat.

"You should'a sent him," Ana said to Bella.

"Excuse me?" Bella asked as she turned around to see her daughter lean against the island.

Ana pulled the taped-back together pamphlet out of her workout pants pocket and held it up.

"Where did you get that?" Bella asked, standing up. *How the hell?*

"Being home didn't help like you said it would," Ana spat. "He's got a secret stash, Mom. Look at him. He's not any better. His eyes are glassy again. He's getting mean again."

"That's enough," Bella said.

"Wait, what's going on? What is that?" Johnny asked as he looked at Ana.

"It's rehab, stupid," Piper said as she glanced at it from her spot closest to Ana.

"Piper don't call him stupid," Bella criticized.

"Rehab? For Dad?" Johnny asked.

"No. It's nothing. Jesus, Ana." Bella glared at her daughter. *Seriously, what the fuck?*

Ana smirked and walked away.

"He's fine," Bella said to anyone who was listening. "Your dad's fine."

Bella smiled tersely and walked out of the room, up the stairs, and slammed her bedroom door. Then she quietly opened it and listened.

"Seriously, dad's in rehab?" Johnny asked.

"No, dummy," Piper spat. "But he should be."

Bella closed the door as Piper walked upstairs.

She glanced at Mike's sketch of her. Simpler times. Easier problems.

What was she going to do now?

26

Career Suicide

Hendrix glanced around at the team, tired and defeated as the plane prepared for takeoff back to Columbus. He flicked an annoyed look to Mike, who sat by himself in the back.

The guy had everyone fooled. He had been good for about a day or two after the Stache laid it out for him, and then Teddy had seen him pilfering pain pills into his sports drink and sucking on it during practice.

Teddy quickly shut his eyes as Mike turned in his direction. He waited a beat, then reopened his eyes and turned to see Mike reach into his jacket and pull something out, then slide something into his mouth and chew.

Mother fucker.

"Alright, off tomorrow," Coach said. "Practice Saturday. Get some rest and come back ready for game five."

Mike fidgeted as the Coach eyed him. The minute Coach turned away, Mike finished chewing, took a long swig from his water bottle, then shut his eyes as he stretched his knee.

Hendrix quickly picked up his phone. He pulled up a contact and started to text, then stopped. He put his phone down. If he did this, he'd be putting his whole career at risk; betraying his brothers. He looked

around at the boys. These were the guys he battled
for every night. He'd be a fucking traitor.

He picked up his phone and scrolled through his
photos to the one with the last words from his dad.

Luv u.

He glanced at Mike then wrote the text.

* * *

Dani Ashton exhaled tiredly in the airport terminal
as she waited for her plane to board while talking to
Ed.

"No, no confirmation Mike was in rehab or wasn't,
or anything," she said into her cell phone. "Just some
bullshit about grief or something."

"So, no story," Ed said loudly as she held the
phone away from her ear.

"I guess. I, uh," Dani said, then paused as she
heard a ding. "Hang on a second, Ed."

Dani pulled the phone from her ear and looked
down at it as she read the text that had come through.

Hendrix: *No rehab. But he needs it. Pain pills.*

"Ed? Give me a minute. I'll call you back."

"Alright."

Dani stared at the text for a second as she thought
through the information she was getting. Was
Hendrix a reliable source? Yes and no. On the one
hand, the kid had proven himself to be a fairly stand-
up guy. Down-to-earth, for the most part. He was a
bit of a scoundrel when it came to the ladies, but

176

overall, decent. On the other hand, it was no secret him and Mike were at each other's throats. Would the guy do anything to get Mike out of the game and take his spot? Like leak a fake story to the press?

Tread lightly.

Dani: *Career suicide anyone finds out this was you.*

Dani nervously looked around as a long pause ensued. Finally, her phone dinged again, just as they started boarding the plane.

Hendrix: *Then keep it to yourself. Just make sure he doesn't take another pill.*

Dani texted her questions and got herself ready for the ire about to come her way from every direction.

And she wouldn't be the only one.

27

Hat Trick

PHL Cup Playoffs
Round Two, Game Five

Columbus v. Pittsburgh
Series: Three-One
Columbus, Ohio

Mike slowly glanced around at the Columbus arena crowd from the Thunder bench. His body was in more of a relaxed hunch than it probably should have been. Fans held "Beat Pittsburgh" signs against the glass next to signs bearing his name and number. They were glad to have him back at this crucial moment. If the team won tonight, they'd be in the Eastern Conference battle, the last stop before the PHL Cup Finals.

"Let's go!" the Stache yelled. The excitement was building on the bench as the second period ticked down with one minute left and them leading by one.

Mike leaned forward on the wall and spit on the floor as he slowly glanced in Hendrix's direction. He thought the guy was looking at him, but things were a little fuzzy. His knee was acting up, but not nearly like it was.

He turned to the action on the ice. Who was out there again? Tuck. Cots. Glaz. Cots rushed down the ice and Mike knew in his bones that the kid was gonna score.

Boom!

The goal cannon sounded as Mike grinned. The group huddled, smacking Cots' helmet. They had a two-goal lead as the period ending buzzer sounded and they headed down the tunnel. He took his time, ignoring most everyone. He thought he heard Tuck. Maybe. Maybe not.

Mike went straight to the bathroom as the team's enthusiasm filled the locker room. He closed the stall door and pulled his baggy out from inside the toilet cover holder. *Good spot.* No one fucking used those things. He grinned at how smart he was.

Mike quickly dumped four pills out into his hand and tossed them in his mouth as he started chewing.

Wait, what's that?

Concern crossed his face as he noticed how badly his hands were shaking.

"What the fuck?" he said quietly. He shook his hands in the air, trying to stop the involuntary movement, but it didn't work.

What the hell is that?

The stall door swung open, pushing Mike back as the baggy dropped. "Someone's in here, asshole," Mike yelled. He couldn't believe he forgot to lock the door.

"Makin' sure you stay in the game?" Hendrix eyed him.

"Fuck off," Mike spat.

He shoved Hendrix into the door as he walked out and into the locker room. He sat in his stall as Tuck walked over.

"Hey man, we need to talk," Tuck said.

"Fuck off," Mike said.

"What the fuck did you say to me?"

Mike looked up at Tuck. This was the last fucking thing he needed right now. "I said, fuck off."

Tuck stepped back in surprise as the coaches walked in and launched into some bullshit about the game. Mike just sat and waited for the calm to come.

The next thing he knew, guys were cheering and heading out the door. He grabbed his shit and focused enough to stand as he followed them back to the ice.

"Mike, get your ass out there," Coach yelled.

Mike shook his head. When had he gotten to the bench? He glanced at the Coach and nodded, then hopped on the ice into the face-off. He could do this blindfolded in the dark. He quickly swept up the puck and before the defense could even move, Mike whipped it up and netted the goal.

Boom!

The goal cannon sounded as his teammates banged his helmet. That was his second of the night. When had he scored the first one? Apparently, he was one goal away from a hat trick. It would cement him back into the team. They'd love him again if he could bring back the guy they all knew.

He glanced at Hendrix, who was giving him the evil eye from the bench.

Yeah. Suck my dick.

Mike took his love from the team and the crowd as he hopped on the bench with a wide, hazy grin.

* * *

Bella watched the game from the player's wives' room. She couldn't take the crowd tonight or the questions. She just wanted to be here for Mike. And if she was honest, to see what was happening in the rink.

She stood nervously at one of the television screens by herself as the other wives and girlfriends talked quietly amongst themselves. She'd been so excited to see Mike get his second goal, but when she turned to smile at the other women, they had given her half-ass, tepid looks.

Their partners are telling them something about Mike. What?

Bella stayed off to herself as she watched the screen. The television showed Mike and Hendrix near each other on the bench. Coach waved them out together and the two jumped on a line.

"Hat trick, baby, come on," Bella said under her breath.

The Scorpions had the puck as Mike and Hendrix got into the rush. Mike picked off a pass and rushed to the net with Hendrix in tow. Mike passed it to Hendrix as Scorpions' defenders moved in. Mike headed to the doorstep for the pass.

"Come on, baby," she whispered.

Hendrix gave him a look then held the puck until a defenseman covered Mike.

"What the fuck?" Bella hissed. *That asshole.*

Hendrix took the shot himself through heavy traffic and the red light flared.

Anger and fear rushed through Bella as the goal cannon sounded.

This would set Mike off again. And she'd be the recipient of his ire. Her and Ana. Maybe she could talk up the fact that they were headed to the conference finals and that would satisfy him; keep his rage at bay.

She glanced around the room as the other ladies filed out, giving her concerned looks.

Her breaths came heavy and hard as her heart ticked up.

Fuck.

She turned back to the television and watched as the team circled up and gave a nod to the fans.

28

Better Vision

Teddy walked into the locker room and went straight to his stall, undressing as sweat poured down his body. He checked his phone quickly: a few texts from a couple hotties he might bang later, Cots letting him know they were going to Glaz's place after the game, and one from Dani two minutes ago.

Dani Ashton: *Was Mike taking pills in tonight's game?*

He glanced at Mike as he turned the phone repeatedly in his hand. The captain was already undressed and sitting dejected in his stall.

What am I doing?

He opened his phone and deleted the texts from Dani, then threw it back in his stall.

Teddy had never acted this poorly toward a teammate. Never. Ratting him out to the press? Stealing a hat trick? Being a dick, generally? *Fuck.* He shook his head. His dad's death had triggered the shithead that lived inside of him. Off the ice it had been skipping out on events, not hanging out with teammates, keeping to himself. On the ice it had been poor performance, unnecessary fights, and dumb penalties.

He threw his clothing in the bin and sighed. He flicked his stare at Mike again.

Teddy had never been like this though, the way he was with Mike. Then again, most guys didn't fight as hard as Mike to ignore their fucking problems. When was Mike going to get the hint and get help?

All Teddy could see when he looked at Mike was Carter fucking Jenkins. How many fucking people had been in a position to change the outcome of what happened to his dad that night and didn't do it?

Teddy felt his blood run like hot oil in a car. He wouldn't be able to live with himself if Mike hurt someone like that and Teddy had a chance to stop it.

As if on cue, Mike turned a stony stare to Teddy. They shared a glare as Cots walked in and slapped Mike's shoulder.

"Next time, Cap," he said as Chary followed up.

"Yeah man, next time."

Tuck strode in and hollered, "Playin' for conference champs!"

The room cheered as the guys started celebrating. Tuck glanced at Mike with a concerned look, then anger. Teddy's brow furrowed. That was unusual for Tuck to ignore Mike. But here he was, getting undressed and talking to everyone in the room except Mike.

Did Mike cross a line with Tuck?

A vibration in his stall made Teddy grab his phone and glance at his texts.

Dani Ashton: *I just have a couple questions.*

Teddy deleted the message and threw his phone back in the stall, harder this time, and stripped off the remainder of his gear as Mike headed to the showers.

"Mike, media's gonna wanna talk to you," Howie said as he breezed in.

Mike stopped, sighed, and came back.

184

"You, too, Hendrix," Howie said.

"Yep," Teddy sighed.

The two eyed each other as they grabbed their stuff and went to talk with the media.

"I fuckin' love you guys," Glaz said as they walked out.

Teddy half-laughed as the room erupted in celebration. Teddy wasn't doing any of his teammates any favors by keeping up this bullshit rivalry. His dad would never approve of this kind of behavior.

Teddy had to find a way to get through to Mike without fucking with him anymore.

* * *

The locker room was mostly cleared out as Mike walked back in with only a slight limp, his fogginess wearing off. The media satisfied with their pound of flesh. The boys were probably already out celebrating without him. He shrugged his left shoulder and cracked his neck.

Hendrix walked in after him and they both went to their stalls to finish up. Mike would just shower at home. Fuck staying here with this asshole.

He eyed Hendrix as the kid's phone went off. He looked irritated when he deleted the message, then he shut off the phone, and threw it back in his locker. Mike shook his head.

"So, what? Didn't have a fuckin' lane tonight?" Mike smirked. "Thought you had better vision than that."

Mike glanced at Hendrix as the kid paused for a moment and let out a sigh.

"Scored, didn't I?"

"Selfish," Mike said. "That's why you're on your third team in three years."

"You have everybody fooled, don't you?" Hendrix asked as he turned and faced Mike.

"I could say the same for you. Mr. Nice Guy comin' in. Bullshit." Mike faced Hendrix and gave him a little push.

Hendrix stumbled a little but stopped as he glanced at Mike.

"I don't wanna dance with you, Mike," Hendrix said. He raised his hands in a stop motion.

Punk mother fucker. First, he was on Mike's ass, agitating him, then he stole his hat trick, and now that piece of shit was acting like the good guy?

"Oh, fuck you," Mike sneered as he lunged for the kid.

"Mike, stop," Hendrix said as he stepped aside. Mike caught the side of Hendrix as his knee buckled underneath him, and he fell to the ground.

"Fuck!" Fuckin' knee had a nasty habit of spasming at the most inopportune times.

"Shit," Hendrix sighed as he slowly moved to help him. "Let me hel—"

Mike slapped Hendrix's hand away as he gingerly stood.

"Get off me."

"Mike, listen, I—"

"Go fuck yourself, Hendrix," Mike snarled as he grabbed his stuff and stormed out of the locker room as best he could with his sore knee.

"Mike, come on," Hendrix yelled, but he didn't follow.

Good. I don't need him. I don't need anybody on this fucking team.

Mike glanced down and halted. He held his visibly shaking hands in front of his face.

"What the fuck?" he whispered.

He grabbed the second stash of pills from a hidden compartment in his bag and looked around. It was empty save a few faint voices and footsteps further into the bowels of the arena. He took four, chewed them up, swallowed. There were only three left. He shrugged his left shoulder and cracked his neck. He dumped the remaining three into his mouth and chewed those down, too.

He violently shook his hands until he felt he'd shaken out the vibrations, then stuffed them into his pockets.

It wasn't the pills. He was just upset. Yeah, that was it. He just needed to get home and everything would be fine.

29

Cover Your Ears

Ana gave Johnny a dirty look across the kitchen island as she leaned back on the bar stool and smirked.

"You two are conspiring against me," she said. She flicked a frown to Piper, who laughed like an evil genius. The television blared in the background. They were talking about tonight's big win and the team heading to the Eastern Conference Finals. Hendrix and her dad both had good games and their interviews with the media afterward were great, like nothing was wrong.

Oscar-worthy performances.

Ana was a player. She knew Teddy had held the puck on purpose and prevented her dad from getting a hat trick. She didn't know what was going on there, but she did know that her dad would be pissed, her mom would be to blame, and Ana needed to get her siblings to bed so they didn't see any of it.

"We can't help it if you're terrible at Monopoly," Piper quipped.

"Yeah," Johnny added. "Dad won, you lost. Get over it. Now go get us our ice cream bars."

"Fine," Ana said. "Clean this up, go to your rooms, and I'll bring you your ice cream. Then, bed."

Ana gave them a stern look that they laughed off as she went out to the freezer in the garage to get the cheery treats. She shuffled through the various flavors.

"Mint chocolate chip Klondike or Magnum dark chocolate and strawberry?" she pondered. She jumped as the garage doors opened simultaneously. "Holy shit."

Ana stepped off to the side to avoid the cars as her dad pulled in first, erratically, almost hitting the freezer.

"What the hell?" Ana said as she moved back further.

Her mom came in next as her dad put his car into park then pulled something from his glove box and fidgeted.

Her parents glanced at each other as her mom shut off her car and her dad put whatever was in his hands into his jacket and quickly got out.

"Great game, babe," her mom said as she got out of the car. "You looked more like yourself."

Her dad moved hastily into the house.

"Mike?" she yelled as she followed him in.

"Oh shit," Ana whispered. She followed behind them, moving past them undetected through the other rooms, then up the stairs, and getting into her perch at the top of the railing.

"Mike, stop," her mom said as she chased him through the kitchen.

"Good game, Dad, congrats," Johnny said.

"Yeah, Dad," Piper echoed.

The two looked confused as their father practically ran past them up the stairs.

"What's wrong with him?" Johnny asked their mom, who was pursuing him.

"Nothing. Everything's fine," she said hastily as she threw her purse on the island.

Her mom trailed her dad as he rushed up the stairs and into their bedroom. She was right behind him and slammed the door as she hurried in.

Ana closed her eyes against the screaming coming from inside their bedroom.

"What the hell, Bella?" Mike yelled.

"I was talking to you; didn't you hear me?" she shouted.

Ana peered down over the staircase as Piper and Johnny walked to the bottom of it. Ana whispered down to them.

"Piper. Get Johnny and go to your room. Now."

Piper grabbed Johnny and moved hurriedly up the stairs.

Ana tip-toed to their parent's door and listened as Piper and Johnny ducked into Piper's room.

As the arguing intensified, Ana crossed the hall and peered into Piper's room. Piper and Johnny sat down against the wall and Piper held Johnny.

"Cover your ears," Piper ordered him.

"I'm scared," Johnny whispered.

"It'll be okay. Cover your ears."

He did as he was told. Piper held him tighter, then covered his hands with her hands.

A look crossed between the sisters.

"Stay here until it's quiet," Ana said.

"Okay."

Ana shut the door and went back to her parent's door and listened.

* * *

Bella couldn't believe they were back here again. It was like being trapped in a small, dark room with no light, no door, and no way out.

"Gimme them," Bella ordered.

"No." Mike pulled off his suit jacket and tie and tossed them on the bed.

"I got a call today. Someone asking for you. Saying they had your medication ready. Said he was a friend of Maize. What the fuck, Mike?"

"Why the fuck did you answer it?" He ripped off his dress shirt and threw it at her as she swatted it away.

"Not the point, and you know it. I'm worried. So is Tuck."

"Fuck Tuck." Mike started pacing.

"Jesus, Mike," Bella said tearfully. She shook her head at him. "The other wives look at me like something's up. Like they know something I don't."

"Fuck them, they don't know anything, Bella."

"A few days off…it didn't help, Mike. I know you're taking them again," she said. She steeled her nerves against the anxiety rushing through her veins. "Are you faking the prescriptions? How are you getting them?"

"It's easier than you think."

She quickly noticed that he couldn't control his body fidgeting or the shaking of his hands. *My God, his hands.*

"Mike," she said, reaching for them. He swatted her away.

"You can't stop, can you? The pills. You can't quit. Mike!"

"I just need to take—"

"No! I should have taken you," Bella yelled. She blocked his way to the bathroom.

"Bella!"

As he shoved past her, she grabbed the pills bulging out of his pocket. He grabbed them back as she grabbed them again. She tried to pull them out of his grip.

"Bella, stop!"

"I'll take you myself."

Just then, Ana cracked open the door to check on them.

"Ana, leave!" Bella ordered, distracted by her daughter's sudden appearance.

Mike jerked her close, his elbow raised.

"Bella, stop!" he screamed.

"Let go!"

The next few seconds moved like some super slow-motion movie clip. Bella had enough awareness to know the pointy part of his elbow had been right near her right eye. She thought he had enough awareness to know that, too. But, when he tried to jerk the pills out of her hands, he boxed her out like she was an NBA player with the ball.

The pain of her husband's elbow was unlike anything she'd ever felt before. He was twice her weight and six inches taller, and he put all of it behind the elbow bone that cracked into her small face.

First, she saw a bright light like an explosion in her retina, then she tasted enough blood that she needed to swallow it, and finally, she could feel the warm, gooey liquid spilling into her hands from her nose as they covered her face.

"Oh shit, Bella..."

"Get away from me," Bella screamed as she dropped like a stone then crawled away from him.

"Mom!" Ana shouted.

Bella collapsed on the floor, writhing in pain, as she gripped her face and Ana came through the door. Bella looked up at her and blood poured from her nose.

"No, Ana, stay back," she yelled as blood poured into her mouth and down her sweater onto the carpet.

"What did you do?" Ana screamed as she turned toward her dad.

"I saw you!" Ana screamed.

"It was an accident, Ana," Mike said, shaking his head. Bella could see he was panic-stricken at what he'd done. "Bella..."

Ana ran over and pushed Mike.

"Stay away from her!"

"Ana, stop!" Mike yelled.

He grabbed Ana's fists and she jerked away, shoving him.

"Don't touch her, Mike!" Bella said, trying to get up, but her head wouldn't allow it. It was spinning and anything vertical was making her want to puke.

"You gonna hit me, too?" Ana screamed. "Get out! Now!"

Johnny rushed in with Piper right behind him. Johnny gasped at what he saw and froze in place.

"Johnny, no, wait!" Piper yelled.

Piper got to the door and took in the scene.

"Oh my God. Mom!"

Piper shoved past Johnny, who backed into a corner. Piper ran to Bella as Ana got in Mike's face.

"Get out! Get the fuck out. Now!"

Ana squared up to her father as he stumbled back, surprised.

"Ana, stop…" Bella mumbled through her bloody hands now covering her nose and mouth as her vision blurred from the pain.

Mike raced out the bedroom door and down the stairs as Ana grabbed her phone and started to dial 911.

The media.

Bella moved quickly and slapped the phone away from Ana as she grabbed Mike's shirt from the floor and put it to her nose to stop the bleeding. The world spun as she tried not to vomit.

The kids were stunned.

"You need an ambulance," Ana said.

"Tuck'll know what to do," Bella responded. "Phone."

She reached out her bloody hand to Ana, who just stood there. "Ana. Phone!"

Ana finally relented as Bella took it and dialed Tuck's number with bloody fingers. Ana shook her head.

"You'll do anything to protect him."

"I'm protecting *you*. You call the squad, Dani fucking Ashton follows. Just get me ice and open the door for Tuck."

Ana shook her head in disbelief.

"Fine."

"Tuck?" she whimpered.

Ana started to leave.

"Ana, wait," Bella said tearfully. "I know what you saw, but this…this was an accident."

"No such thing."

Ana left the room as Bella heard Tuck say, "I'm on my way."

"Okay, thanks, bye."

Piper stared at Bella as Bella hung up the phone.

"It was an accident, Piper…Johnny…I swear to you."

"I believe you," Piper said quietly. Bella wasn't sure that she did, but she could tell that Piper wanted to.

"Take Johnny back to his room until Tuck gets here," Bella said, trying to regain control of the situation. "It's fine. It'll be fine."

Piper nodded as she took a speechless Johnny out of the room.

After they left, Bella threw the phone against the wall and tried not to throw up.

30

We All Know Better

Mike stumbled from the kitchen into the garage and tried to get in his car. His heart pounded and his shaky hands dropped his keys. He picked them up, dropped them again, grabbed them a second time. He jerked on the door handle once, twice, three times, before he finally opened it. He hopped in and sat back in his seat as he shut his door.

He clenched and unclenched his fists. *What did I do?* All he could see in his mind was the blood pouring from Bella's face. Then his daughter throwing him out. *His daughter. Christ.*

He glanced down at his hands. They were shaking uncontrollably. He squeezed them shut, opened them. Again. Again. They still shook.

He reached into his jacket and pulled out a flask. He struggled to open it as his fingers quivered wildly. He finally tumbled the cap off and took a swig. Another. He was calming down. One more.

He reached back in his jacket and pulled out the baggy he'd jerked from Bella. Grabbed two pills, swallowed them with the whiskey in his flask. Two more. Swallowed them.

He started the car, opened the garage door, and pulled out before the door was even up, breaking off the bottom of it. A piece of the door crashed onto his car hood then slid off when Mike backed onto the road of his spread-out suburban neighborhood. No

one was close enough to hear the commotion. He
took another swig.

Just calm down.

He hit the gas and screeched into the darkness.

* * *

Teddy sat at a red light just outside the arena as
Old Blue's blinker anxiously clicked right for home.
He leaned his head against the back of the seat and
pushed air slowly out of his lips.

"Teddy!"

He glanced down at the car that pulled up beside
him and saw none other than Bones waving his arms
around from the front passenger seat of a tiny sedan,
his blue wig still on, and Hendrix's jersey draped
over his painted chest.

"Ah, shit," Teddy said. He laughed as he rolled
down his window.

"Bones," Teddy said with a nod.

"Holy shit, you know my name," Bones yelled
with excitement as his buddies rolled down their
windows and started cheering. "Can I get your
autograph?"

Teddy glanced at the red light and then his side
mirrors. No one was behind him. "Sure," he said.

"Holy fuck, this is the greatest night ever." Bones
grabbed a sharpie from his jean pocket and ripped off
his wig, then his jersey, with a grin. He handed the
pen and jersey to Teddy. "I always come prepared."

Jesus, this guy.

Teddy grinned as he signed his name, then handed the pen and jersey back to Bones as a car that had pulled up behind Bones started honking.

"Gimme a second!" Bones yelled.

Teddy looked at the green light. "You better go," Teddy said. He nodded at the light.

"Yeah, yeah," Bones said. He nodded as the car started to pull away. "You and Olsky were fire tonight, baby! Bring the Cup home!"

Bones hollered that last word long and loud as the car behind them pulled up and several girls flashed Teddy as they drove past. "We love you, Teddy!"

"I love *you*," Teddy yelled. "Damn. Thank you."

His wide grin quickly faded as he glanced up to the light and started to turn right. He stopped at the bare intersection and sighed. He owed Mike an apology. Maybe all the captain needed was for Teddy to give him a fucking break. Like Tuck had done when Teddy had arrived.

Either way, the team had to come first at this point, and the shitshow between him and Mike was making winning harder. Teddy's stupid issues tonight were proof he needed to take control of his own fucking behavior.

He shook his head and clicked his blinker to turn left. He moved Old Blue to the turning lane then into the intersection and quickly got out of downtown. He made it to the side roads leading to Mike's house within minutes.

He tapped his fingers against the steering wheel and turned the music up. *Those girls were hot.*

198

Teddy flew down the open two-lane highway and got stuck almost immediately behind a Honda Pilot.

"Oh, come on," he whispered. He squinted in the darkness and could see the shape of a man at the wheel with a girl in the passenger seat.

"Let's goooo," Teddy said impatiently. He wanted to get this fucking over with before he lost his nerve.

Teddy picked up his speed and passed the SUV on the dotted white line. He glanced over as the man shook his head. Teddy gave him an apologetic wave, then he noticed the girl in the passenger seat looked familiar.

Shit. He'd seen her at the rink with Mike's daughter before. Her name was…something to do with paper. Or books or something. He quickly slowed down and pulled in behind them. He didn't want to be a total asshole, especially if they happened to be on their way to Mike's house.

Teddy sighed with annoyance as he looked ahead and saw the entrance to Mike's neighborhood. A little further back, he saw Mike's SUV.

"What the fuck?" he said slowly.

Mike's car was swerving all over the neighborhood, taking out mailboxes, and gnomes.

"Oh shit," Teddy whispered.

He quickly started to move his truck around the Honda on the right side as dirt and pebbles kicked up from the grass and gravel. Mike was to the entrance now, about to zoom onto the road like a race car driver.

"No, no, no," Teddy said as the man in the Honda started to brake and swerve just before Mike T-boned him. Teddy sped up and raced around them.

"Fuck." Teddy made sure his seatbelt was tight, then laid on his horn, and aimed right for Mike.

* * *

Mike shook his head in disbelief. He could swear a gnome had just dropped onto the hood of his car.

"What the fuck?"

Is that a horn? His eyes drooped as the pills took hold. Then, headlights, bright, coming right at him.

"What the fuck?"

The lights side-swiped his SUV, pushing him into a stone pillar at the entrance gates. His car came to a sudden halt as Mike's head slammed into the airbag as it deployed.

"Fuck!" he yelled. Hitting an airbag was like hitting a cement wall. The white powder from its release filled the SUV like flour in a baker's shop. Mike tried to push the airbag away as his head swam. When he looked out the driver's side window, he swore he saw a familiar face.

"Hendrix?" Mike questioned. His eyelids drooped as his head spun. Darkness crawled into his brain and put him to sleep.

* * *

The first thing Mike heard before he opened his eyes was a heart monitor, then he smelled antiseptic and cold air. It was just like the room his dead father had been in.

Mike startled awake, grasping the sides of the bed in fear. Tuck stood there staring at him.

"What the fuck?" Mike asked. His eyes blinked as they adjusted to the bright, white room. "What happened?"

Mike looked to the other side of the room where the Stache stood next to a banged-up Hendrix. Dominic, the team's attorney, stood with them, still dressed in his suit and tie from the game.

"Why are you here?" Mike asked roughly.

"Keeping you out of jail," Dominic said.

"Dominic worked it all out," Tuck said quietly. Mike looked at Tuck's serious face. Tuck was pissed and irritated.

Mike looked back to Dominic. "Worked what out?" Mike questioned.

"You could have killed that girl and her—"

"Killed?" Mike interrupted. His heart monitor beeped wildly as he glanced to Tuck, then Hendrix.

"Yeah, Mike, killed," Dominic said. "You were barreling toward them when Hendrix, stupidly, stopped you," Dominic said. "Do you remember the accident at all?"

"Accident?" Mike shook his head. *This can't be happening. Killed someone?*

"The police have agreed not to charge Hendrix for being an idiot. You, on the other hand."

"Who?" Mike asked. He looked at Dominic.

"Who, what?" Dominic asked confused.

"Who did I almost ki…" Mike couldn't say the word. *Jesus.*

"It was Paige and her dad," Tuck said quietly.

Mike shook his head at Tuck. Tuck slowly nodded as Mike felt the words sink into his bones. He frantically looked at Dominic.

"I'll apologize. I'll—"

"No, we're done with that, Mike," Dominic said. "This is serious for you and the team. The prosecutor is willing to work with us since no one, except you, was hurt and you never made it out of the neighborhood onto the roads. And, technically, Hendrix is the one that caused the accident. No one's being charged. Yet."

Dominic moved closer to him and shoved his hands in pockets.

"Here's what you're gonna do—"

"Are they okay? Paige and her dad?" Mike asked.

Dominic nodded as he said, "Yeah, they're okay. I don't think they realize what's going on. Hendrix made up something about swerving to miss an animal and jumping the curb. So, they're fine. They think Hendrix is the asshole."

Mike glanced at Hendrix who shifted uncomfortably where he stood next to the Stache. Coach wouldn't even look at Mike.

"But we all know better, don't we?" Dominic smirked. "So, Mike, you're gonna—"

"Does Ana know?" Mike asked Tuck. He searched his friend's eyes for any sign he knew what happened at his home tonight.

Tuck leaned close to Mike and whispered, "Pay attention, Mike."

Tuck's icy stare chilled Mike's body. His friend pulled back as Mike looked at Dominic.

"Like I was saying," Dominic said. "You're gonna have to pay for the property damage you caused in your neighborhood. And you'll do any other damn thing the prosecution wants including a large donation to several of their programs."

Dominic bounced his stare between Mike and Hendrix. "And neither one of you will speak about this to anyone, unless I'm present, understood?"

Hendrix nodded as he glanced to Mike, who twitched his lip. The room felt warmer and smaller. He nodded.

"Now, Hendrix said he pulled some shit out of your car," Dominic said. "I don't know what and I don't wanna know."

Mike glanced to Hendrix, who looked away.

"All the cops have right now are the blood tests. Alcohol, pain pills."

Dominic crossed his arms.

"We can explain away both. Pain pills for the knee. Alcohol for the celebration. You didn't realize how they'd mix," Dominic said. He shrugged. "At some point, someone's gonna ask why there was so much of each in your system. We'll cross that bridge if we get there."

Dominic waited until Mike looked at him. Mike tried to look away, but he couldn't. *Christ, I could have killed Ana's best friend tonight.*

"So, for now, here's what happened, according to Hendrix's statement to the police," Dominic said. "Hendrix swerved to miss an animal, ran up over the curb, and hit Mike. It was an accident."

Dominic shoved his hands in his pockets.

"Hendrix was there because, according to the team," Dominic nodded to the Stache, "Hendrix was on his way to help Tuck take you to the Pathway to Hope Center for a little bit of treatment to avoid the *possibility* of addiction. You and the team were being proactive."

Mike nodded and looked away. His chest was constricted as his breath came and went in deep, tight breaths. *How had he gotten here?*

"So, you're going to go to that treatment center and you're going to clean yourself up, Mike," Dominic warned. "Because if you don't, the prosecution will re-evaluate this case and when they do, the team will end your contract."

Mike snapped his stare to Dominic's face.

"And you won't spend another day in hockey for the rest of your life."

31

No Comment

Tuck drove in silence as Mike sat quietly in the passenger seat. Tuck glanced in his rearview mirror at Hendrix in the backseat. The kid checked his phone, shook his head, and put it away in his pocket.

Dani fucking Ashton had been asking a lot of poignant questions recently. She'd seen the brawl at the wake, but she had more information than she should from only that event. *Is it the kid? Is that her source now?*

Tuck tapped the steering wheel. Teddy, that fucking idiot, had probably saved Mike's life and career by doing what he did. Not to mention Paige and her father. One minute the kid was cool, the next he was a dick. Tuck wasn't sure what to think of him anymore.

Tuck sighed and glanced at Mike. He winced at his friend's bandaged head. He had to hold back from saying anything right now because Mike needed help and Tuck wasn't going to do anything to prevent that. *If he takes it.*

When Tuck had heard Bella's broken voice on the phone earlier, and the kids upset in the background, he wanted to tear into Mike. He still wasn't entirely sure what had happened at the Olsky house before the accident, but he'd know soon enough. When he talked to Bella the second time to tell her about the accident, she could barely speak for the injuries to her face.

Tuck gripped the steering wheel until his hand turned white. Bella was like a sister to him. *Goddammit, Mike.*

Tuck had texted Jaime after that, and Jaime called Bella to tell her what to do until he and Tuck got there. And on top of all that, the team had him keeping an eye on Hendrix like a fucking babysitter.

He shifted uncomfortably in the driver's seat as he exited the interstate. "Turn right," the maps app said from the speaker. As Tuck brought his car to a slow roll, he caught a glimpse of Mike's face. *He's scared.*

Tuck's forehead furrowed as he turned into traffic. "Stay in the left lane," the directions ordered.

Tuck didn't think he'd ever seen Mike scared a day in his life.

"You have arrived," the app said.

Tuck let out a tightly held breath as he pulled into the Pathway to Hope Center and parked around back. The team already had a security guy there and waiting. The former FBI agent stood watch as the head doctor stepped out from the building and Mike and Tuck climbed out of Tuck's Escalade. Mike's limp was nearly gone now.

Tuck grabbed Mike's bag from the back and came around to meet his friend.

"Tuck, I—"

"Just get better, Mike," Tuck interrupted.

"Bella," Mike said.

"I'm headed over there after this," Tuck said.

Mike nodded, his eyes were swollen and tired, his face was pinched and drawn. He looked nothing like the best friend Tuck had known for years. Jaime had said to give Mike support right now. *Do it.*

"I'm still your best friend, eh," Tuck said. He gave Mike a light slap to the arm.

Mike's eyes were downtrodden as he said, "My only friend right now."

Tuck shifted his weight as he slung Mike's bag over his own shoulder. "Focus on healing. Team needs you. Bella needs you. Your kids."

Mike nodded. "Thanks."

"Yeah," Tuck said. Mike turned to the doctor and slowly walked inside as Hendrix got out of the backseat and slid into the front.

Tuck took the opportunity to fire a warning shot at Hendrix in case he was thinking of leaking this shit to Dani, "No one knows about this. Got it?"

Hendrix looked surprised as he replied, "Yeah, yeah. Got it."

Tuck eyed him for a second, then Hendrix looked away. Tuck smirked and walked inside the facility. He handed Mike's bag to a nurse with a nod, then glanced around the clean, quiet hallway in the back of the building.

Where'd he go?

Tuck saw the doctor and hustled up to him.

"Hang on, hang on," Tuck said as the doctor stopped and turned to him.

"So, uh, what happens next?" Tuck asked.

"Detox," the doc said matter of fact. "If he makes it through that, then he gets therapy."

"If he makes it through?" Tuck asked.

"Detox, withdrawal, it's a painful process," the doctor said. "Some people check out and leave before therapy even starts."

"Oh," Tuck said. "Gotcha." Jaime had told him that, but it was different hearing it now that he was in the facility. He ran his hand through his hair as the doctor waited patiently.

"Will you call when he's ready to leave?" Tuck asked.

"No," the doctor said. He held his clipboard to his chest. "He checked himself in. He can check himself out any time. It really depends on how well he wants to be."

"I see," Tuck said. "And the media?"

"It's all confidential," the doctor said. He gave Tuck a single nod. Tuck could see he was itching to get going, so he stopped.

"Okay, yeah, thanks." Tuck shook the man's hand, then walked out of the rehab facility just as Dani mother fucking Ashton walked up. The team's security guy stepped in front of Tuck.

He glanced over to his car and glared at Hendrix as he thought of about ten different ways to tell Dani to kiss his ass.

* * *

Dani knew when she saw Tuck's face that she was crossing a line she might not be able to bounce back from.

"Oh, what the fuck, Dani? Seriously? No fucking comment," Tuck spat as the security detail attempted to detain her.

"Touch me and I'll call the cops," Dani said as the guy stepped back but kept her from getting too close to Tuck.

He was incensed and she didn't blame him. If the shoe was on the other foot, she'd feel that way, too. But after more than a few nights of sipping tequila with Tuck and talking about his life over the years, she felt the two of them could handle this.

"Tuck, come on," she said.

Dani knew about Tuck. She had found him and his then-boyfriend out to dinner. She swore to him she'd never tell, and she never did. And that had always earned Tuck's respect. This was different, of course. This was betrayal of his friend. His team. And Tuck was a team-first guy, all the way.

But in this case, Tuck's loyalty was misguided.

"How long you gonna cover for him, Tuck?" she asked.

"No comment. How'd you even know he was here?" Tuck glanced over to Hendrix as he moved around his car keeping security between him and Dani.

Dani glanced to the Escalade and saw Hendrix in the passenger's seat nervously watching them. He was off the hook on this one. A certain beat cop who was pissed off at the deal that was cut with Mike, had tipped her off.

"Not the point and you know it." She peered around the security guy. "You can't protect him after tonight."

"I don't know what you're talking about," Tuck said with a superiority she didn't appreciate as he opened his door. "Mike had a prescription for the meds. He was celebrating the win with a drink. He didn't realize they'd mix like that. And besides, Hendrix was the one who hopped the curb, not Mike."

"Don't give me that bullshit," she spat. "Did Dominic write that shit? Tuck?"

Dani tried to touch his arm, but the security bulldog held her back. She swatted at the guy as he shook his head. She yelled at Tuck as he ducked into his car. "You need to be his friend, Tuck, not his P.R. machine."

Dani shouted, "Tuck! He has a real problem here. You know it." She stopped in frustration as he looked at her from inside his car, the door still wide open.

"How do you sleep at night, Dani?"

"I could ask you the same question," she spat.

They stared at each other for a second. She had an enormous respect for Tuck, but the facts didn't change just because he wanted them to.

She said, "He could o' killed two people. One of them was seventeen years old. And whether you like it or not, not everyone agrees with your team-first mentality on this one." She shook her head. "I know Mike. He's better than this. And so are you."

Tuck huffed a laugh.

"You don't know anything, Dani," he said. "We're done here."

* * *

Tuck slammed the door of his Escalade and eyed Hendrix for a second. Immediately Hendrix twitched. Tuck started the car and watched as Dani pulled out her phone and called someone. *Probably that fucking asshole, Ed.*

He shook his head. Tuck knew Dani had a job to do, just like he did, but it didn't stop him from being pissed about it. The worst fucking part of the whole thing was the fact that she was right. Mike was in the wrong. There was no doubt about that. But, fuck, his life wasn't her fucking story to write.

He turned his ire to Hendrix.

"Funny how fuckin' Dani knew we were here," Tuck said. "And at the back entrance, no less."

"Yeah," Hendrix said nervously. "Reporters are a real pain in the ass."

"They're not the only ones."

Tuck eyed Hendrix as he put the Escalade in gear and headed for Bella and the kids.

<h1 style="text-align:center">32</h1>

<h2 style="text-align:center">Hit This</h2>

Mike walked into the dimly lit rehab room with its one window and twin-sized bed like a man going to prison. Gone was the opulence of his home replaced by bare, bone-colored walls.

It's exactly where he deserved to be.

He switched his weight side-to-side, his hands shaking. He walked gingerly to the bed and dropped his camel leather bag onto it with a light thud. Mike had no idea what was in it. Someone from the team had picked it up from his house and brought it to the hospital. Bella had probably packed it.

Bella. He winced then looked over his shoulder to the door as someone knocked. A tall, black, muscled male nurse took up almost the entire doorframe. Jesus, the guy had to have been an athlete at some point. He was like Jack fucking Reacher.

"They sent the big guns, huh," Mike quipped.

The man laughed as he slapped his hands together. "You've got a sense of humor," the man said as he pointed at Mike. "You're gonna need it in here."

Mike nodded as the guy strutted into the room with an affable smile. Mike noticed the phrase, "Semper Fi," tattooed on the thirty-something's forearm.

"I'm Carson, Mike. I'm your nurse," he said as he met Mike at the bed and shook his hand. "Whenever you need me, hit this call light, here."

Carson picked up a tan tube with a red button on the tip of it. "Don't be afraid to ask for help while you're in here. 'Cause you're gonna need it. I promise."

Mike cleared his throat as he squeezed his arms. His body ached in places he didn't even know he had. Carson glanced at him and smiled as he went through Mike's bag item by item, removing the razor and ibuprofen, among other things.

"Yeah, everything's gonna hurt for the next twenty-four to forty-eight hours," Carson said. "Real bad."

Mike asked, "You play footb—" when a violent wave of sickness lurched from his gut to his throat. He doubled over and dry heaved.

"Whoa," Carson said as he rushed to Mike and slid a small trash can under his mouth. Mike dry heaved once, twice more, then violently vomited. As he spit out the foul taste in his mouth, Carson patted his shoulder.

"Started with an injury, right?" Carson asked.

Mike nodded as he held his head near the trash can until he was sure the sickness had passed.

"You aren't the first," Carson said. "You won't be the last. It gets hold of people before they even realize. I've seen it happen."

Mike turned his head to Carson, who smiled.

"And, yeah, football." Carson knelt next to him. "I was in the Marines, too. I saw this happen to a couple veterans who served in the Middle East. Saw combat. Bad injuries. The meds…they're like a virus. You don't even know you're infected until it drops you like a stone."

Mike nodded as the sickness returned and he dropped his head into the acidic-smelling trash can. He was grateful Carter was here. Finally, someone who knew about the thing that crawled inside of him.

"Anyone is susceptible to addiction to these meds," Carter said. "They don't give a shit who you are."

Mike vomited again in the trash can and weakly glanced at Carson.

"I do have good news," Carson said. "This first part won't kill you." He patted Mike's shoulder.

"But, unfortunately, Mike, it's gonna hurt like hell."

33

I Used to Say That

The guilt rose in Hendrix's gut as soon as he followed Tuck into Mike's home. It worsened once he saw the kids gathered around the island in the kitchen. His father's wake came to mind. After everyone had left, his Boston Bears' teammates had gathered in the kitchen and stood by Hendrix as he grieved.

That's what it looked like right now. Grieving. And Hendrix was responsible for a portion of that.

Fuck.

His reasons for putting Dani on Mike's trail wouldn't matter to them. It would only matter that he'd done it. *Betrayal.*

"Uncle Tuck," Piper said as she ran to the "A" and grabbed hold, tears falling down her face. Tuck kissed her head and squeezed her tight. She was joined quickly by Johnny, who wrapped his arms partially around Piper and partially around Tuck, and then Ana, who grabbed Tuck from the side.

"It's okay, guys," Tuck said quietly. "It's gonna be okay. I promise."

Hendrix swallowed hard as his heart rate ticked up and his chest tightened. His guilt was competing with his grief. If he had it to do all over again, would he change anything? The scene unfolding in front of him now would be ten million times worse if Mike had struck and killed Paige and her father; or himself.

Hendrix had caused a little pain now to save a lot of pain later. He didn't feel bad about that.

The kids stepped away from Tuck as Hendrix shoved his hands in his pockets.

"Where's Bella?" Tuck asked.

"Upstairs," Ana said quietly. "I helped her clean up. She's in bed. She's okay for now." Ana wiped the tears from her face and crossed her arms. She glanced to Hendrix.

"What's he doing here?" she spat.

He deserved that. Ana was a hockey player. A good one, too. If she'd seen the game earlier, she'd know that Hendrix had purposely held the puck.

"Helping," Tuck said. Hendrix nodded at Tuck's intense stare.

Hendrix knew why he was here. It wasn't to help. The team had him and Mike on a short leash now and Tuck was the netminder. Tuck's new job was to stop the bullshit.

Tuck looked back to the kids.

"Your dad…he didn't mean it. You guys know that, right?" Tuck said. "That's not who he is."

Johnny and Piper nodded as Ana grimaced, then walked out.

"Ana?" Tuck called.

She was angry. Hendrix understood that. The anger he held toward the man who'd gotten drunk and killed his father was palpable. It was an anchor in his chest. Hendrix glanced to Piper and Johnny, who glared at him. Yeah, he'd fucking hate him, too, if he were them.

"Im'ma check on your mom," Tuck said.

Johnny and Piper nodded as Tuck ascended the staircase. Hendrix half-smiled at them.

"Come on, Johnny," Piper said. She grabbed her brother's arm, and they followed Tuck up the stairs.

Hendrix let out a deep breath and sat down at the island as he started scrolling through social media. The story was fucking everywhere and written just as Dominic had scripted.

Hendrix checked his email and texts. Reporters from various hockey publications were hitting him up personally. Hendrix huffed. *They can't get past the team's communication guys.*

Just then, a text popped up from Dani Ashton.

Dani: *Any more on Mike?*

Hendrix eyed the staircase and then a family photo on the wall. He shook his knee as he pondered what to do next. He had done everything he could within the limits of what he was willing to sacrifice to get Mike the help he needed.

Now that he'd done what he intended, and Mike was getting help, there was nothing left to say.

Hendrix: *We're done.*

* * *

Bella opened her eyes as Tuck walked in. She adjusted the ice pack on her aching jaw and nose as she tried to pick up the tissues lying all around her, on the bed, on the floor. She tried to throw them

away, but every time she moved, the pressure in her
eye and face caused streaking pain.

"Don't," Tuck said as he shut the door behind him.
He shook his head and winced as he looked over the
bruising and swelling. He said, "This is my fault. I
should have—"

"It's not," Bella said. She pushed herself up
against her pillows a little bit more and smiled at him
with the side of her face that worked. "He's there?"

Tuck nodded as he came further into the room. He
glanced down at the blood-stained carpet.

"Jesus," he whispered. He shook his head.

"It was an accident, Tuck," she said matter of fact.
She knew Tuck would understand that in a way the
kids couldn't right now. The man who did this to her
was not the same man she married. "We were
fighting over the pills. I got distracted."

Tuck nodded as he sat down at the edge of the bed
and took Bella's hand. She appreciated the concerned
look in his eyes. Tuck was her family. She needed
him right now.

He reached up and touched her face, studied it like
he was a doctor. When he was satisfied, he dropped
his hand.

"Jaime's going to come by after his shift," Tuck
said. "You talked to him?"

Bella nodded. "I just love him," she said. Tuck
smiled. Him and Jaime were perfect together, and
Bella could tell it was real, true love. Something
Tuck deserved in his life.

"He thinks you need to get a cat scan," Tuck said. "Check for a concussion. Make sure no bones in your face are fractured."

She nodded and said, "He mentioned that. All of it feels broken right now."

"He should be here in about an hour," Tuck said. "He's going to take you through urgent care. Privately. Through the back of the facility. I'll stay here with the kids."

"Thank you," she choked out. She couldn't stop the rush of relief and the tears it brought with it.

Tuck nodded as he squeezed her hand. She stopped the tears quickly. It hurt her face too much to cry.

"You must love him," Bella said. She looked over Tuck's face and saw his eyes light up.

"I do," he said quietly. "I trust him."

She tried to smile, but that was also too painful. She reached up and touched the scrub on Tuck's face.

"Playoff beard."

"Jaime hates it," Tuck said.

Bella started to smile again, but tears came instead. *Fuck it.* Her whole face pounded in pain as the tears fell. She couldn't stop it in front of Tuck.

"I should have taken him myself," she said. She grabbed the tissues and wiped her face as she cried, painfully blowing her nose in between sobs. "I feel like I've betrayed him somehow. It never occurred to me he could have a real problem. It's Mike. This kind of stuff doesn't happen to Mike. To us."

Tuck nodded in agreement.

"He was at the top and then…Jesus, when did we get old? I don't think he…we…ever thought it would actually have to end someday. And then Hendrix."

Bella stopped crying and looked right at Tuck.

"Watching Hendrix is like watching Mike when he was that age. So much promise," she said.

"It's uncanny," Tuck agreed.

She tucked a hair behind her ear. "And then Pops. Everything. All of it."

Tuck took her hand again and squeezed it. "This isn't your fault. And I know it doesn't seem like it right now, but I promise, it will be okay."

"You can't know that Tuck."

"I guess," he said. He shrugged. "But I do know Mike. And I know you and Mike. That's enough."

Bella nodded with a half-smile. She asked, "Does Dani know?"

"She was there."

"Fuck...the kids," Bella said. She closed her eyes and put the ice to her jaw and nose again. She shook her head. "It's probably everywhere already, isn't it?"

She opened her eyes and peered at Tuck.

He said, "They're tough. They can handle it."

She whimpered in pain. "I used to say that about Mike."

34

The Red Button

Mike squeezed every inch of his body as he curled into the fetal position on the scratchy blanket draped across his jail-sized bed. His body had never felt like this in his whole life. Not after bag skates, not after PHL Cup Playoffs, never. It was a dull, painful ache that pulsed like a drip of water on his forehead in a prison camp.

There wasn't a single thing on his body that wasn't crying out for relief.

"Oh, God," he whimpered as he fidgeted and squeezed. Fidgeted and squeezed. He rolled off the bed to a standing position and started to pace, disillusioned by the idea that movement would help. Instead, the sickness gripped his stomach and he dropped to his knees.

"Oh my God."

He crawled to the bed and grabbed the trash can, dropping his face into it and vomiting once, twice, three times. The acid tore at his throat and mouth as he gripped his stomach in pain.

He was eye level with the red button now.

You mother fucker.

It was taunting him. All he had to do was press it and help would come. Carson would appear from thin air like an angel of mercy and find a way to ease his pain.

What pain?

Now, see.
That's what got you here in the first place.

What the hell was that thought breaking through?
It sounded like something Bella would say. Bella.
The fucking love of his life. He'd die for that woman.
The woman he'd left bloodied on their bedroom
floor.

It was an accident.

You're lying to yourself.

What the fucking hell? What was that? His guilty
conscious? Was he losing his mind?
"Ahh...," he moaned as his body seared with pain
and his gut wrenched vomit out through his mouth
into the trash can again.
"Fuck," he spat. He looked at the red button. His
newest adversary.

Just press it, Mike.

Don't you dare!

Ask for help, please!
You're in pain!

What pain?

Stop it!
Press the button!

He stared at it as he writhed like a man possessed.
"Oh my...fucking...ahh...," he groaned.

All he could think of was Bella. His mind drifted to that moment in the gallery. Her eyes. Her smile. The way she had looked at him. The feeling he had in that moment.

He had been a desperate man that day. Bella wasn't like any woman he'd ever met, and he wasn't going to leave without her number. He'd tried a few things on her, the stuff that normally works, the bullshit. But she was a bona fide bullshit detector.

It wasn't until he had showed her who he was, sat down and sketched her, that she let him in. He knew then and there he had to marry her. Even through the tough stuff, he never regretted the day he said, "I do."

It wasn't just that he loved her, he did. It was that Bella saw everything inside of him that no one else ever had. She saw him for who he was and loved him anyway.

If Pops had poisoned Mike, Bella was the elixir who had set him free.

I love you, Mike.

"I love you, too," he said quietly.

He gave a hard stare at the red button, reached out, grabbed the tube, and pushed it.

35

Don't Sweat It

Dani tapped her voice recorder against the seat of the arena as she observed morning skate from her usual spot. There were a lot of rolled pucks, stick slams to the ice, and "fucks" across the board. The team didn't look bad, but they didn't look good, either. They were gassed and distracted, especially Tuck and Hendrix, who probably hadn't slept yet after the night they had. Hendrix was pretty banged up from the accident.

It wasn't the look you wanted when you were playing for the conference title.

Not that Dani could say much about any of that. She was exhausted after chasing down the story, then getting it turned in and out on social media as breaking news. She only got a couple hours of sleep before ending up back here again.

"Alright, bring it in," the coach said.

Dani tucked her dark hair behind her ear as she glanced around her. Bobbi was nowhere to be found. His vet appointment for Piccolo must have gone over. She glanced to the other media, who smiled politely at her; the team brass and communications people were in a completely different area today. They weren't happy with her right now.

She turned back to the team gathered around Coach Jackman and absentmindedly ran a finger over her press badge.

"We fly out tonight and face Tampa Bay in two days. Not much of a break, I know," he said to a few groans. "Olsky isn't joining."

A few of the players glanced in her direction and she felt the heat rise in her throat.

Yeah, they hated her, too. But, tomorrow, there'd be a new story, and something new to be mad about. She just had to ride it out.

"Time to step it up, boys," Coach demanded. "Get ready to win."

As the group glided off the ice, Dani stood up and straightened her white button-down shirt and black pants, then walked with the others to the locker room.

"Don't sweat it," Grines said as he patted her back and walked past her to the locker room.

"Yeah," Dani said as she got a sympathetic smile from Gary's broadcast partner, Rick. She didn't really need the encouragement, but she did appreciate it. Dani had never sweated doing her job. She understood the repercussions of inking stories that pissed people off. And this was one of them.

Nothing felt worse than walking into that room after you've just written the story that had the potential to bring the whole team down and trying to interview players that had closed ranks, ostracized you, and treated you like a lepper.

But mostly, she hated having to go to Tuck in this position. She respected him for his loyalty, even if it was misled. And she knew he was a good guy, even if it showed up in ways she didn't agree with.

She took a deep breath and walked up to him as he stripped off his practice gear.

"How is he?" Dani asked.

Tuck huffed a laugh.

"Come on, Tuck, you know it's my job."

"Fuck your job," Tuck said quietly.

She shook her head and turned to walk away when a light shoulder tap made her turn and face him.

"Hendrix, right?" he whispered. "Your source."

"A lot o' people knew about this, Tuck," Dani said. "And a hell of a lot of people care that Mike could have killed someone. You just don't seem to be one of them."

Tuck shook his head, threw his shit in the laundry at the center of the room, and walked out.

Dani glanced over to Hendrix, who didn't look her way. He didn't even shower, just grabbed his things and left.

She glanced around the mostly cleared room except for those players still talking to Gary and Rick. Howie breezed by.

"Howie," Dani said as he turned to her. "Any other players available today?"

He gave her a once over and smiled. "Not today."

He politely turned and walked away. Dani smirked as she shook her head. She knew what he really meant when he said, "Not today," was "Not for you."

She banged her recorder against her thigh and walked out.

36

The Hard Stuff

Mike laid on the cold floor of his room, shaking and chilled. He hadn't vomited in several hours, but he couldn't keep anything down just yet, either. He heard his new favorite person come through the door with a cheery, "Doin' great, Mike. Almost there."

Carson.

The big man with a big heart sat down next to him with a glass of clear soda and crackers.

"I promise," Carson said, his voice warm and deep, "you're nearly through the worst of it."

Mike couldn't do anything except nod as Carson put the straw to Mike's mouth. Mike took hold of it with his tongue, closed his eyes, and took a small sip, then another. He spit the plastic out and gripped his stomach as the fluid struck his gut and caused it to sour.

"Fuck," he choked out.

"You gotta keep it down or I'm puttin' an I.V. in you," Carson said calmly.

Mike held it down as his body shook. Carson grabbed a blanket and laid it over him.

"We'll try and get you in bed in a bit. Get some sleep," Carson said. "Then the hard stuff."

Mike flicked his tired, questioning eyes to Carson.

"Time to start talkin'."

37

Don't You Dare

Bella shoved her hands into her jean pockets as she walked up to Pops' grave. Ana put down the roses in her arm, then cleaned up cut grass and other dirt from his stone.

"I would have come sooner," Bella said as Ana tensed. "Jaime wanted to triple-check my tests."

"And?" Ana asked quietly.

Bella touched her swollen face. "No fractures."

"What about a concussion?" Ana asked.

"No," Bella said. "Not that, either. It'll just be a nasty bruise. A headache. Painful for a bit."

Ana was quiet for a moment and Bella appreciated the silence. It had been a long night and morning. Jaime had picked her up and taken her in for her examination sometime after midnight. They hadn't gotten back until seven in the morning. Tuck had the kids up and off to school while he headed for morning skate.

"We're gonna get you through this," Tuck had said when he had hugged her.

"Thank you," she had said as she cried. After Tuck had left, she thanked Jaime profusely, took ibuprofen, and slept the rest of the morning. When she had woken up sometime after lunch, Jaime had still been there.

"What are you doing?" she had asked. She had glanced around at her clean house, the homemade soup and rolls, chocolate chip cookies, laundry in the wash, and fresh flowers in a vase on the island.

"You need someone to take care of you for a little bit," Jaime had said. And Bella had started crying. She hadn't stopped for quite some time as Jaime held her. He'd left shortly after that, and she had texted Tuck almost immediately.

Bella: *Don't lose that one.*

Tuck: *I won't. Trust me.*

Jaime had said he had helped Ana pick flowers for Pops' grave when she came home for lunch, the same roses he'd cut and put in the vase. So, Bella went to the gravesite and found her daughter.

Bella glanced at her now. "Pops loved having you around."

Ana glanced back to her. "I hope you're not here to defend dad."

"I'm not here to defend him," Bella said. "I'm here to check on you. We need to talk about what happened last night."

Ana turned to Bella, her eyes were red and swollen.

"Oh, Ana," Bella said. She reached for her daughter's face, but Ana swatted her hand away.

"No." Ana cut her off. "You're here to get our stories straight."

"That's not—"

"I'm going to Paige's for dinner," Ana said flatly as she walked away and to her car.

Bella let her go. They all needed time and space for healing, and in their own way. That included Bella. Ana didn't understand the nuances of marriage and these kinds of situations. A huff of air escaped her lips.

I don't even fully understand.

One minute she was in a heated argument with Mike and the next, he's in rehab after almost killing someone and she's bruised and broken. Their family was falling apart right before her eyes, and she couldn't stop it.

Could I have stopped it?

That question was nagging at her. Where had it gone wrong? What had she missed? Should she have taken him before? It just hadn't seemed like addiction then. Dependency, maybe, but the doctors had warned them about that. It was an expected consequence and manageable with tapering.

Until it wasn't.

She shook her head as she glanced at Pops' grave. Even before his injury, Mike hadn't been happy. He'd been worried since training camp about his knees and getting older and whispers about retirement. Had he been going into some kind of depression then? Had she? Was she anxious about his retirement and losing the life they had built? Was September the point when they should have addressed this?

She touched her face lightly. The pain was coming back, and she needed to lay down. She crossed her arms over her chest and started for her car.

There was a reason for the phrase "Hindsight is twenty-twenty." She was living it right now. And she didn't like what she saw.

The signs had been there. Her and Mike just hadn't done anything about it. They thought they were invincible. It couldn't happen to them, right? And then it did.

She felt the tears slide down her face and she winced. Crying was painful. The pressure it created inside her face made the injury thump like it had its own aortic artery.

She pushed a focused breath out of her mouth and tried to think about herself in this moment. Their children.

First things first, she needed to heal, and so did their kids. The space from Mike right now would be good for all of them.

Mike was going to have heal himself if there was going to be any hope for their marriage and their family to survive this.

38

You and Me

Hendrix glanced around the plane in the early morning as they prepared to fly to Florida. He sat down awkwardly next to Tuck.

Might as well get this over with.

"Have you talked to him?" Hendrix asked hesitantly.

Tuck said quietly, "I know it was you."

"I—"

"I won't tell the team. They need to be focused. But you and me?" Tuck looked right at Hendrix, then put on his headphones, leaned his head back, and shut his eyes.

Jitters permeated Hendrix's body as the jet started moving. He looked around at his teammates and back to Tuck as he tapped his toe nervously.

Tuck was nowhere near ready to talk this through and Hendrix couldn't blame him for that. Especially after seeing Tuck with Mike's family. He hadn't realized how close they actually were. Uncle Tuck? The kids had called him that. Like Tuck and Mike were brothers.

Hendrix gave a side-eye to Tuck.

He didn't give a fuck if Tuck hated him, and yet, he did. He swallowed down the twisted emotions, leaned his head back, and closed his eyes.

Not caring was how he'd survived since his dad's death.

Fuck.

He opened his eyes and glanced again at Tuck. He turned and looked over his shoulder at Cots and Chary coming up with a new bar game; Frenchie and his wavy locks ready for a photoshoot; Glaz in another terrible fucking suit, this one hot pink with a white, 1970s serial killer tie.

Jesus with that. And that asshole got more chicks than any of them. Well, except for Hendrix.

Hendrix shook his head with a grin and turned back to face the front of the plane.

There was a way to fix this. He just had to figure out how.

* * *

PHL Cup Playoffs

Eastern Conference Championship
Game One

Columbus Thunder v. Tampa Bay Waves
Tampa Bay, Fla.

Tuck sighed as he looked around the arena and the rabid Tampa Bay fan base. They were loving this. He peered at the scoreboard and shook his head. They were getting trounced two to zero.

They were gonna lose.

Fuck.

He banged his stick on the ice, breaking it, as the players skated to their benches during a TV time out.

Tuck flicked a heated look at Hendrix as the trainers got Tuck a new stick and cleared off the broken one.

He wasn't sure what to do about the kid. The coach was on his ass to do *something.* Hendrix was a decent guy and a hell of a player that had helped them get here. And yeah, before John Hendrix's death, the kid had been a leader in the room and on the ice. Tuck wasn't fucking blind. He could see that in him. The team followed him willingly. Blindly, even. Pied-fucking-Piper.

But ratting out a teammate to the press? It was unheard of. Dead dad or not. It was a traitorous act. All Tuck had to do was pull the trigger and tell the team and it would be over for Hendrix. The kid had put himself above all of them. It was unacceptable.

He swallowed hard as he glanced at Hendrix and took a long pull from his water bottle. Then again, the kid hadn't been fucking wrong, either. Tuck swirled the water in his mouth and spit it out.

Fuck. Fuck. Fuck.

The only thing Tuck knew right now was that he had to figure something out, and fast. Because if they didn't get their shit together, they were going to lose. And Tuck wasn't about to lose again. Not this year. The boys had worked too hard for this. Losing because they were the worst team on the ice was one thing.

Losing because they couldn't get their off-ice shit together was inexcusable.

He had to find a way to get out of his own head and get Hendrix out of his fucking head and into team mode. He just wasn't sure how the fuck he was supposed to do that with the current captain down and the next captain still learning how to be one.

He tossed his water bottle and glided back on the ice as the game started back up. He grimaced as he waited for the puck drop that would lead to their first loss in the conference finals.

39

What Kind of Person

Mike shifted in the plastic, cactus-green office chair trying to find any position that didn't make him feel and look like a rusty tin man.

"Fuck me."

He crossed and uncrossed his arms over his chest, jiggled his legs, twisted his fingers, and peered around the small, cramped room with a single office table and empty, tan walls. Someone had tried to lighten up the space by adding one of those bullshit inspirational posters, but all it did was make him want to throw something.

"Fuckin' stupid."

Mike needed help, but he had some serious fucking doubts this place was going to provide it.

"Morning, Mike. Sorry to keep you waiting."

Dr. Rosten.

Mike smirked as the big man's glasses slid down his nose, and then were pushed back up by his hairy, Hulk Hogan fingers. He did it twice more as he sat down across from Mike.

Mike held his breath. *No way that cheap piece of shit plastic can hold him.*

When it didn't break into smithereens, Mike exhaled as the doctor organized the papers inside what Mike presumed was his patient folder.

Yeah, that's me. I'm your fuckin' head case today.

He twisted his hands, shifted again.

"Glad to see you're still here and wanna talk," said Dr. Rosten. He finally looked at Mike with his curious eyes and clean-shaven, chiseled face.

What was it with this place and football players? Or maybe this guy had been into rugby. *Or maybe they're here for guys like me.*

Mike stood up as Dr. Rosten eyed him with curiosity. Mike sat back down. He sighed and tapped his fingers on the table. *Pfft.* How much fucking money was he paying for this place and the table was some kind of laminate?

"So, you catch the game last night?" Dr. Rosten asked cheerfully.

He was trying to find common ground with Mike. Mike knew that move. He'd use it on rookies and new guys to get them comfortable in the room and on the ice. Connection. Familiarity.

Mike huffed and stood again. This time he found a worn, two-foot by two-foot spot on the rug and helped make it worse. He squeezed his arms with his hands. The deep aching was persistent. Maddening.

"Must be tough, huh?" Dr. Rosten asked. Mike glanced over as the good doctor sat back in the weak green chair. *How long until that piece of shit breaks under that dude's weight?*

"Being isolated from your team for so long. The knee," Dr. Rosten lamented. "Then gettin' thrown back in the fire. A lot o' pressure, I'm guessing."

Even if this guy had played sports, what did he know about this level of competition? There were only so many people in the world who got to do it. This asshole wasn't one of them.

Mike turned to the one window in the room with all the morning light streaming through it. He got his nose within an inch of the warm pane. Bella was probably getting ready for her day right now.

He winced.

She was probably using that special make-up to cover up the bruising on her face. The make-up she used to cover varicose veins and "unsavory" lines.

He leaned his head against the glass as his eyes squeezed shut to erase the memory.

It didn't work. He could still see the blood.

"Look, Mike, I get it. We don't have to talk." Dr. Rosten stood suddenly and gathered his things as Mike stood straight and peered over his shoulder at the bear of a man.

"You're not gonna make me?" Mike asked.

"Make you?" Dr. Rosten made a "that's stupid" face and half-laughed. "You're a grown man, Mike."

He paused. "Is that what the kids say? Grown man?"

"I think it's grown-ass man you're thinking of," Mike corrected.

"Ah, right," Dr. Rosten said. He shook his head. "You checked yourself in, you can check yourself out."

He smiled at Mike. "Either you wanna get better or you don't. I'm here when you do."

The doc shoved his glasses up his nose then held out his big paw across the table. "Nice meeting you, though."

Mike slowly reached out to shake the man's hand. He was impressed by the good doctor's grip. The direct eye contact. The unwavering stance.

Respect.

Dr. Rosten let go and turned to leave. *Rule number one of any negotiation: be willing to walk away.* This guy was good.

"You know I could have killed a seventeen-year-old girl," Mike said.

He winced at the thought.

Dr. Rosten stopped and turned back to Mike.

"Tough to hear it out loud?" he asked.

Some kind of noise escaped Mike's throat as he nodded.

"My daughter is seventeen, too. It was her teammate. Paige," Mike said quietly. "My daughter…Ana…she plays hockey."

"Like you?" the doctor asked as he made his way back to his chair. Mike tried not to grin at that big man standing next to that tiny chair.

I like him.

"Ana is…she's more like her mom. Thank God," Mike said. Warmth flowed into his bloodstream. "She's smart. Really smart. And funny. She's a winger. Pure goal scorer. And then there's Piper, she's artistic and kind of hippie chick. And my youngest, my son, Johnny. The clown. Kid can cook. It's like a five-star restaurant in our house most of the time. I try to keep up."

Mike shook his head and shrugged lightly.

"You're smiling," the good doc said.

Mike flicked a glance at him. "Am I?"

Dr. Rosten nodded.

The happiness started to slide away again. He tried to catch it, but it was already through his body as the black stickiness emerged. The thing inside him was on the move. His body was heavy again, the aching returning. He squeezed his arms. Shifted his weight.

"She's scared of me," he choked out.

"Who's scared of you, Mike?"

"Ana," he whispered. "Bella."

Dr. Rosten rapped the table and Mike faced him.

"I've read your intake form," the good doc said. "My guess is that they're not scared of *you*, exactly. But of who you've become."

"Semantics," Mike said.

"Not semantics," he said. "There's you and there's you on drugs."

"Oh Christ," Mike shook his head. "Like the fucking egg commercial?"

Mike made a face and with a mocking voice said, "This is your brain; this is your brain on drugs."

He laughed as he waved off the doctor and turned to the window. When Dr. Rosten said nothing, he turned back to him. Mike examined his face, patient and waiting. They stood like that for a second as Mike swallowed hard. He could feel the thing wiggle around in his gut, pinching and snipping at it. He crossed his arms over his chest as the doctor's stare pierced his heart.

"Alright, what if I entertained this bullshit you're spouting?" Mike asked.

"You would have to admit you're an addict."

Mike bent over and laughed, then stood up. Dr. Rosten nodded his head until Mike felt the tears coat his eyes. He swallowed again until they went away.

"Your family, Mike, they knew you before your addiction," Dr. Rosten said. "They don't know the guy who came after. Unpredictable. Angry. Grieving. Lost. Always on the hunt for the next high to get him through the day. Willing to beat up teammates, loved ones. Anything to get rid of the pain. Anything to—"

"Stop," Mike ordered. It was less of an order than the sound of a dying animal lurching from his gut.

Mike searched the room with his eyes, then the window, and finally the good doc's stare. He wasn't an addict. But the doc was right. He needed some help.

"What kind of person does this?" Mike asked. He shifted his weight and fidgeted more.

"You'd be surprised how many people are one really bad day away from this."

Dr. Rosten used his folder to wave up and down Mike's form, then he raised his eyebrows as if to say, "Are we gonna do this?"

Mike slowly sat back down in the cheap chair as Dr. Rosten followed suit at the same pace, almost like his mirror image.

The good doc shoved his glasses back up his nose as Mike crossed and uncrossed his fingers, bounced his toe rapidly against the floor.

"Tell me about your really bad day, Mike," Dr. Rosten said.

"How long you got?" Mike asked.

"As long as you need."

40

You Don't Know

Tuck sat quietly in the Florida hotel bar with its rich, black leather seating, shiny mahogany surfaces, and smartly dressed service staff. The tall, blonde server with green eyes kept giving him the tap. She'd be his type if that's what he was into. She looked Swedish, maybe German, and she was reserved, cool, and calm.

He smiled at her as she sauntered up to the bar and put in a drink order for her table.

"Two Cosmos and one margarita with a side shot of tequila," she said coolly. She winked at him.

Yeah, she'd definitely be my type.

She glanced away flirtatiously as he watched the bartender make up the drinks. Tuck's guess for those lightweight cocktails was a trio of ladies in their forties, probably on vacation. He bet at least one of them was getting a divorce. He grinned just as Sweden looked at him again.

"Hi," she said.

"Hello, Sweden." He took a sip of his own tequila, savoring the thick earthy taste as it slid down the back of his throat and coated it with an agave-tasting comfort he knew and loved.

"Sweden?" she asked.

"Mmmhmm," he mumbled.

"I like that," she said low and quiet.

"I bet you do," he said, flirting back. He grinned at the beauty, just as the bartender put her drinks down.

"Don't miss me too much," she quipped as she grabbed the tray and walked away with a cute little swing in her ass.

"Damn." He shook his head, then turned away as he closed his eyes and exhaled.

This was the point of a road trip when him and Mike would come to the bar and talk shit about everything from partners and hockey to teammates and life. They'd flirt like assholes with beautiful women just like Sweden, then laugh that neither one of them could partake. The last time they'd had a moment like this, they had talked about kids.

Mike was the only person, other than Bella, who knew Tuck wanted to get married and adopt. Mike had told him to go for it once he found the right person. And then they had scrolled through Coach Stacheman's Instagram posts and laughed their asses off.

Tuck drained his tequila, put the glass down, and tapped the bar. The handsome twenty-something bartender with his rich, brown eyes nodded.

"I get off at ten." Sweden was back.

Whoops. He'd pushed this one a little too far.

"Sorry, beautiful," Tuck said. He grinned, softened his gaze, and looked her right in the eye. "And you are beautiful, Sweden. But I'm taken."

She made a sad face, then smiled. "Lucky girl."

She ran her finger up Tuck's arm, then strutted away. Tuck followed her ass to the table with three older women and chuckled.

Nailed it.

He glanced back to the bartender, who smiled at him. Guys always knew which team he was on; women rarely did. It was always just easier to let them believe what they wanted. Plus, at least two other people at the bar saw them flirt. It'd help to shoot down any rumors out there about him until he was ready for them to transition from their cocoon of simple chatter to bona fide truth.

"Diet Coke."

"Fuuuuck," Tuck hissed under his breath.

Hendrix.

"And?" the bartender asked.

"Just Diet Coke."

Hendrix sat down next to him, taking up a shit ton of Tuck's personal space as the bartender put down another tequila and walked away.

"Killin' my vibe, kid," Tuck said. He took a long sip of the clear liquid and checked his phone. Nothing. Jaime was on call tonight.

"I'll call when I can," Jaime had said earlier. "Love you."

"Love you, too," Tuck had said.

Hendrix's long sigh interrupted his thoughts as the bartender came back and put down the soda. Tuck let out a noisy sigh and rolled his eyes. He took another sip of his drink and made a face. He tapped the bar and the hottie returned.

"Tastes like shit," Tuck said.

The bartender walked up, picked up Tuck's drink, sniffed it.

"It's the same as your last one, sir."

Tuck glanced at Hendrix. "Must be the company then."

The bartender grinned and took the glass. "I'll get you a new drink, sir."

Hendrix took a sip of his soda as the bartender walked away.

"Fuckin' hilarious," Hendrix said.

"Ba-domp, ching," Tuck said as he made a motion of banging the drums. "Next show in an hour."

Hendrix just shook his head as Tuck looked right at him.

"You probably already know that, though, right? Probably already tipped Dani off. She'll be in the crowd, front row, I'm sure."

Hendrix shook his head. "I didn't tip her off about rehab."

"Bullshit."

"That wasn't me," Hendrix said. "But everything before that...yeah. Alright? Yeah. It was me. And I'm not sorry I did it, either."

Tuck huffed a laugh as the bartender set down his drink. Tuck nodded at him and took a sip.

"Nobody did anything. You included," Hendrix quipped.

"You ratted out your teammate," Tuck said, holding his drink mid-air as he shot Hendrix a glare.

"Kept your secret, didn't I?" Hendrix chirped, turning to meet his stare.

Mother fucker.

"Tread lightly," Tuck said quietly.

Hendrix flicked his stare away as Tuck turned back to his drink and took a sip. The kid was a

question mark. *Why he couldn't find a team.*
Teammates couldn't get a read on him, so they stayed
away. Tuck sat his drink back down on the bar.

It didn't matter. The kid was his responsibility
now. He had to solve the Rubik's fucking cube that
was Teddy fucking Hendrix.

"There's a way to handle things," Tuck said. "You
haven't learned that yet, apparently."

"Don't gimme that bullshit, team-first line,"
Hendrix said. "I'm all about the team. But Mike
needed help. And he needed his team to help him, not
coddle him."

"He's gettin' help, you asshole," Tuck said.

Tuck made a writing motion to the bartender for
his bill as he stood up.

Hendrix stood with him. "You didn't push him
hard enough, Tuck."

"And you pushed him over the edge," Tuck said
low and gravely.

"Nobody pushed Mike," Teddy said. "He
jumped."

The bartender dropped the bill between them and
walked away.

"You don't know what it's like," Hendrix said. He
shook his head as his eyes softened. "To lose your
dad. The way I did. Manslaughter. A fuckin' DUI.
Senseless, just one minute there, the next one, gone."

Tuck relented. He didn't know what that was like.

"I'm sorry about your dad, kid," Tuck said. "I
really fuckin' am. But you're young. You don't know
what it's like yet. Being Mike. Guys like Mike. Who
live and die for this game. Sittin' in that fucking

246

suite. Watching the guy who's gonna take your place. Knowing this is your last dance."

Hendrix sighed as he looked away.

Tuck felt fuckin' bad for the kid. But it paled in comparison to his friendship with Mike.

"Mike went the wrong way, and honestly, your idiotic move the other night probably saved his whole fucking career," Tuck said. He shrugged as he glanced at the bill, then pulled his wallet out from his back pocket and opened it up, thumbing through the cash. "But know this. Mike *will* come back. Because that's who he is. And when he does, you'll realize you aren't half the leader Mike is. And you never fucking will be."

Tuck dropped a bundle of money on the bar.

"Drink's on me, kid," he said as he walked out of the bar.

Hendrix needed to get his mind wrapped around the truth of the situation. And if he couldn't, there'd be no place for him on this team, or any team, ever again.

That was how you played the game.

And fuck you if you didn't.

41

Trained for This

Mike glanced around the noisy lunchroom of the rehab center and took note of the various folks in attendance. Some clanged their forks against their trays as they ate while others mumbled about one thing or another. They were all in varying stages of alcohol or drug withdrawal and therapy; a few of them were repeat offenders. One of them, Jackson Paulson, had been a "mathlete," turned drug dealer, then pain med addict.

The twenty-something swore his third time was the charm.

"Relapse is a bitch," the mop-haired twig had said. "But now I know how to get extra pudding."

Mike grinned at his tray with its three puddings stacked on high, found Jackson's face in the crowd, and gave him a nod. Jackson raised his pudding cup and grinned.

"How was group therapy?" Dr. Rosten asked as he sat down next to Mike, his tray banging against the round, brown wood.

"Why do I have to do group sessions?" Mike asked. He leaned forward to Dr. Rosten and whispered, "Some of 'em are…you know."

Mike glanced around for Henrietta. He spied her two tables over, in her sixties, staring at him with googly eyes. She was never hard to find; her heated gaze was always on Mike.

"You think you're not…you know?" Dr. Rosten asked as he organized his food.

"No, no, I'm not judging," Mike said.

Dr. Rosten raised an eyebrow as he cracked open his Snapple and took a drink.

"I'm not," Mike said defensively. He cracked open one of his puddings and dunked his plastic spoon inside pulling out a large mound of vanilla goodness. "I'd have a drink with anyone here."

"Come on, man." Dr. Rosten gave him a "wtf" look as he unwrapped a turkey sandwich.

"You know what I mean," Mike said. He shoved the pudding in his mouth and swallowed. "This is more like an H.R. violation. Harassment."

"So, Bella has competition?" Dr. Rosten grinned as he opened his corn chips.

"Dude," Mike said, sitting back, dropping his pudding. "It's not funny. I feel like a piece of meat around here."

Mike glanced at Henrietta, then ducked forward as Dr. Rosten chuckled warmly.

"Maybe they think *you're*… you know."

"Press has said worse," Mike said. He flicked the plastic spoon making it do a back flip from his tray onto the table.

"That why you're so angry?" Dr. Rosten asked. He shoved his glasses onto the bridge of his nose, then took an enormous bite of his sandwich. Mike admired how one swift chomp took almost half of the half.

"I'm not angry," Mike shrugged nonchalantly. "Who said I'm angry?"

Mike crossed and uncrossed his fingers. Sat forward, then backward. Dr. Rosten eyed him quietly as he chewed noisily on his sandwich, waiting patiently for Mike to answer.

"Okay, alright, I'm angry, alright? Okay?" Mike banged the table. The noise level dropped around him as he looked over to see the other patients staring at him. Henrietta turned her gaze away.

Mike smirked and leaned in further, hissing "I'm furious. I trained for this my whole life. It's all I know."

"Did you think your life would always be rose-colored glasses?" Dr. Rosten asked. He polished off the first half of his sandwich in another large bite, grabbed his drink and took a long gulp.

Mike stood up and spied Henrietta staring at him again. She smiled and the lipstick on her teeth looked like she'd eaten a bloody animal for lunch. He sat back down with a hard thud and started fidgeting again.

"I mean, yeah," Mike said. "Fuck."

He slammed the table again and turned his ire toward the do-good doctor.

"Why wouldn't I think it would all be perfect?" Mike asked. "My career has been…well, fuck. Perfect."

Dr. Rosten stopped mid-bite, looked at Mike, and sat his sandwich down.

"Mike. Perfect is extreme language," he said. "Has it really been perfect?"

Mike shrugged. "Yeah. I guess. Yes."

"Oh, okay, I see," Dr. Rosten said as he shrugged, grabbed a napkin, and wiped his hands, then threw the napkin on the table. "So, you're the lucky S.O.B. who has *never* fought with his wife. *Never* thought about cheating or leaving."

"Okay, alrigh—"

"And you must have the one wife in the world who never thought about leaving *you*," Dr. Rosten interrupted.

Mike flicked an offended stare to him.

"Your kids are the only kids in the world who *never* annoy the shit out of you."

Mike cleared his throat and shrugged his left shoulder.

"Oh, and you've got the group of friends who *never* get on your nerves."

Mike looked at his tray, picked up his spoon, started tapping it. The good doctor was making a little too much sense.

"I suppose *you* are the one hockey player in history who has never, ever been pissed off at the team during contract negotiations. Never seen bad shit happen to good players. *Never* wanted to tell your coach to fuck off. And, never, ever wanted to take a night off from the game."

Mike tapped his spoon harder.

"I guess you're that one son in all of human history who *never* got angry with his father for coming between him and his wife."

"Stop," Mike said.

"The one guy with a father who *never* pushed him too damn hard."

"I said stop," Mike yelled. He pushed down hard on the plastic spoon, snapping it in half, as the loose part spun up and smacked the doctor in the forehead.

Mike glanced at the doctor, who smirked. "There's no such thing as perfect, Mike."

Dr. Rosten took the broken spoon from Mike's hand and set it aside, then gave Mike the clean spoon from his tray. Mike slowly took it.

"I'm sorry," Mike said. Dr. Rosten grinned at him.

"You trained for hockey, Mike," the big man said. "Sports. Athletics. The challenges of the game and the business of the game. Not this. Not addiction or retirement or your dad dying or life changes with you and Bella. Your kids growing up, preparing to leave your home and then what? Life is not perfect. It doesn't stay the same. Ever."

Mike grabbed his second pudding cup and yanked the foil off the top. He shrugged his left shoulder and cleared his throat. "It does for me."

Mike ignored Dr. Rosten as the man's head shook in disbelief and instead sunk his spoon in the chocolate pudding. He shoved a huge bite in his mouth.

"Clearly," the doc said. Dr. Rosten smirked, shoved his glasses back up his nose, and started in on the other half of his sandwich.

Mike swallowed the goopy sweetness and sighed.

The good doc *may* have made a couple good points.

Mike's dream was to do exactly what he had been doing for the last forty years of his life, with the exact person he was doing it with. He had hockey and he had Bella. And that, to him, *was* perfect.

To be his age and have to imagine there was some other dream after that was…there was no other dream. The playbook—Mike and Bella's playbook— didn't have any other pages.

The only thing they'd thought about was money. The union had been good at helping all its players with financial information and he'd taken advantage of that at his father-in-law's encouragement.

"Generational wealth," the union had called it. Mike bought into that, so the mathematician and Mike's financial advisor had correctly surmised how much to put away and when, so him and Bella, and their children, and so on, would be set.

And they were.

Outside of that, though, what had they prepared for? What had Mike prepared for?

Nothing.

The union had encouraged them to think beyond the game. Mike had thought that was spot-on.

For everyone else.

Mike had thought, "Yeah, just look at all those stories of guys who made millions and then went bankrupt or didn't have a plan after hockey and ended up on shit creek. Poor sons of bitches. Pity for them."

But he, Mike Olsky, would never be beyond the game. Not like those guys, right?

Mike glanced at Jackson.

Three times. Jackson had lied to himself three times about why he was here. And what did the repeat offender have to show for it?

Mike glanced at his pudding cup, dropped it, and started to fidget.

42

Not Watching

Bella paused outside Ana's room and steeled herself against the onslaught of anger her daughter was sure to spew at her as soon as she walked in. Ana needed time to work through what was happening, so Bella gave ger a long leash of space to rage.

She took a deep breath and knocked lightly on the door. No response. She checked her watch. Hockey practice was in thirty minutes. The club schedule was brutal, and Ana hated to be late.

She cracked open the door and peered in. Ana was lying on her bed with her headphones on. Her eyes were closed, and her brown curls looked like mermaid hair spread across her blue blanket.

Bella leaned against the door frame as her hand found her heart. Ana looked so young, so innocent laying there like that.

Ana had always been a serious, responsible child, and when Piper had come along, Ana pretended to be her mom and take care of her along with her other dolls. When Bella would paint in her studio, Ana would bring her babies in one-by-one and line them up next to Piper's playpen so she could feed them all lunch and put them down for their naps.

By the time Johnny had come along, Ana was already into pee-wee hockey and idolizing her father. She had wanted to be just like him, which wasn't a stretch. Ana was the most like Mike in mannerisms and personality, as well as on the ice. The similarities in their playing style and passionate approach to the game was uncanny. Which meant that, of all three children, this situation was the hardest on Ana.

For Piper and Johnny, it was confusing and hurtful. But for Ana, it was a betrayal of the father-daughter bond they had built for seventeen years.

"My girl," Bella said quietly as she stared at her teenager. And now, Ana was about to go away for college. Mike wouldn't really talk about it, but Bella knew it was hurting his heart for his first baby to be leaving.

Bella moved her hand from her heart to her face, touching it gingerly. She had used the good pancake make-up to cover the bruising that extended from the point of impact at the corner of her right eye, across her nose, up into her forehead and right eyebrow, the right eye itself, and across her right cheek almost to her right ear.

Yeah. Betrayal.

Bella cleared the anger out of her throat. "You've got practice in thirty minutes."

Ana flicked opened her eyes and shot a look at Bella, then took off her headphones.

"What?" she asked.

"You've got practice in thirty minutes," Bella repeated as she walked further into Ana's room. She picked up Ana's bag and put it on the foot of her bed. "I know you hate being late."

"Not going." Ana turned on her side away from Bella's stare.

"Come on. Let's go," Bella clapped her hands together. This wasn't her area of expertise. Ana always pushed herself to be timely and ready, and when she had down moments, Mike would get her fired up. This kind of morale, coach-you-up boosting wasn't typically her job.

"You can't let your team down, Ana," Bella said. "They need you. You know that. Your dad taught you that."

Ana half-laughed.

"What?" Bella asked. "Why is that funny?"

Ana grabbed her phone, clicked open an app, scrolled through to a certain point, then handed it to her mom over her shoulder.

"What's this?" Bella asked as she took the phone and peered at it. *Oh, shit.* "Ana, what the hell is this?"

It was some kind of social media channel that Bella had never heard of, and it was set up like a forum that, based on the language and comments, wasn't being moderated by anyone.

She read what Ana had centered it on: a forum called "Like Father, Like Daughter," and a string of comments about Mike, his stint at rehab, that he was an addict, and that the team was lying about it. It then went into comments about Ana being just like him and "no wonder she's good," because she was "probably taking doping meds."

Bella said urgently, "We need to report this."

Ana shook her head and jumped up, grabbing her phone from Bella, and throwing it into her hockey bag.

"It's nothing, never mind," Ana said. She started gathering up her things.

"I can talk to the principal or the coach—"

"God, mom, no," Ana said. She looked at Bella with an exasperated sigh. "You'll make it worse."

"But—"

"No," Ana said firmly. Her cheeks were turning hot pink as she turned from Bella and finished packing her bag.

Bella wasn't going to push the conversation with Ana right now, but she was definitely going to call the coach later and the school tomorrow.

Fucking kids. She pushed air out of her lungs through her mouth, then took a breath through her nose. She exhaled purposefully one more time and swallowed as she re-focused on Ana.

"So," Bella said. She tucked a hair behind her ear. "After practice, should we go to the game or watch from home?"

"Not watching."

"I know you're not in a great place but—"

"I have to change my clothes," Ana interrupted. She began a staring match with Bella that she easily won as Bella relented.

"Okay," Bella said. She turned to leave, then turned back to Ana. "I think you should delete that app. And stay off social media for a while."

Ana glanced at her and gave a single nod.

"Okay," Bella said. She turned to leave and stopped again.

"I love you," Bella said quietly.

Ana nodded. "I love you, too, mom."

Bella smiled then walked out of Ana's bedroom, quietly closing the door behind her. She took a deep breath and leaned against the door frame, then exhaled it out slowly as she heard Ana sob on the other side of the door.

"Mom?" Johnny said.

Bella turned her teary stare to Johnny as he walked over from his bedroom.

"Hey," she said tiredly as she tucked a hair behind her ear and wiped her eyes. "Homework finished?"

Johnny nodded. "I was gonna play Call o' Duty but…"

"But?" Bella asked.

He shifted his weight and scratched his head. "I miss dad."

"Me, too, buddy," she said quietly.

Bella opened her arms and nodded Johnny over. A smile turned up at the corners of his mouth as he moved quickly to her and wrapped his arms around her waist. She pulled him in and kissed his head as she rubbed his back.

Bella glanced to the side at the creak of a door and saw Piper peek out. She leaned against her door.

"When's he coming home, Mom?" she asked.

Tears formed in Bella's eyes as she shrugged. "Soon."

Bella opened her right arm to welcome Piper over, and she accepted, moving quickly down the hall, and joining in the hug.

Bella wasn't sure how much more she could take without the man she loved and married, for better or

worse. But she knew she was willing to fight like hell
to get them all back to good, if Mike was.

43

There's No Mystery

Mike wiped the sweat from his brow just as Dr. Rosten passed him the basketball. He caught it as it hit his gut.

"Uhh," Mike muttered.

"Sorry, there," Dr. Rosten said breathlessly. He doubled over, putting his hands on his knees.

"Are you?" Mike asked. He grunted suspiciously at the good doctor as their fifth game of PIG was about to end. "What letters do you have again?"

"I think you keep asking me that so you can remind me that I'm losing." The doctor stood and put his hands on his hips as he tried to catch his breath.

"Well, you're the therapist, so you'd know my motivations." Mike grinned as he squared up to the rehab center's only hoop in its small gym.

"P and I," the doc said. "I suspect I'm about to get a G."

Mike looked at the big man and smiled as he shot at the hoop without even turning to see it.

Swish!

"That's bullshit," Dr. Rosten said as he shook his head.

Mike laughed as the ball bounced away and the doctor slowly moved to get it. Mike reached down and adjusted his knee brace. His body was still sore, but better. Without the haze of pain pills and alcohol, Mike realized his knee was in decent shape. A bit overworked, but basically healed. It was a strange feeling to still crave something he didn't need for the reason he initially needed it.

He'd been shoving all that shit down his throat for ghost pain. And now his body kept sending him real physical signals for physical pain that didn't exist. It was a constant alarm going off. Mike still hadn't found any switch to shut it off.

Infuriating.

Mike put his hands on his hips as the doctor grabbed the ball and tried to twirl it on his finger. Failure.

"So, you always wanna shrink people's heads?" Mike asked.

"Race car driver."

"Shut the fuck up," Mike said with a laugh.

"Seriously," Dr. Rosten earnestly. He smacked the ball then passed it to Mike, who caught it easily. "Loved it."

Mike laughed as he took a shot.

Swish!

He winked at Dr. Rosten, who gave him an annoyed look and retrieved the ball again.

"But it was too damn hot in that car," the doc said as he came back to his spot near the hoop and held the orange leather. "And tiny. Look at me."

Mike laughed and flicked his hands at Dr. Rosten, who passed him the ball. Mike squared up.

"And then one day, one of my buddies was racing—"

Swish!

Mike grinned as the doctor shook his head and quickly retrieved the ball. He stood again under the hoop.

"He wrecked; it was bad," Dr. Rosten said. "Paralyzed. Waist-down. Talk about a life change."

Mike's smile dropped. "I'm sorry. Really."

"He's okay, Mike," the good doc said. He passed Mike the ball. "He saw a therapist. And now he's doing more with his life than he did before the accident."

Mike flicked the ball between his own hands and nodded. "That's great."

"It's better than great. It was a miracle the way he brought my friend back from that." Dr. Rosten shrugged. "I thought it was kind'a cool, you know? How he made him whole. Like super glue to a cracked vase that could hold flowers again."

Mike couldn't help the smile that appeared without much prompting. He eyed the burly man in front of him. The guy had heart. No, no, that wasn't quite right.

Dr. Rosten is all heart.

The doc shrugged and said, "I thought, hey, maybe I can do that, too."

Dr. Rosten shoved his uncooperative glasses onto the bridge of his nose and grinned sheepishly at Mike. "So, here I am."

Mike nodded, then shifted his weight, shrugged his left shoulder, fidgeted. His body was gnawing at him again.

"You okay?" Dr. Rosten asked as he stepped to Mike. Mike held up his hand and the doc stopped.

"Gim'me a sec," Mike said. He gripped the round ball and shoved concentrated breath through pursed lips. *Bella.* Her blue eyes and blonde hair permeated his thoughts. Her smile. The way she smelled good all the time. How she tasted when he kissed her. Her laugh and the way it rang his eardrums like church bells on a Sunday morning.

He pushed another breath out, doubled over, dropped the ball, and grabbed a large pack of spearmint gum from the pocket of his long, baggy shorts. The ball smacked the hardwood floor several times before coming to a stop as Mike pulled a stick of foil-wrapped deterrent from the green package.

He stood and unwrapped it with precision then shoved the soft, powdered stick into his mouth. He chewed hard and fast. Another stick. *Another.* The cool mint tasted good as it permeated his tongue buds and filled his sinuses.

Another. Another. Another.

He pushed air out of his lungs like a player getting a cortisone shot mid-game right in the center of the joint.

Another. Another.

The memory of Bella's lips moving and saying, "I love you," was on a loop now.

Another.

The signal from his brain started to weaken. The alarm was quieting. The pulsing urge was passing. His body was calming itself. He could smell the basketball court again. Heard the sounds of the rehab center. Felt the doctor's presence. Looked at him.

"You good?" Dr. Rosten asked.

Mike nodded. He glanced down at the mess he'd made. "Sorry."

"No apologies."

Mike nodded as he shoved the pack of gum back into his pocket next to a few small suckers. He bent down and picked up all the wrappers, turned, found the trash can, spit out the enormous wad of chewed stickiness, and tossed in all the shiny foil. He took a deep breath, then exhaled quietly.

He turned back to Dr. Rosten. "The rest of my life with that, huh?"

The good doctor nodded. "Yeah."

Mike slowly walked to the ball, picked it up, and handed it to the doctor. As Dr. Rosten took it, Mike held on.

"My name…," he said deliberately, "…is Mike Olsky."

Dr. Rosten looked him over as an understanding passed between them.

"And?" Dr. Rosten asked, encouraging him forward.

Mike paused as he looked into the man's eyes. "I'm an addict."

"Welcome, Mike." Dr. Rosten nodded.

"I'm nine days sober."

"How'd you get here?" They locked eyes for a second as Mike inhaled a sharp breath.

"I'm still workin' on that." He let go of the ball and took a step back as the doctor took it.

"You're off to a great start."

Mike shifted his body; squeezed the aches in his arms.

"Say it with me."

Mike nodded as Dr. Rosten said, "God grant me the serenity…"

"To accept the things I cannot change," Mike joined in.

"Courage to change the things I can," they continued.

"And the wisdom to know the difference," Mike said quietly.

The gym was suddenly peaceful as Mike stared at the basketball.

"My dad would be so pissed right now," he said. He looked at Dr. Rosten.

"Why do you think that?"

Mike twisted his left shoulder.

"The last time I saw him. I thought..."

"You thought...?" Dr. Rosten pressed.

Mike cracked his neck side-to-side.

"I should'a stayed with him that night. Taken him to the doctor myself, but…I couldn't, you know, I was high off my ass," Mike said. "But I knew...I knew something was wrong."

Mike dropped his gaze to the hardwood floor.

"He...he said he liked something I drew," Mike said quietly. He looked up at Dr. Rosten. "He never said that in his whole life. Ever."

"You draw? Any good?"

"Pretty good." Mike nodded.

Dr. Rosten shook his head. "God really gave with both hands when he made you, huh?"

Mike cracked a smile. He appreciated that sense of humor from the good doctor. Especially at times like this.

"So, did you ever wannna be an artist? Like make a real go of it?"

Mike nodded. "I thought about it. Put together a portfolio. Applied to the big art school in New York." He shrugged. "I didn't get in. That's what Pops told me."

"Believe him?" Dr. Rosten asked.

Mike let out a breath. "I wanted to believe him."

"Ah, I see," Dr. Rosten said with a knowing nod.

Mike shook his head and smiled. "Oh yeah?"

"Mmmhmm," Dr. Rosten tried to spin the ball on his finger again and failed. He pulled the ball to his side and held it with his elbow. "You had already made your choice. Hockey. Art school was a…back-up?"

Mike tilted his head side-to-side. "I suppose so."

"So, your dad helped you do exactly what you wanted to do."

Mike shifted his weight and put his hands on his hips.

"I suppose." Mike glanced at him.

Dr. Rosten grinned and wiped the last of the sweat from his brow as he said, "You did, Pops did, what you both thought was right in the moment. Regret is useless unless you can allow it to be a catalyst for learning and moving on. Isn't that what you do in hockey?"

Mike grinned at the comparison, then nodded.

"I'm right, right? When you lose, you wanna hurry up and play again?" Dr. Rosten smiled as he flipped his hand up toward Mike. "Because you're only as good as your last set of choices. And then, luckily, you get to make new ones in a new game. Right?"

Mike huffed out air. The good doctor was making sense again.

"You're in your next game right now, Mike. What have your regrets allowed you to learn?"

Mike sighed as Dr. Rosten searched his stare.

"You know what, let me ask you in a way that makes sense to you," Dr. Rosten said. He grinned. "What do you think Pops would want you to do with this next set of choices?"

"Easy," Mike said. He shrugged. "Win."

"Feel good about that?"

Mike tilted his head, nodded.

"Uh-oh, I see hesitancy," Dr. Rosten said with a smile. "That looks like…oh shit, learning."

Mike laughed as he shook his head.

Dr. Rosten pressed harder, "Come, on, what? Tell me. What has regret taught you, Mike?"

"I wanna win," Mike said.

"But?"

"Not at any cost."

"Oh, shit. Ladies and gentlemen," the good doctor exclaimed. He slammed the ball down and held up his hands like a champion. "Progress!"

Mike laughed as he picked up the ball and shook his head. He walked back to what would be the three-point line.

"Settle down," Mike cracked.

Dr. Rosten did a lap with his hands in the air then slowed down and stopped under the hoop, breathing hard from his exertion as he grinned. Mike glanced at him.

"I wanted to ask my dad...I wanted to know...nah, never mind."

"No. Don't do that. C'mon. Talk to me. Let's keep this hot streak going," Dr. Rosten said as he clicked his fingers. "What did you wanna know?"

"What happens when I'm not a hockey player anymore?" Mike asked. "When I'm not me. And there isn't another game to prove myself?"

Dr. Rosten grinned. "There's always another game, Mike."

Mike gave him a questioning look.

"When you're done with hockey, yeah, you won't be this version of you, anymore. Good," the doc said. "Because tomorrow, you won't be the same you anymore, either, hopefully. Or the next day, or the next day. Like I said before. Life…you…none of it stays the same."

Mike took a deep breath. The words started to burrow inside of him. Hockey was coming to an end. Tears hit the back of his eyes. He didn't try to hide them.

Dr. Rosten took note and smiled.

"Look, Mike, you're older. Your Dad died. Your life isn't where you want it to be at the moment. And it scares you," he said calmly.

Mike let out a guttural noise as the truth started to take root in his body.

"It should scare you," Dr. Rosten said. "You could o' killed two people."

The words melted into his skin as a bitter feeling rose in his gut. He turned a hard stare to the good doctor.

"You didn't acknowledge your pain, so it ate at you, and you ate pain pills. There's no mystery there," Dr. Rosten said. "But, Mike, you have to feel that pain, that regret, to move past it. Feeling pain allows you to grieve. And grieving turns into healing, which becomes learning. And after learning is the next version of yourself. You missed all those steps. We're taking them now."

Mike nodded as he rolled the ball in his hands and acknowledged the sickness in his gut. He used the sleeve of his left shoulder to wipe away the remaining wetness in his eyes.

"Any good news in all this?" Mike asked.

Dr. Rosten grinned. "Yeah. All that good stuff you earned for yourself; what you meant to your dad, and what he meant to you. What hockey means to you and what you mean to the sport. That killer family of yours; how much you love Bella. Those are all good things."

"And the bad stuff?"

"It can transform and become something else, if you're willing to learn from it."

Mike took a deep breath as he looked at the doctor, took the ball, and spun it on his finger with a grin.

Dr. Rosten shook his head. "That's bullshit right there, Mike. Total bullshit."

Mike laughed as he squared up to the net.

Swish!

Mike glanced at the doc. "I think that's gonna be a P for you."

"I'm done," Dr. Rosten said. He walked to the door.

"Don't leave mad, Doc!" Mike yelled as he laughed.

The good doctor threw a hand up at Mike as he walked out the door.

"See ya at group," Mike hollered.

"Yep," the doc yelled from the hallway.

Sore loser.

Mike hustled up the ball and turned back to the hoop.

"Okay," he said quietly. "I make it, we win the Cup."

He squared up to the basket and took his best shot.

44

All You Can Do Is Ask

PHL Cup Playoffs

Eastern Conference Championship
Game Six

Columbus v. Tampa Bay
Series: Three-Two
Columbus, Ohio

Bella sat on the edge of the comfy leather couch in their living room as Johnny and Piper sat on either side of her. A big, cozy blanket covered all three of them. The announcers talked about the incredible comeback at Columbus' arena thanks to Teddy Hendrix. Bella was trying to stay cool as they discussed how the Thunder were going to play for the Cup if they could just close this game out.

Come on, Tuck. Make it worth all this.

"I hope dad gets to play for the Cup," Johnny said as he chomped down on his "special" popcorn. It had a one-of-a-kind seasoning mix he'd created. "I mean, you know, when he's back."

Ana walked into the kitchen from her workout and lazily got a drink from the fridge. Sweat dripped down her face and glistened across her bare arms and stomach as she huffed a laugh.

"Yeah. When's that gonna be?" she asked
sarcastically as she slammed the refrigerator door and
walked up the stairs to her room.

Johnny and Piper looked to Bella. She smiled as
she rubbed the soft sleeves of her fitted lavender
shirt.

"Tomorrow," she said. "He'll be home tomorrow."

Bella turned back to the television. Her anxiety
was brewing like a fine tea about Mike coming home.
Which man would it be who walked through their
door tomorrow? And what would that man want for
his future? Her? Some twenty-something? A whole
different life? A different family? Or maybe the
worst scenario possible, which would be that he
hadn't changed at all. She sucked in a sharp breath as
she glanced at Piper.

"She'll be okay, you know," Piper said as she
nodded at Ana. Piper pulled down the sleeves of her
pink, oversized sweatshirt and wrapped her arms
around her chest. Her fluorescent pink nails
shimmered with glitter.

"Yeah," Bella said. She tucked a hair behind her
ear and smiled. She thumbed her wedding ring
nervously.

"Think she'll ever forgive dad?" Johnny asked. He
stopped eating for a second to look for Bella's
reaction, then wiped his seasoned hands on his white
T-shirt. She grimaced at the stain she'd have to wash
out.

"I hope so, buddy," she said. She reached out and
rubbed his head as she smiled.

"Think dad's watching the game?" Piper asked.

Bella let out a half-laugh. "I'd like to see them try and stop him."

* * *

Mike crunched down on the strawberry-flavored sucker in his mouth and closed his eyes as he waited for the nagging sensation from his brain to subside. It had started up in the shower and then again while Mike was trimming up his playoff scrub. He obviously wasn't going to have the full beard, but he couldn't walk baby-faced into the locker room, either.

He scratched the groomed follicles as the pulsing desire for pills subsided with the melting sucker. He tossed the stick in his trash can and glanced over to his camel-leather bag sitting by the door, packed and ready to go. It was hard to believe how different he was from when he first brought that packed bag into this ugly fucking room.

He grinned as he looked around. God, he missed home.

Bella.

"Open," he said at the knock on his door.

Dr. Rosten walked in with a grin and a gift bag.

"I heard there was some kind of important game going on," he said as he pushed up his glasses.

Mike's chest rumbled with joy. "Yeah, you could say that."

Mike stood and extended his hand as Dr. Rosten took it. Mike pulled him into a fond hug as the announcers chatted over the game action.

"We're in the second overtime of game six as the Thunder battle to win the Eastern Conference Championship tonight," said play-by-play announcer Grines.

"And what a comeback it's been in this chippy series," said color announcer Cotter. "Hendrix has been on fire."

As Mike and Dr. Rosten gave a final shake of their hands, the doc handed him the gift bag, "A little somethin' to remember us by."

"Thanks," Mike said as he took the bag and glanced in. "Oh, get the fuck outta here."

Dr. Rosten laughed as Mike pulled out a bouquet of plastic spoons wrapped with blue ribbon and a six-pack of pudding.

"I'll cherish this for about a day," Mike cracked. "And then it'll be gone."

"I figured."

Mike grinned as he sat the bag on the bed.

Dr. Rosten asked, "Mind if I catch this O.T. with you?"

He glanced at Mike as Mike sat down on the edge of his bed. "O.T. is the right way to say it, right?"

Mike grinned. "You've watched sports before, yeah?"

Dr. Rosten laughed. "Sure, yeah. Not super familiar with hockey specifics, though."

"O.T. is the same in every sport," Mike cracked.

"Right, good."

"Sit," Mike said.

Dr. Rosten grabbed one of the green, plastic chairs in Mike's room and sat down, his big body making the thing disappear underneath him.

"You know we all have bets on when that damn thing is gonna break, right?" Mike asked.

Dr. Rosten glanced down at his body surrounding the chair. "What do you win?"

"Pudding."

A belly laugh shook Dr. Rosten's body. "Shit's like gold in here."

Mike laughed. "Yeah it is."

Dr. Rosten smacked the chair legs. "It's tougher than it looks."

"Uh-huh," Mike said as they both turned to the game action. The boys were in a mad rush down the ice.

"I see why you love it so much," the good doctor said. "Exciting stuff."

Mike nodded as he sat back, proud of his team.

"So, what quarter are we in again?" Dr. Rosten asked hesitantly.

Mike shook his head. "Period, not quarter, man, Jesus."

"Gotcha, period, right, I knew that," Dr. Rosten said as he furrowed his brow. He crossed his left leg over his right knee and drummed his fingers against it. "And, uh, is that the rubber disc thing, there?"

Mike closed his eyes in disbelief, opened them, and looked at the doctor.

"Puck."

Dr. Rosten nodded. "Yep, puck, lost the word for a second."

A brief silence settled over them. Mike could feel the doc looking at him.

"What?" Mike asked.

"The, uh, blue line—"

"You can quit now," Mike said.

"Oh, thank God," Dr. Rosten said as he pushed his glasses up the bridge of his nose. The camera panned to the upper deck. Mike grinned.

"Oh, wow, who's that guy?" the doc asked as he pointed at the blue-wig character.

"Bones," Mike said. He glanced at the doctor who gave him a side-glance as the game got back in action. "Don't ask."

"Yep," Dr. Rosten agreed.

They watched quietly as Cots fired a heavy shot through traffic that rebounded and was quickly scooped up by Hendrix, who roofed it for the win.

The Columbus cannon sounded, and the camera panned the arena, the crowd now on its feet, just like Mike and Dr. Rosten.

"That was incredible how he put it in the end zone net thing, there," Dr. Rosten said as he tried to visualize what he was saying with his hands.

"It's not...," Mike started to correct him. "You know what, never mind."

Mike slapped Dr. Rosten's shoulder.

"Very cool," the doc said.

The camera panned in on the team as they circled up at center ice and raised their sticks to the crowd. Mike dipped his head and glanced at the ground.

God, he missed that.

He took a deep breath and looked back to the TV as a deep ache filled his gut. He was going to miss it when it was gone.

"That's so cool how they circle up like that," Dr. Rosten said as he crossed his arms over that barrel chest of his. "Love it."

"We do, too," Mike said quietly.

As the teams lined up and shook hands, Mike grabbed a piece of gum and started chewing. Dr. Rosten glanced over, and a look passed between them. The good doctor gave him an encouraging smile.

"So, you're leaving tomorrow?" he asked.

"Yeah," Mike said.

"And you signed up for your outpatient therapy?"

"Done."

"You have my notes, the lists I gave you? The tips and tricks for when you feel you wanna relapse?" Dr. Rosten turned a little more toward him and smiled.

"Got 'em."

Mike glanced at the big man and gave him a grateful smile.

"You did good in here, Mike."

Mike's throat started to swell and contract with emotion as he nodded. "I have something for you, too."

"If it's a basketball, I politely decline."

Mike laughed as he grabbed an envelope from the small desk in his room and handed it to the good doctor.

"Yeah, uh, do me a favor and open it some other time," Mike said as Dr. Rosten took it from his hand and smiled. He lifted it in the air like it was a vodka and he was giving a cheer.

"I will," the doc said. "Thank you."

Dr. Rosten held out his big paw. "It's been a pleasure, Mike."

Mike took his hand and squeezed. "Thanks for bringing me back to life, Doc."

Mike saw the tears fill the good doctor's eyes as he pulled his hand back and shoved his glasses up his nose. "You're welcome."

He nodded at Mike and turned to leave.

"Hey Doc," Mike asked as Dr. Rosten stopped and turned to look at him. "Will my family...team...will they forgive me?"

"All you can do is ask, Mike," he said. He gave one final nod and was out the door, closing it quietly behind him. Mike turned back to the post-game broadcast.

He grabbed a sucker from his pocket and shoved it in his mouth as his ghosts came calling.

45

Full Responsibility

Mike stood at the edge of the tunnel and stared at the stealthy Zamboni as it finished its job in the cold Columbus arena. He shrugged his left shoulder to bring the weight of his leather bag closer to his chest. Every cell in his body responded to the frozen tundra with tingling excitement as the smell of the ice filled his senses.

The Zamboni driver nodded at Mike as the large steel machine passed by and revealed "PHL Cup Finals" written in the ice. A wide grin swept across his face. It was quickly followed by an acknowledgment in his gut that his team had done this mostly without him.

He had to give an unwilling nod to Teddy Hendrix. He was a huge part of why Mike was standing on the cusp of this ice at all.

"You ready?"

Mike turned to see Coach Jackman, Dominic and Howie waiting inside the tunnel for him. Howie smiled warmly as Dominic straightened his tie. Coach looked…well, like Coach.

Mike nodded as he turned to them. Dominic and the Stache headed down the tunnel as Mike reached out and gave Howie's jacket sleeve a tug. Mike nodded for him to hang back.

"Yeah?" Howie asked.

"Listen, can you do me a favor after this?"

"Sure, Mike," Howie said.

"There's a guy. A fan. Kirby Clark. He—"

"I know Kirby," said Howie. His grin lit up his eyes. "We all know him. Him and his daughter, Casey. Children's Hospital, right? They use the special suite we have for those families. Sometimes they're down near the locker room for special events."

"Yeah." Mike reached in his pocket, pulled out a piece of gum and unwrapped it. He popped it in his mouth. "Can, uh, you find out how she's doing? Casey? Maybe send some tickets to them, on me. For as far as we go. The home games."

"Sure, no problem," Howie agreed.

"Thanks. Appreciate it."

"Yeah, man." Howie turned down the tunnel and Mike followed. He grabbed another piece of gum, unwrapped it, shoved it in his mouth. His heart was hammering against his chest. He grabbed another piece of gum. *Another.*

He was grateful they were doing this after morning skate and the team was gone. He didn't want to see anyone just yet. He needed to get this part out of the way and get home to Bella. He didn't want his mind wandering off and worrying about this shit while he was making it right with her.

Another. Another.

He stepped into the elevator with the other three men and chewed hard and fast on the gum. As the door closed, his heart beat harder. He squeezed his hands and waited for his brain to stop throwing red flags. He squeezed his eyes shut and quietly pushed air through his lips.

The elevator doors opened, and Mike could hear the quiet mumbling of the press corps as they waited for him.

"Let me take that," Howie said. He reached for Mike's bag and took it off his shoulder, putting it on his own.

"Thanks," Mike said.

"Sure."

Mike stepped off the elevator and slowed as Coach and Dominic walked around him. The other elevator dinged, and Doc, the general manager, the VP of communications, and the team president walked off and over. They nodded politely at Mike as Mike chewed harder on his gum.

"Doc?" Mike queried. Doc stopped and turned around to Mike. He looked…hurt wasn't the right word. But, yeah.

"I'm sorry," Mike said. He extended his hand.

Doc glanced at it. He finally reached his own hand out and took Mike's. "I hope you take this seriously, Mike."

"I understand," Mike said. "I am."

"Good," Doc said. He finally smiled and gave Mike's arm a slap. "Glad to have you back."

"Thank you," Mike said.

The Doc turned and caught up to the brass. As they took the lead into the press conference, Mike went to the nearest trash can and spit out the chewed gum. He glanced at Howie, who gave him an encouraging smile. The two started down the hallway.

Mike could hear the cameras clicking before he saw the phones and broadcast cameras turning on as he walked in. The space was small and overlooked the ice. He saw Dani Ashton and turned away. He wasn't ready for that, either.

He inhaled sharply as he took his seat at the press conference table, the microphone prominently set up in front of him.

He glanced at his Coach, who nodded at him.

"Thank you all for being here," Mike said. The tension ratcheted up as the press corps quieted down. "I want to start by saying that I take full responsibility for my actions the night of the accident. I—"

He glanced at Dominic. "I didn't realize that alcohol would interfere with my pain medication in the way that it did."

Just keep toeing the line. Just keep going.

"I'm lucky Hendrix was there that night while I was on my way to get a few things before I left," Mike said. The cameras clicked. He stared into the sea of red, blinking lights and microphones. He glanced at the press. An image of hyenas came to mind. He cleared his throat. "He was there, of course, to help Tuck take me to the Pathway Center for a preventative stint to ensure I wouldn't become addicted to the pain meds, which I felt I'd become a little too reliant on as my knee healed."

Keep going. You're almost done.

"The good news is that an MRI revealed my knee is healed." He nodded to Doc who acknowledged that truth to the press. "And the stint did what it was supposed to and helped me before it became unmanageable."

Get the last part in. The part I believe in.

"I'll be visiting athletic camps over the summer to talk about pain pills and their inherent dangers and how to prevent issues," Mike said. "I'll also be discussing the importance of therapy in sports."

As soon as the press realized he was done, the questions began. Dani was always first. Even hockey media had an off-the-books hierarchy.

"Are you concerned about a relapse?" Dani asked.

He sighed as he looked at her and his fingers twitched. *Stupid fucking question.* Of course he was concerned, goddammit. And just like that, without warning, the thing inside of Mike was on the move again. His whole body was flooded with sirens blinking and banging for relief.

"Thanks, guys." Mike stood up and saw that Coach and Dominic weren't happy he was leaving. He didn't care. He had to take care of himself. If he didn't, his ass was going to be right back in that center, just like Jackson fucking Paulson and his stupid fucking puddings. Mike wasn't going to play fast and loose with his family or his life, anymore.

He strode past all of them as Howie said, "Thanks, everyone." The only person who gave him a knowing look was Doc. Mike gave him a nod, which Doc returned as his lips shot up at the corners.

This was Mike's new reality. The day had finally come.

The game wasn't number one anymore.

He grabbed the gum from his pocket and started chewing.

46

Just Like This

Bella looked out her bedroom window into their spacious backyard with its deep turquoise pool and carefully manicured lawn. Mike would be home any minute now.

She thumbed her wedding ring as she scanned the roses, the slick patio furniture, the expensive finishes, and the stainless-steel grilling and cooking area. Everywhere her eye wandered, something was beautiful, shaped, or made to look as though it were perfect.

Her chest tightened as she turned back to their bedroom and studied it. A contractor had come in and ripped out the blood-stained carpet and replaced it with a beautiful hardwood floor. She'd picked out a cream-colored, blue, and slate gray rug to cover most of it. The bed had new sheets and blankets. She'd gotten new tile in the bathroom.

Like nothing happened.

Her chest tightened as her breathing intensified.

She rubbed her sternum as she tried to breathe through it. Deep-seated emotions rose in her throat, threatening to ruin her freshly done hair and make-up.

Breathe.

She tried to suck in air as fast as she could. She wasn't getting enough of it and her head started to spin. She stumbled to her dresser by the door and

searched her image frantically in the mirror attached
to it.

Am I dying?

She caught a look at the sketch Mike had done of
her hanging on the wall and her breathing slowed.
She looked back in the mirror. *Fully done hair. Fake
eyelashes. Red lipstick. Pancake make-up to cover
the light bruising on my nearly healed face.*

She looked back to the sketch and shook her head.

"Fuck this," she whispered.

Bella caught her breath and stormed into the
bathroom. She frantically turned on the faucet and
peered in the mirror. She ripped off the fake
eyelashes and pulled her hair into a ponytail. She
bent over and splashed the hot water on her face.

"Fuck," she hissed. She flipped on the cold water
and grabbed another cupped hand full of water and
threw it on her face. The mascara and make-up were
all over the sink and floor.

A mess.

Her chest loosened.

She reached over and squirted face wash into her
hand. She glanced in the mirror at the varying shades
of color running down her cheeks and neck.

Better.

She bent down again and rubbed her hands
together until they soaped up, then she attacked her
face with the stringent and scrubbed until her skin
was raw. She splashed water on her skin and
removed the suds. Then she did the whole thing all
over again.

Bella stood up and looked at her reddened face in the mirror, the green-ish bruising on her right eye, the plain face and pulled back hair. The water dripped from her skin to the floor as she shut off the faucet. Everything was quiet. Mike wasn't here yet.

She grabbed a towel and wiped her face and chest dry, peering for a moment at the mess of make-up it had captured. She went to hang it back on the rack but stopped herself. Bella threw it on the floor instead and quickly grabbed all the towels and wash clothes from all the surfaces and the cabinet and threw them all on the floor. She left them there then marched into the bedroom.

Her first stop was the bed. She ripped off the sheets and covers and pillows and threw them in a pile outside their bedroom door in the hallway, leaving only the plain, silky mattress.

Good.

She blew a loose hair off her forehead as she grabbed the bed by the frame and pulled and shoved until it was against the wall. She lifted its legs one at a time, yanking the rug out until it was loosened from the things that held it down. Her shoulder scrunched up and wiped the sweat from her face as she dragged the rug out the door and tossed as much of it as she could onto the stairs with a warrior's yell.

"Bella?"

As the rug dropped, she saw Mike's handsome face with its carefully groomed scrub and tired eyes. His look made her catch her breath. It was twisted into confusion at what she was doing. She felt that way, too.

"Mike." Something cracked inside of her as a long-held sob lurched from the deepest parts of her body. She dropped to her knees and a split-second later Mike's arms were around her, his body stiff and tight against her own, steeling them both as the headwinds of their situation rose and fell.

"I'm sorry." His voice cracked when he said it and he buried his face into the crook of her neck meeting her heaving sobs with his own. The storm was upon them. The rain was coming down. And they held fast to each other.

"It hurts," she choked out.

He squeezed her tighter. "I know."

He rocked her in a slow, gentle motion, never loosening his grip, as her sobs became a gentle weeping, and then a sniffle. She turned her bare face to him, knowing she looked worse than she ever had in all the years of their marriage.

His eyes were red and swollen, and he was sniffing back the snot running out of his nose. She noticed a touch of crow's feet and a few wrinkles in his brow. There was a nip of gray in his hair.

A slight smile touched the corner of his lips.

"You're beautiful," he said quietly.

She nodded as another round of tears threatened to escape. "I missed you."

"I missed you, too," he said as another round geared up in his eyes. He leaned his forehead against hers and held her just like that until they both leaned into the pile of sheets and blankets she'd thrown on the hallway floor.

"I'm scared, Mike," she cried.

He latched his body to hers and his arms wrapped around her chest until her breathing slowed.

"Me, too," he said quietly into her ear. His breath against her neck sent warm heat down her body as they laid like that for a moment. Mike broke the silence and said, "I want to fight for us and our family, if you do."

She grasped his arms and nodded as she pulled him tighter. Relief escaped her body in measured sobs.

The man who came home to her was the man she had married all those years ago. They were starting over again, like all the times they had over the course of their relationship.

Mike and Bella, the fifth, sixth, whatever iteration they were in now, would always find a way.

And now she was certain, they would find it this time, too.

47

There's More to You

Mike watched Ana from a distance as she cleared the cut grass from Pop's headstone and straightened the flowers around it in the late afternoon sun. She took the old, dead blooms and walked them to a trash can a few graves over, then came back and sat down cross-legged in front of his headstone. Mike blinked his eyes to clear the tears as she reached out and touched the shiny, black engraved marble.

Bella had left him a note that Ana would be here: *Picking up Johnny and Piper. Ana headed to Pops' grave after hockey practice.*

Mike knew his wife well enough to know that was her way of saying, "Go see Ana."

There was a lot of work to be done to fix his relationship with his wife; there was even more to fix it with his children, especially Ana.

The truth was, Mike had thought his marriage was over when he had arrived home from the press conference and saw Bella throwing everything out of their bedroom into the hallway. His gut had lurched into his throat thinking that was the end of his family. But when she had looked at him with those eyes and said his name, he had known there was still hope. He had rushed to Bella then and hadn't let go, rocking them both to much-needed sleep and comfort.

He hadn't heard her get up and leave, so he was grateful for her note.

He watched Ana now a moment longer, then took
a deep breath, swallowed a few times, put a piece of
gum in, and slowly crossed the distance between
them. His heart ticked up a notch the closer he got.
When he was within earshot, she said, "I don't wanna
talk to you."

Mike stopped and exhaled. You couldn't get
anything past Ana. If she didn't make a career of
hockey, she could have one in the FBI.

"I wouldn't wanna talk to me, either," he said. He
continued his march until he was standing next to
her. "Thanks for takin' care of Pops."

She yanked a blade of grass from the earth and
ripped it into twenty pieces.

"I'm not proud of myself, Ana." He sat down next
to her. He pulled out his own blade of grass and
twisted it in his fingers. He dropped it and sighed.
"I'm here to make it right with you."

He reached out and lightly tapped her arm. She
flinched at his touch and stood up.

"Don't bother." She turned and walked toward her
car.

"Ana." He stood up and followed. "Ana, please,
I'm sorry, I—"

She whipped around and faced him like a wounded
animal. His gut clenched with a sickness he didn't
know existed.

"Don't you get it?" she spat. "I'm not gonna
forgive you. Not today. Maybe not ever. I just want
you to leave me alone."

She yelled that last word from the depths of her
gut as her eyes filled with tears. Helplessness seared
through him.

"Ana—"

"No," she yelled, cutting him off and walking
away.

Mike tried to catch his breath as the thing inside
him moved and swayed, creating pain, and causing
his body to ache. He reached into his pocket and
pilfered one stick of gum into his mouth, then two.
Another. Another. Another.

He faced his father's headstone and remembered
the way he and his father had fought like this.

"Another, son! You think you're gonna make
Juniors with that look? Do it again," Pops had yelled
over and over at varying times throughout Mike's
life. The only word that changed was Juniors to PHL.

"I'm tired. I wanna eat," a ten-year-old Mike had
said. That time it had been two o'clock in the
morning and Mike still hadn't been allowed to have
dinner following the game. Pops wouldn't dare. Not
until Mike had put one hundred pucks past him into
the net. "Daddy, my feet hurt."

"They hurt, huh?" Pops had sneered at him.
"You're talkin' to me about pain? What pain? Do it
again!"

"Ana!" Mike screamed as he turned toward her.
The guttural pitch of his voice caused her to look
back at him suddenly. She probably thought he was
dying the way he said it.

In a way, he was.

Her alarmed face looked him over for signs she needed to call emergency services. When she didn't see anything that needed an ambulance, she searched his face, now twisted with some kind of anguish, he was certain. She finally settled into annoyed curiosity. She was angry at him. He understood that.

"If you never listen to another thing I say," Mike said, "Please, just hear this."

She shifted her weight and glared at him. He deserved that.

"There's more to life than hockey," he said.

A huff of air escaped her lips as she rolled her eyes and walked away again.

Yeah, that sounded cheesy, he knew that. Who was he to say it anyway? He'd made his family's whole goddamn existence about hockey. And with Ana, who was so much like him, it had been the entire foundation of their relationship. That was the real problem.

Fuck, I said the wrong fucking thing.

"Ana, wait, please," he said.

She turned to him and asked, "Are you kidding me with this?"

"I'm sorry, it's not what I meant," he said taking a step toward her. He spit out the gum in his mouth.

"Then what did you mean?" she asked. A warmth crossed into his chest. The older Ana got, the more she looked like her mother, especially in the eyes. They were questioning him now.

"I meant, there's more to *you* than hockey," he said.

There it is. That's exactly what he wanted to say. And she knew it. He could see that. *And one more thing.*

"Hockey isn't the reason I love you, kid," Mike said. "You're my child. You're stubborn. Funny. Responsible. Smart as hell. I swear to God you need to work for law enforcement or the FBI or something the way you always know what's up."

He let a small laugh pass through his lips as her eyes got shiny with tears.

"Anyway, I know you hate me right now. I know, I deserve it," Mike said. His eyes felt heavy with tears as hers tumbled over down her cheeks. "But I hope…I don't want it to be like this with us. I don't even want it to be like it *was*, with us."

He searched her eyes as she dried them, rubbing them until they were red and swollen, then crossing her arms against her chest. She turned a hard stare his way.

"I don't know, Dad," she said tearfully.

He nodded as she sniffed and wiped her face.

"I just," she said, trying to find the words to express all the hurt he'd caused her and their family. "I just don't know."

"I understand," Mike said. "My friend, Dr. Rosten…he could, maybe." He cleared his throat. "Maybe we could do family counseling, or something."

She gave him a questioning glance. "You'd do that?"

He nodded. "Of course," he said.

She wiped her face again as the tears slowed. She nodded at him. "Maybe."

"Okay," he said. She was still angry and…what was that? Hurt. Wounded. He grabbed a piece of gum and shoved it in his mouth. She gave him one last look, turned, and walked to her car.

His phone dinged just as Ana got in and drove away. He glanced down.

Hendrix: *6203 Gale Rd.*

Mike glanced up and watched as Ana's car disappeared down the road. He walked to the trash can and spit out his gum, then grabbed a sucker from his pocket and put that in his mouth instead.

He was one for two today. What were his odds he'd go two for three with Hendrix?

48

I'm Sure You Already Know

Teddy roamed the old junk yard looking for parts and pieces to fix Old Blue. The truck was busted up after the accident and needed some TLC. He'd already done the windshield and the tires, now he was working on the engine and the frame. He was psyched to find the same model tucked in the very back of the auto graveyard.

Teddy grinned as he flipped open the hood and searched the engine.

"Ah, winner." The alternator in Old Blue basically worked but after the crash it was loud as hell. This beauty would be a good replacement. Teddy quickly disconnected the battery and checked for other electrical components on the alternator itself. He carefully removed the drive belt.

"You're gonna need this."

Teddy peered over his shoulder at Mike, who was holding a socket wrench. Teddy took it from him and started on the mounting bolts.

"Thanks for hearing me out," Mike said.

"Mmmhmm," Teddy uttered as he worked. He could smell spearmint gum coming from Mike. He'd already heard through the rumor mill that gum and suckers were Mikey's new little helpers.

As long it's not pills and whiskey.

"You looked good against Tampa," Mike complimented.

"Thanks," Teddy said. He finished the last bolt and put the socket wrench back in his toolbox at his feet. "I like it here."

"You have a funny way of showin' it."

Teddy flicked a side-eye at Mike as Mike reached into the engine bay and grabbed hold of one side of the fifteen-pound alternator. Teddy grabbed the other side, and they carefully worked it out of its spot and placed it on the ground.

"Where'd you learn how to work on cars?" Mike asked.

"My dad. He was a mechanic," Teddy said as he peered back in the engine and continued looking for anything else he might be able to salvage. "Owned his own shop. I used to help. When I wasn't playing."

"Just you and your dad?"

Teddy nodded. "Never knew my mom."

"I'm sorry," Mike said. Teddy sighed as he combed through the engine. There wasn't much else he needed from this truck, except the bumper, but he wasn't ready to fully engage with Mike yet either. So, he kept his head low to the bay.

"I know Tuck was pissed," Mike said. "He picked me up this morning. Took me to get a rental car since mine was totaled. Should'a brought it to you, I guess, huh?"

Teddy huffed a laugh and stood up. He sighed as he absentmindedly looked over the engine.

"I told him to ease up," Mike said. "Trust me, if Tuck hated you, he would'a thrown your ass under the bus already. So, consider the fact he's only being a dick, a gift."

Teddy put each of his hands on either side of the engine bay and leaned on them. He dropped his head. Teddy knew Mike was right about Tuck. He shifted his weight.

His dad would want him to make this right. To find a way. And if he was honest, he wanted to find a way, too.

Teddy looked up and right at Mike. "You remember it? Me hitting you?"

Teddy appreciated that Mike didn't turn away from his stare. "I used to read the police transcripts from their interview with the guy who killed my dad," Teddy said. "I read 'em over and over again."

Teddy stood straight and grabbed the rag out of his back pocket, wiping his hands.

"The morning after. When he sobered up. The cops asked him: 'Did you remember it?'"

Mike took a deep breath as Teddy eyed him. "I'm sure you already know what he said."

Mike nodded.

"He didn't even brake. Neither did you."

Teddy put the rag back in his pocket and shut the hood.

"Have you talked to the family?" Teddy asked. "The ones you could have killed."

Mike shifted uncomfortably. He said, "I'm starting with you."

Teddy started in on the bumper as Mike went to help him.

"I got it." Teddy brushed him off as Mike took a step back. They were quiet for a moment as Mike pulled out a piece of gum and started chewing.

"Deterrent," he said.

Teddy nodded.

"I'll leave you to it." Mike turned and walked away.

Teddy sighed and banged the truck hood. He turned to Mike. "He wrote me a letter, you know. From jail."

Mike stopped and turned back to Teddy.

"Did you read it?" Mike asked.

Teddy looked around the junk yard and back to Mike. "Nope."

Mike tilted his head side-to-side. "Maybe you should."

"What's it gonna say?" Teddy asked.

Mike shrugged. "I can't possibly know that."

Teddy watched as Mike started away again, only to turn back to him.

"But you know what," Mike said. He scratched his scruff, then dropped his hand to his side. "My guess…it's got something to do with forgiveness."

Mike gave Teddy a single nod then turned, got in his rental car, and left as Hendrix banged the hood of the truck and tossed the rag into the junkyard.

49

A Good Game

PHL Cup Finals
Game One

Eastern Conference Champs Columbus Thunder
v.
Western Conference Winnipeg Ice
Columbus, Ohio

Hendrix skated onto the ice from a TV timeout as Cots joined him.

"Crowd's tight tonight," Cots said with approval.

"Fuckin' love this," Hendrix said. He took in the PHL Cup signs that permeated every square inch of the arena, the excited faces, the energy. A few signs bore his name and several fans sported his sweater. There wasn't anything like seeing people walk around with his name and number on their backs. Truly something special.

Especially on that brunette who wore it the other night. His body stirred from the memory.

"You see the blonde?" Cots grinned as he nodded at the glass and put his hands in front of his chest.

"Am I dead?" Hendrix asked with his best movie star smile. "You see Bones?"

"Jesus, that guy," Cots quipped.

Hendrix's chest shook with laughter. "That whole section needs cut off."

Cots laughed as the crowd started chanting: "Ol-sky! Ol-sky!"

Hendrix looked back to the bench to see the captain take the ice along with Tuck and Glaz. Frenchie was already in position at the net.

Hendrix dropped his face shield as Mike took his place in the face-off circle. The puck dropped and Mike swept it out and over to Hendrix as they moved into the Ice's zone.

Mike, Hendrix, and Cots sat up in front of the net as they cycled the puck and looked for an open lane.

Mike got a break and drove in, wristed it, and it got kicked back into the crease by Sampson's pad. Hendrix picked it up and took a shot as Sampson's stick batted it away like it was nothing. Cots was waiting at the doorstep and roofed it past the wall that was Sampson, solving the stoic force with sheer will and little bit of that golden puck luck.

Boom!

They all circled up and bumped Cots' helmet as the crowd gave the team a standing ovation. Their roar made his skin pimple with excitement. He glanced up to the scoreboard. They were winning three to one.

He nodded his head with a stifled acknowledgement to Mike. Hendrix couldn't deny that when the captain was on the ice, and sober, he had something otherworldly that helped the team push through and win. Hendrix wasn't sure what it was, exactly, just that little extra thing you can't put into words. And Mike had it.

He gave the captain a look as they skated to the bench for the congratulatory receiving line. He nodded with respect, and Mike returned.

Hope surged through Hendrix as he went through the line banging gloves. They still had time to fix this rift on their way to the Cup.

If Mike could face his demons and let go, Hendrix could fucking do it, too.

* * *

Mike stepped out of Tuck's Escalade and took a long pull of cool night air as he stretched his knee. A lightness filtered through his body as he eyed his home. The warm light from the windows were welcoming against the dark night. He glanced back to Tuck's car and laughed as the unrecognizable singing and yelling coming from inside got louder for no obvious reason.

"What the fuck?" he said. He turned and looked back at Tuck, who shrugged and shook his head. Mike laughed and finished the sucker in his mouth. He put the stick into his pocket and left the passenger door open as he walked up to Cots' head hanging out the back window on his side.

They'd won the first game of the finals. That was a reason to celebrate.

"You gonna be alright, Cots?" Mike asked as Hendrix came around the back of the car and stopped on the other side of Cots' head.

"Cots!" Hendrix yelled.

Cots made an unintelligible sound as the group inside sang louder.

"I got him," Hendrix said.

"Good." Mike nodded. He could tell Hendrix had something to say, so he gave the kid space to say it. But nothing came out, so Mike slapped his arm and turned for his house as Hendrix headed for the front seat.

Tuck had bristled at Mike's suggestion for Hendrix to ride shotgun, but it was necessary for the three of them to get their shit straight during this final push. There was no time left. They could deal with the rest of this nonsense on the golf course.

"It was a good game."

Mike stopped with a sigh then turned back to Hendrix. The kid had that thing. That hockey thing. People wanted to follow the guy. Probably because his core was good, even if he hadn't figured out how to lead just yet.

It was now Mike's job to get him there.

"It was," Mike finally said. He nodded at Hendrix, who gave it back.

That was a good start.

Hendrix got in the passenger seat as Mike turned and walked into his house.

Everything was quiet as he walked through the front door and entryway into their spacious kitchen. Bella had been very specific about this room, from the things she needed to cook with, to the open design to keep them all together. It was his favorite space in the house.

Everything that woman touched became like gold to him.

He pushed air through his lips as the memory of her bloody face made an appearance. He reached quickly for the gum in his pocket, unwrapped a piece, shoved it in his mouth. *Another. Another.*

The thing was awake and searching for relief again.

Another. Another. Another.

It was an unspeakable hell to know that if another man had touched his wife like that, Mike would have fucking killed him. But he was the man who did it. He couldn't reconcile that simple fact.

Another. Another.

He pushed out more air. Again. The thing began to retreat. Another push of air. Deep inhale. Exhale. Deep inhale. Exhale. He could hear the quietness of his house again. Opened his eyes. His breath was back to normal. The thing was settled.

He stretched his knee. *Ibuprofen.*

He moved toward the cabinet, opened it, grabbed the bottle, and spun the cap off. He shook out two of the orange pills, closed it back up and put it away.

Bella. He'd know her vanilla-based perfume anywhere.

"Hi baby," he said without even turning around.

"Creepy how you do that," she said. He grinned and turned to face her. Damn, she looked good in that red, silk nightie.

"I'd know your scent anywhere."

She glanced at his cupped hand with the pills.

"Knee?" she asked. She slid onto the bar stool at the island, and he couldn't help but notice the way the lacey edge of that short little number crept up her thigh. God, he wanted her.

Mike nodded as he popped them in his mouth and turned back to the faucet, turning on the cold water and cupping it in his hand. He drank from the well and swallowed the pills, then shut it off and turned back to her.

She had a look in her eye. She wanted him, too. He knew all her signals. But something was holding her back. He understood that. There was a myriad of roadblocks between them right now. They had to be removed before they got the green light.

"How long will the cravings last?" she asked. She tucked a hair behind her ear. "I read they sometimes use Methadone."

"They can." He leaned against the sink. "I didn't."

She nodded. "Was it awful?"

He shifted his weight and crossed his arms against his chest as he thought about her question. "The pain was, yeah," he said. "But the therapy was good."

"What?" she asked. She grinned. "You hated marriage counseling."

"I didn't hate marriage counseling. I hated fighting with you."

She nodded. "I hated that, too," she said quietly.

He uncrossed his arms and put his hands against the sink.

"I have to go to outpatient therapy for a while," he said. "They taught me some stuff to help prevent relapse."

"So, you'll still crave it?"

Mike nodded.

"How do you know you won't relapse?" she asked. He could see the worry in her eyes.

He shook his head. "I don't."

A moment passed between them as she took that realization in and then she said hesitantly, "Okay."

Tears began to form in her eyes.

"Bella," he said quietly as he started to move.

"No," she said, putting her hand out to stop him. He stood there, helpless. She took a deep breath and exhaled.

She asked, "Should I have taken you?"

"Nobody knew what to do." He took another step toward her, and she let him this time. He stood in front of her. "This isn't your fault."

"Isn't it?" she asked. "I knew you weren't right."

"I knew I wasn't right, too. I could have asked for help, I didn't."

"I—"

"Bella," he interrupted. "I need you to hear this...it was never your problem to fix in the first place. It was mine. It *is* mine. Not yours."

"We're a team."

"We are. And my half of it is healing right now."

It hurt somewhere deep inside him when he saw the pain in her expression.

"How did we get here, Mike?"

"I've been trying to answer that," he said shakily. He cleared his throat.

"You know, when I got injured, it was just my knee that hurt. But then...Hendrix. And I knew when

I saw him, I was done. And then dad…". He had to
stop and catch his breath. She reached out to him then
and took his hand. "I couldn't tell anymore which
part of me was hurting. Which part I was treating
with the pills, the alcohol. They just…numbed
everything. And I just...felt lost. All the time."

She stood up and slid her hands up his chest and
around his neck as she pulled him into an embrace.
He held on to her for dear life.

"Am I gonna lose you, Bella?" he asked in her ear.
"Once I'm not me anymore?"

She pulled back sharply from his embrace and
looked him right in his eyes as she touched his face.

"You haven't been you for a while now, Mike.
And I'm still here."

A smile touched the corner of his lips. "For better,
for worse," he whispered.

"Always," she said quietly.

He searched her blue eyes and found what had
always been there: not just love, but devotion. He had
given Bella his heart a long time ago. And she had
kept it safe and sound ever since.

"I've never really thanked you for keeping
everyone's shit together," he said. "You know, said
it. Really. I haven't made it easy on you. I'm sorry."

She grinned as she stood on her tippy-toes and
gave him a light kiss.

"You're my favorite teammate," he said quietly.

"You're just sayin' that 'cause I look better in
lingerie than Tuck."

"Ah, fuck, Bella," he cracked. "Now I've got that
image in my head."

She laughed as she slid her arms around his neck
and writhed her body seductively against his.

"No, seriously, I actually do have that image in my
head. It was Vegas, and there was a dare and...you
don't wanna know."

"You guys are idiots," she said.

"That's true."

He moved his hands down her body and pulled her
tight. He kissed her gently. "I'm sorry, Bella. For all
of it. Your face—"

"Stop," she said. "We're looking forward now.
Okay?"

He nodded.

"Mike, I'm proud of you for going," she said
quietly. "But more than that, I'm proud of you for
staying. Taking the help. Getting your shit together.
That's...a lot of people can't do it, you know?
Addiction is...," she shook her head, "...every day
you don't use, you win. I'm proud of you for that."

Those words hit his gut in a way he didn't expect.
It was something like relief and love and gratefulness
that he married a person who had that kind of grace
and strength.

He didn't deserve it. And that made it even more
perfect.

"I love you," he whispered. "That real shit."

"I love you, too, Mike," she said. "That real shit."

"Yeah." They grinned at each other as she rested
her forehead against his.

"Now," she asked. "What do we need to do for
you to win that Cup?"

He nodded in earnest. He knew exactly what he needed to win. A lot of players abstained from all sex during the playoffs, and he'd been one of them in the beginning of his career. The energy was needed elsewhere. But he'd grown out of that in recent years, and right now, he needed to be close to his wife.

He needed Bella.

"I think the best way to win the Cup—"

"Yeah?"

"Is for us to have smokin' hot sex right fucking now."

Bella's laugh filling their kitchen was music in his soul. If he had her, anything was possible.

50

You Can Let It Go

PHL Cup Finals
Game Two

Columbus Thunder v. Winnipeg Ice
Series: One-Zero
Columbus, Ohio

Tuck was doing his best to make amends with Hendrix as Mike had requested. Now that Mike was back, the task of "setting Hendrix straight" had been relegated to Mike at Mike's request and Tuck had agreed.

For Tuck, the best place to heal wounds was on the ice. And he had been doing his best to pilfer the puck to Hendrix and get him on the board, but no such luck. Sampson's glove was hot tonight.

Lucky for them, so was Frenchie's.

"Fuck," Tuck hissed as he glided near Hendrix and Chary during a pause in the action.

"Jesus, man," Chary said. "Fuckin' on top of us."

"No more extra workouts for Frenchie tonight, boys," Hendrix quipped as he skated to the face-off circle.

Tuck took his familiar stance and smirked as Hendrix lost the face-off. Within seconds, it was another shot on Frenchie, another rebound.

Enough of this shit.

Tuck picked off the puck and passed it out to Chary. Chary made a sweet pass to Glaz, who zipped past a defender to the net and dropped it to Hendrix, who took a shot at Sampson. Gloved again.

"Fuck," Tuck spat. Hendrix had the same reaction, banging his stick on the frozen surface and jumping the board to the bench next to Mike.

Tuck skated over and took a spot on the other side of Mike as he grabbed his water bottle and took a long drink while he caught his breath. His legs were on fire.

"Look," Mike said to Hendrix, "I know I'm the last person you want advice from—"

"If you know how to beat him, I wanna know," Hendrix interrupted as he sucked down his sports drink.

Tuck glanced down the other side of the bench and caught the Stache watching Mike with Hendrix.

Interesting.

Line change. Mike, Hendrix, and Cots hopped on the ice and immediately got in the rush. Mike skated to the net and picked up Cots' saucer pass with Hendrix in tow. Mike faked a shot and drop-passed to Hendrix just as an Ice defenseman tripped up and crashed into Mike's knee, bringing him down.

"Ah, fuck," Tuck said.

Hendrix picked up Mike's pass and quickly shot then solved the Sampson puzzle as he roofed it glove side. Quick glance to the scoreboard showed the Thunder going up by one with a minute and ten seconds left.

Tuck looked back to Mike, who started to move. He waited for Mike's nod but instead Hendrix was on the scene. Mike and Hendrix eyed each other for a second, then Hendrix reached down his hand and helped Mike up and off the ice along with Cots.

Holy shit. Did Hendrix just help Mike willingly?

Mike sat at the end of the bench as the trainers attended to him. He glanced at Tuck and grinned. Tuck shook his head. Whatever kind of snake charm bullshit he was working on Hendrix to get the kid out of his head and into his groove was working. And Mike knew it.

The captain knew his team. Knew how to read guys the same way he could read the ice. That's why Mike was Mike.

"One minute of play remaining in the period."

Tuck took another shift as they fought to keep their win. With around thirty seconds remaining, Tuck glanced to the bench. Mike was talking to the guys, encouraging them, giving them tips as the ice pack smothered his knee. Again, Tuck caught the Coach watching Mike with the team.

I wonder.

The final buzzer sounded, and Columbus led the series two to zero.

* * *

Mike took a sip of water and shook his head at the guys as they worked the bar. A few of them were shooting pool, a couple were at the dart boards, most of them were looking to get lucky. Cots and Chary had a set of brunettes flanking them and were starting up another game of credit card roulette, while Glaz chased down a blonde. Hendrix chatted up a quiet, raven-haired beauty.

Mike reached into his pocket and grabbed a stick of gum. This scene of brotherhood in front of him was ripping his fucking heart out.

"You okay?" Tuck asked as he sat down on the stool next to Mike.

Mike nodded as he put the gum in his mouth and started chewing. He dropped the foil wrapping on the bar. "Yeah, good."

"Good." Tuck took a sip of his tequila. Mike smiled. Being in love looked good on Tuck.

"How's Jaime?" Mike asked.

Tuck smiled. "He's good."

"Yeah?"

"Yep." Tuck grinned at him.

"Glad to hear that man," Mike said. He slapped Tuck's arm and took a sip of his water. "We'd like to have you two for dinner after all this. A thank you. To both of you."

Tuck glanced at him and smiled. "We'd like that."

"Jaime pissed at me? What happened. Bella." Mike shifted in his seat.

"He's an N.P., Mike. He's seen much worse." Mike winced.

"I didn't mean it like that," Tuck said. "I meant, he knows why it happened. That it was an accident. And you got help. He's good."

Mike nodded. "Okay, good."

Mike looked Tuck and up and down and swallowed. "Are you still pissed at me?"

Now Tuck was the one shifting uncomfortably in his chair. He looked Mike dead in the eye.

"I'll lay you the fuck out if you ever touch her like that again, Mike."

Mike sucked in a breath. He could see in Tuck's eyes that he meant every fucking word he had just said. And why wouldn't he? They were family; Bella was like Tuck's sister.

"I won't," Mike said.

"Then we're good," Tuck said quietly.

Cots yelled, "What the hell, Hendrix?"

Mike and Tuck glanced over to the skirmish and saw Hendrix had ripped Cots' credit card roulette hat from his hands and was now rifling through it. Finally, Hendrix yanked out a credit card and slammed it into Cots' chest.

"You lose, bitch," Hendrix said as his raven-haired girl laughed. "Drinks on Cots!"

The guys laughed at Cots' stoned, surprised face.

"That's bullshit, Hendrix!" Cots incensed. He turned to Chary. "What the fuck are you laughin' at?"

A laugh tumbled out of Mike as Tuck grinned.

"Idiots," Tuck said.

"I'm gonna miss it," Mike said quietly. His chest was tight with nostalgia remembering all the moments just like this one that had made up his entire career.

Tuck sighed as he looked at his drink, then Mike. "When did you decide?"

Mike glanced at Tuck. "Bella and I talked about it a few days ago. I had to…adjust to the news."

Adjust was an understatement. Mike had been pretty broken up. He practically had a meltdown. Dr. Rosten had to be called. It was fucking terrible.

He winced at the memory.

Tuck nodded, started to take a sip of his tequila, but then put it down on the bar without taking a drink. "Shit, man." He blinked away his emotions.

Yeah, Mike felt that, too. Mike and Tuck had been on this ride together for years. There hadn't been a day that had gone by since Mike could remember that Tuck hadn't been a part of his everyday life in some shape or form. Tuck was his brother.

"I could probably get another season or two out of my knee," Mike said. "But…"

"Yeah," Tuck said as he nodded. "I get it."

"I can't risk relapse," Mike said. "I can't do that to my family. That includes you."

Tuck glanced at Mike and nodded. "I knew."

Mike bowed his head, then glanced back to Tuck.

"I just kept hoping…" Tuck shrugged, "I don't know what I hoped."

"Same thing we all do," Mike said as Tuck looked at him. "That it'll never end."

Tuck grinned. "Yeah."

Cots was still giving everyone hell as they glanced back to the team.

"Hey, I've already got a goal and two assists through two games, assholes," Cots said, defending himself against some argument the boys were having. "Abstinence works."

"Don't you have to be having sex first to abstain from it?" Chary jabbed.

"Chary!" Cots hollered. "Dick."

The guys laughed as the brunettes who were hanging out with Cots and Chary walked away.

"Oh, baby, come on, he's abstaining, not me," Chary said as he chased them. "I can handle both of you."

Hendrix let out a low laugh, then glanced at Mike and Tuck.

"Fuck," Tuck said as Hendrix excused himself from his arm candy and made his way to them.

"You need to give him a break," Mike said. "I'm not saying what he did was right. But he lost his dad to an asshole like me. If you can forgive me. You can let it go for him. It's over."

Tuck smirked as Hendrix closed the distance, then gave him a nod that Tuck reciprocated.

"So. That defenseman on your knee," Hendrix said to Mike.

"Don't you worry about him," Tuck said. "I got it."

Mike grinned as the two talked strategy in game three, which basically amounted to kicking Winnipeg's ass for railing on Mike.

He sighed as he listened to them. This was his last ride to the Cup as a player. The thing inside of him knew it, rearing up, then settling back down.

Mike planned to enjoy every second of this ride, absorb it in his skin, and take in every memory. All so that he could walk away from the game and know he had left nothing on the ice.

51

Now or Never

PHL Cup Finals
Game Three

Columbus Thunder v. Winnipeg Ice
Series: Two-Zero
Winnipeg, Manitoba, Canada

Bella watched the game with a different lens now, knowing that she and Mike had made the decision he was going to retire. It hadn't been an easy one.

"Mike," she had said and wrapped him in her arms as he had started to spiral. It was twenty-four hours of sponsor calls and going through a lot of gum and suckers before the deterrents just stopped working all together. She'd had to call Dr. Rosten for an emergency session. It was a stark reminder of why he needed to retire in the first place.

"Tuck's getting revenge for dad," Johnny said excitedly.

Bella tuned back in to the television in Pops' and Marie's living room as Piper and Johnny snuggled around Marie.

"Oh, Tuck lights him up again," said play-by-play announcer Grines over the action.

"Yeah, Gar, brutal out there tonight," color announcer Cotter agreed, as a replay showed the fight between Tuck and the defenseman who had slammed into Mike's knee the game before.

"Get him Tuck," Marie said, smiling.

Bella took a sip of her diet soda as she eyed Marie. Pops' death had been as hard on her as it was on Mike. Bella had spent a lot of time with Marie teaching her how to pay bills online, file paperwork for the attorneys, and transfer ownership of the cars.

"How do you know how to do all this?" Marie had asked in a moment of being overwhelmed to tears.

"Well, Mike is gone all the time, so I handle all the bills and the mortgage and, everything," Bella had said. "Plus, I have my own business, the gallery, and an agent and, well, yeah."

Marie had given Bella a look of admiration that had warmed her heart, and then it had quickly faded into uncertainty. Marie came from a different time. Women took care of the kids and the house, and men handled the money and the business.

"Bella, would you mind getting me some tea?" Marie asked, interrupting Bella's thoughts. Marie pointed to the kids cozied up around her.

"Of course," Bell said as she put her glass down. "Mint?"

"Chamomile," Marie said with a smile.

"Got it," Bella said.

Bella might know how to do bills and business, but doing life without Mike? Her heart raced as she thumbed her wedding ring. If the last few months had taught her anything, it was that losing Mike, their love, their family, would be devastating. She wasn't sure she'd be able to handle it as well as Marie was.

"Bones!" Piper and Johnny yelled as the nutty fan and his friends were televised for fighting with the opposing fans.

Bella shook her head and stood up as Ana walked in sweaty from her run.

"Dad barely played tonight," she said.

"You watched?" Bella asked.

"Radio," she said, waving her phone with the station app that broadcast the game.

"Ah," Bella said. "Well, his knee is sore from that hit so he's taking a beat."

Ana eyed her mom with suspicion.

"What's he takin' for the pain, Mom?" Ana asked. All eyes turned and looked at Bella. The weight of four pairs of them was palpable.

She cleared her throat and said, "Ibuprofen."

"You sure about that?"

"Of course I'm sure," Bella said. She understood Ana was concerned, but it was time for her to start trusting them again and to make up with her father. "He's better, Ana. I promise you."

Bella smiled as she grabbed all the glasses on the coffee table and walked over to Ana.

"You gotta cut him a little slack on this one, kid," Bella whispered. "He made a mistake. He's trying to correct it." Bella gave Ana a peck on the cheek, then turned and walked out.

Bella headed into the kitchen and put the glasses in the sink. She glanced in the mirror at her reflection and touched the right side of her face. The bruise was totally gone now, and her make-up and hair were more natural. The fake eyelashes were gone, and she had stopped doom-scrolling every two seconds on social media looking for their names.

"You seem different," Mike had said in bed after a particularly hot and intimate lovemaking session. "Calmer or something, I don't know."

She had looked in his eyes and said, "I just…I feel more real, or something."

"You've always been real to me," he had said. And then he'd moved a sweaty hair from her eye. "Did I make you feel like you weren't?"

She had thumbed her wedding ring and gazed into his eyes then. "Your career…that life. Just a lot of pressure, Mike. For me; the kids. I mean, a great life. But sometimes it just felt…I felt, boxed in or something. A fishbowl."

"And now that I'm retiring, you—"

"Don't have to grip the stick so tight," she had said quietly as she grinned at him.

"Goddammit I love when you use sports analogies," he had said, and they both had laughed.

Bella knew he had known what she meant. In hockey, the game gets worse the harder you try to control it. That's what she'd been doing for years with their life.

Mike had kissed her then and said, "Me, too, baby."

Bella glanced around Marie's kitchen and tucked a hair behind her ear. "Teacups," she whispered. She went to the cabinet above the dishwasher and grabbed the number one Grandma mug, filled it with water, and popped it in the microwave for two minutes. She walked over to the ceramic chicken on

Marie's counter and searched through it for the chamomile.

First bag she pulled out was mint. She smelled it and felt her spirits life. *My favorite.* She tried again. Lavender? She smelled that one, too. *Relaxing, but no.* She dipped her hand in again and pulled out…*ooo, lemon.* She smelled it and felt a tingle in her nose. *Too bright for the evening hours.*

"Chamomile," she whispered as she pulled out the winner and tore it open. She inhaled the calming floral and honey-scented notes, then set it aside until the tea was hot.

She glanced down at her wedding ring. Mike had told her he would get out of hockey completely if that's what she wanted; if she thought that was best for them and their family. But she didn't think that at all. In fact, going cold turkey might be the absolute worst thing for Mike and cause an even bigger relapse. Maybe one he couldn't recover from.

"Let's see where we're at in a year," she had said. "You have some options. But let's start with the one you really want, okay? I think we'll be okay with it. It's the best choice right now."

He had grinned and raised his eyebrows and she had laughed.

"You're gonna totally fuck with Hendrix, aren't you?" she had asked.

"I don't know what you're talking about," he had said with a laugh. And she had seen pure happiness in his eyes. *Yeah, it had been the right choice for them, for now.*

Hockey was the foundational make-up of Mike's blood and guts. Take that from him and she didn't know what would happen.

Her ringing phone interrupted her thoughts as she pulled it out of her pocket and smiled.

"Hey, baby," Bella said as she answered it.

"Hey, beautiful," Mike said.

"How's your knee?" She turned around and leaned back against the sink as she glanced at the microwave. Thirty more seconds.

"Hurts. Like hell, actually."

"I'm sorry," she said. She paused for a second and shoved her hand in her jeans' pocket. "What are you doing for it?"

"Trainers wrapped it. Ice pack. Ibuprofen. Chewing gum."

"It'll get better, baby."

"I hope so," he said quietly.

"Mike, you're gonna get in the game," Bella said. He was itching to be on the ice. Any player worth his salt wanted to be in the battle when it mattered the most.

"I know," he said. "It's just hard."

"I know," she said. "Do you need me to come to Winnipeg? I will. I'll get on a plane right now, baby."

She heard a low laugh rumble through the line, and she grinned.

"You're something else, baby," he said. "But I'm okay."

"Okay," she said quietly as the microwave dinged.

"You makin' something?" he asked.

"Tea for your mom," she said as she pulled the cup
out and dropped the tea bag in it. "Remind me how
much sugar she takes?"

"Two teaspoons," he said.

"Got it." She pulled out the tea bag and threw it
away, then grabbed the sugar bowl from the cabinet
and a spoon from the drawer. She scooped two
mounds of the sparkling white powder in and stirred.

"Mike?" she asked. "You still there?"

"I'm here," he said softly. "Did Ana watch the
game?"

Bella smiled. The man loved his children,
especially his Ana. It was like a weight on his chest
that he hadn't gotten through to her yet. "She did.
She listened to it on her phone while she was
running." Bella tossed the spoon in the sink.

He asked, "Think she'll talk to me?"

"Actually," Bella said, "I do." She picked up the
tea and walked back to the living room.

* * *

Ana watched the locker room interviews as Bella
walked in and handed the tea carefully to Marie.
Piper and Johnny sat up to give their grandma room
to sit up and drink it.

Then her mom turned and handed her phone to
Ana. "For you."

Her and her mom made eye contact and Bella's
eyebrow raise communicated everything Ana needed

324

to know; it was time to talk to her father. She took the phone as everyone looked at her.

"What?" She scowled and walked out of the room into the hallway with the phone. She made sure no one followed her and then she leaned against the wall and spoke into the slim, black device.

"So, Tuck took care of O'Reilly, huh?"

"Yeah, he did," her father said. She could hear in his voice that he was happy to talk to her. She smiled as she grabbed a piece of hair from her ponytail and twisted it.

"Good." She bounced on her toes as she waited for her dad to speak.

"We gonna be okay, kid?"

"Maybe," Ana said quietly. She stopped bouncing and turned from her back to her side against the wall.

"It would mean a lot to me if you came to the games," he said. "Ana? Ana, I'm not takin' any more pills. I swear to you."

The tears rushed to her eyes as she sharply inhaled a breath. "You can't ever touch her again like that," she said, her voice breaking.

"Never."

"I'm serious, Dad. Not a finger." She regained control as she stood up and crossed her arm over her bare stomach and workout pants.

"Kid, I told you. Never again."

"Okay." She leaned against the wall and wiped away the tears.

"Yeah?"

She nodded.

"Ana?"

"Yeah," she said.

"I love you so much," her dad said. "My first-born. Going away to college."

Tears hit her eyes as she heard her dad catch his breath. "I'm gonna miss you, Daddy."

She heard what sounded like her father start to cry, and there was a brief pause.

"I'm gonna miss you, too, kid," he finally said. After a pause, he said, "I better get going. I need to get my knee up."

"Okay," she said quietly.

"Tell Johnny and Piper I love 'em?"

"I will," she said.

"Okay. Night, kid."

"Wait, Dad?" She stood up straight and played with her ponytail.

"Yeah?"

"Can I ask you something?"

"You can ask me anything."

"I was just curious," she said as she started pacing the hallway. "You know, I'm getting ready to graduate and…I don't know. The future. And you're so good at drawing. And…Pops always said you didn't get into art school."

"Yeah, that's what he told me. Why? Where's this coming from?"

She shrugged. "I don't know. Just curious. I mean, what if you had? Gotten in." She stopped and twisted her ponytail around her finger.

"I don't know, kid. But I honestly don't think it would have changed anything. I love being a hockey player. My body, as we all now know, was only ever

326

gonna last for so long. It was kind of now or never, back then. Whereas art school is always there, you know? There was a choice to be made. Pops, I think, knew that before I did. Does that answer your question?"

"Yeah. Yeah," she said. She paused. "So, will you?"

"Will I what?"

"Go back. To art school?" She started pacing again.

"Can I do that?"

Ana laughed.

"I hadn't thought about it, kid. But now you've got my brain going."

"I think you should." She leaned against the wall.

"I love ya, kid."

"Me, too, Dad."

"Okay, g'night."

"Night."

Ana hung up the phone and glanced down the hallway to Pops' office. She twisted her ponytail, then let go and headed for the door.

As she walked into her grandfather's office, she put her mother's phone in one workout pant pocket and took her own phone from the other. She pulled the case away from the glass and a folded sheet fell out. She picked it up, opened it, and looked at it for a moment.

She grinned as she walked to the shredder and put the piece of thick paper in it. She hit the start button and walked out as the letter with the art school logo at the top and the words *CONGRATULATIONS!*

Welcome to the New York Art School got eaten by the machine.

There was simply no sense in dwelling on the past anymore. Whatever her father was or would become, he was her dad, and she loved him.

Art school might not have meant more to her father than the game, but his family did.

And now she knew it, too.

52

New Bond

Hendrix sat in his Winnipeg hotel room with a bag of ice on his shoulder. It had been a chippy game with very little scoring. That kind of game wasn't what he liked, but in a series like this, it's the kind of game the team needed. Winnipeg had shown their teeth, and the Thunder had come together to respond. A new bond had been formed.

Hendrix glanced at the door as a knock echoed through his room. Probably Cots or Chary with some bullshit about something. If there was a credit card roulette hat waiting for him on the other side of that door, he might kick Cots' ass.

"Hang on," he yelled. He stood gingerly, his body sore and tired, as he hobbled to the door and opened it.

That's not a hat.

"Hey," Mike said.

"Hey." Hendrix shifted his weight. He definitely didn't expect the captain.

"Will you go with me?" Mike asked. His knee was in its brace and the skin around it was red from ice. The guy was perfectly sober and sincere.

"Where?" Hendrix asked.

Mike glanced down the hallway, then back to Hendrix as he let out a sigh.

"Paige's house. When we get back to Columbus."

"Oh," Hendrix said. He wasn't sure why Mike needed him, of all people, to go see Paige and her father. That seemed like a Tuck job.

Hendrix eyed Mike as Mike shifted his weight and waited patiently for a response. Hendrix's brow furrowed. If he knew anything about Mike, it was that there was always a reason for what the captain did. And when it came to the team and its players, when he was sober, it was usually a good one. He'd proven that already with his advice on Sampson.

"Yeah, okay," Hendrix said slowly.

Mike nodded. "Good."

Hendrix nodded back as Mike turned and walked gingerly down the hallway back to his room. Hendrix peered out into the hallway and watched him for a second, then stepped back in his room and shut the door.

"Hmph," he uttered.

He turned back to the empty room with its luxurious finishes and King-sized bed and spied his bag on the small desk against the window. He moved like an old man toward it as he readjusted the ice on his shoulder, then dropped the wet, cold bag on the shiny surface.

He exhaled a deep sigh as he reached for his bag and unzipped it, then started digging around inside. He felt the familiar paper and yanked, pulling the sealed envelope from its cave, and eyeing the corrections facility address and then his own name, who it was addressed to. The handwriting was small, tight, and neat. It took up less space on the letter-sized envelope than it should, which made it look disproportionate.

He ran his thumb over it, then turned it over. He picked at the corner of the sealed back where it had ripped at some point during transit. It slowly began to open. He picked a little more and now it exposed a plain, white letter inside. Hendrix inhaled a breath and held it as he picked a little more and a little more.

"Fuck," he whispered. He stopped and exhaled, then started picking at it again. Now it was halfway open, and his heart was racing. The letter was folded neatly inside.

Hendrix took another deep breath then let it out. He shook his head and stuffed it back in the bag.

He grabbed his ice and went back to bed.

They had another game in Winnipeg, and he needed to be focused. Anything less than his full attention wouldn't get them where they needed to go.

* * *

PHL Cup Finals
Game Four

Columbus Thunder v. Winnipeg Ice
Series: Two-One
Winnipeg, Manitoba, Canada

Mike glanced at the scoreboard in Winnipeg's arena and shook his head. The Thunder were getting their asses handed to them four to one. The Winnipeg crowd was on its feet and letting Columbus know they were walking out of there with a loss. In exactly thirty seconds, the series would be tied two to two, and Columbus would be back on its heels, starting at square one.

A seven-game series would be physically and mentally brutal; and worse, at this very moment, Winnipeg was stronger than they were on both counts. The only thing Columbus had going for it was they were headed back to their home ice. They needed their fans, their friends, and their families to help get them reenergized and on track.

Mike glanced at Hendrix, sweaty and tired.

Who was Mike kidding? There was more to them winning than just a cheerleading section. Mike needed to square things up with Paige and her dad, and Hendrix needed to find a way out of his own head. Mike had a plan to kill two birds with one stone. Not only would he attempt to make things right with Paige, but by taking Hendrix, maybe he could get the kid to let go of his own past.

Maybe, if Hendrix could see Mike ask for forgiveness and hopefully get it, then the kid might be able to find it in his own life, too.

Mike glanced at Hendrix as they got into the face-off circle. They were headed home on the heels of two losses and a lot of regrets. They all had choices to make now. And Mike needed to step up and lead in a new way. A better way.

A way that would finally help them win in more than just the game.

53

I Gotta Go

Mike sat in his brand-new Suburban outside Paige and her family's little white house with a literal picket fence, trying to figure out the car's technology.

"Fuck me," he breathed.

He'd finally ditched the rental car and picked out this new beauty with Bella just before he left for Winnipeg. She'd driven it a few times and set things the way that she liked them, and now he was stuck trying to figure out her launch sequence so he could replace it with his own.

The tech was like the cockpit of a damn fighter jet.

"Where the fuck is the Bluetooth setting?" He grimaced as he pressed a series of buttons just as a loud engine pulled up behind him. He switched his stare to the rearview mirror and saw Teddy pull up on a black Ducati.

"Are you fuckin' kidding me?" Mike shook his head with a laugh as he shut off his Chevy, opened the door, and slid out of the front seat. He popped a piece of gum as Teddy got off his bike, pulled off his helmet and hung it on the handlebar. He grabbed a pair of aviators from inside his leather jacket and slid them on as he turned to Mike.

"So, that's your back-up, huh, Maverick?" Mike shut his car door.

Teddy looked at his bike, then back to Mike, and grinned.

"I'm Rooster," Teddy said. "You're the old guy, Maverick."

"Funny, asshole."

Teddy laughed as he met Mike at his car and they turned to walk up the porch to the front door of the cozy, little, suburban home.

They stood quietly as Mike rang the doorbell and a burst of excited children's voices began yammering inside. Mike smiled as a ten-tear-old boy swung open the red door.

"Hi, Mr. Olsky," the kid said.

"Hey, Christopher," Mike replied. He tousled the young boy's dark hair. Christopher was Ron and his wife's little surprise a few years back. Bella had made Mike go to the doctor shortly thereafter, so they didn't have any more little surprises of their own.

"Christopher! Don't open the door to strange— oh," the man said. He was wearing a blue golf shirt and tan trousers.

"Ron," Mike said with a nod.

"Mike." Ron nodded back. "Christopher, go find your mom and tell her you're ready to eat."

"Okay, Daddy," the tiny tyke said as he ran off.

Mike reached out his hand and waited. He would understand if the guy spit in his face and slammed the door, but he didn't. Ron was one of the good guys. He slowly took Mike's hand and shook.

"I'm sorry for that night, Ron. What could have happened," Mike said. "I feel—"

"I know," Ron said as they closed out their handshake. "Thank you for showing up and saying so. I'm glad to see you went for treatment."

Mike nodded. "It was exactly what I needed."

"I hear recovery can last a lifetime," Ron said as he shoved a hand into his pant pocket.

"It is forever," Mike said. "One day at a time. I know that's cliché, but it's the truth."

"I believe if anyone can make it through, you can," Ron said as he smiled.

Mike nodded and asked, "Did I catch you going to or coming from the golf course?" He waved a finger up and down Ron's outfit.

"From." Ron grinned. "Nine holes."

"Perfect day for it." Mike glanced inside the house and saw a glimpse of Paige going up the steps. "Hey Ron, would it be alright if I talked to Paige for a second?"

"Oh, yeah, of course, come in," Ron said.

As Ron turned to let them in, Mike glanced to Teddy and saw the look of surprise mixed with something like consideration on his face. That's what Mike had been hoping for. Maybe it would help the kid get to the other side of his anger and find forgiveness.

As they walked into the house, Teddy closed the door behind them. Ron yelled up the stairs for Paige, then turned and peered at Teddy.

"You're Hendrix?" Ron asked.

"Yes, sir." Teddy extended his hand as Ron took it.

"Yeah, you're the one who tried to pass me on the road that night," Ron smirked. Mike chuckled as Teddy gave him a side eye.

"I apologize for that, sir," Teddy said.

"Mmmhmm," Ron mumbled. He shook Teddy's hand then let go as an awkward silence descended. Finally, Ron spoke again and said, "The way I understand it, though, you're the reason we're still standing."

Teddy gave a single nod.

"Thank you for that," Ron said.

"You're welcome," Teddy said quietly.

"Your dad would be proud," Ron said. He slapped Teddy's arm and Mike could swear he saw a tear in the corner of Teddy's eye. But as quick as it had come, it was gone. "You're playing some great hockey."

"Thank you, sir," Teddy said as Paige came down the stairs.

Mike peered at Teddy and hoped this was all making a difference for the kid. He couldn't think of anything else that might help him get out of his own way. So, if this didn't work, Mike wasn't sure what to do next.

* * *

Hendrix watched as Paige rushed down the stairs to say hello wearing a "Bears Hockey Team" T-shirt. That was Ana's team.

How in the hell was Paige excited to see Mike? *Why isn't she pissed off? Why isn't Ron?*

"Mr. Olsky! How are you?" Paige asked as she rushed up and gave Mike a side-hug. "Are you okay after the accident?"

"I am, yeah," Mike said. "Are you?"

"Who me?" Paige asked confused. She pulled back and stood up straight. "Yeah, totally fine. You didn't hit us. You got hit."

She flipped a hand at Teddy and grinned.

You're welcome for that.

"You're Teddy Hendrix, right?" Paige asked as everybody moved further into the living room and took a spot on the furniture. It was super homey in the small, gray living room with bursts of yellow here and there. "Didn't really get to talk the other night."

"Right, yeah, nice to meet you," he said. They quickly shook hands.

"You're playing great," Paige said as she waved her hands around in an animated fashion. "We all think so. The whole team."

"Appreciate that," Teddy said.

Teddy nodded at Mike as another silence fell upon them. Mike picked it back up.

"You're a good friend to Ana, Paige," Mike said. "I just…I wanted you to know how sorry I am for the way I've acted."

"Oh, thanks for that," Paige said as she got animated again. "But, really, it's okay. I know you're trying, you know?"

She shrugged as Mike nodded.

"I appreciate that, thank you," Mike said. "You'll still come over and hang, right?"

"Of course. Ana's my girl," Paige said. "It's all good."

"Good," Mike said.

Teddy bounced a questioning look between them. How were these fucking people being so calm about all this? It was like he was in *The Twilight Zone* or something.

"You're gonna be impressed the next time you see her play," Paige said. "Coach put her on the PK. She's killin' it. She's got your moves."

Mike grinned and Teddy could swear the captain's buttons were gonna pop right off of his light blue dress shirt with the sleeves rolled up.

"Can't wait," Mike said. "She's really excelled in the Bears program."

"She really has," Paige said. "She's gonna be amazing at Buckeye State."

"I know, I can't wait to see her play at that level," Mike said as he slapped his knees and sat back.

Teddy glanced at Mike. What was this side of him? This fatherly side. *Look at him.* Teddy knew that look on Mike's face. It was the same way Teddy's father used to look at him. *Pride.* And love.

Fuck. Mike's a decent fucking guy.

"I gotta go, Dad, mom's taking me to practice," Paige said as she turned to her father. "You're picking me up, though, right?"

"You got it, kid," Ron agreed.

They all stood. "Good seeing you Mr. Olsky," Paige said. "Nice to meet you Mr. Hendrix."

"Oh, yeah, no, no Mr.," Teddy said. "Teddy. Seriously."

Paige laughed as she corrected herself, "Nice to meet you, Teddy."

"Thank you," he said. He nodded at her as she left.

Mike and Ron shook hands and talked the series and how Columbus still had a chance. It was surreal to Teddy. He didn't get it. He couldn't imagine standing in a room with Carter, like Ron was, and shaking the man's hand and talking hockey.

Then again, Mike hadn't killed anyone. Teddy shifted his weight.

Did that matter?

"Good to meet you, Teddy."

Teddy snapped out of it when he heard Ron's voice and saw his extended hand. Teddy quickly took it.

"Yeah, you, too," he said.

Teddy turned and followed Mike out the door as they all said goodbye. As it shut behind them, Teddy's chest tightened, and his heart ticked up. He quickly walked down the porch steps and moved fast toward his bike.

"Wait, can we—"

"I gotta go," Teddy interrupted Mike. Teddy wasted no time grabbing his helmet and hopping on his bike. He quickly started it up and sped away as he glanced over and caught Mike's surprised expression.

He had to get out of there.

The sooner, the better.

54

A Little Lost

Mike stepped into his parent's house and for the first time since his father died, he didn't look for the whiskey bottle.

"Mom?" he yelled into the quiet space.

"Bedroom," she answered lightly.

He smiled as he looked around at the perfectly cleaned and settled house. His mother had always taken care of the home and the food and the love since he could remember. Marie's husband and her son were her career and her whole life.

Mike touched a family picture on the wall as he turned down the hallway to his parent's bedroom.

He appreciated how much she had done for him. His mother was the softer side of how he made it to hockey. She cleaned his jerseys, made sure his skates were sharp, fed him, clothed him, put band-aids on him, and drove him across God's green Earth for practices and games. When Pops was on a tear, she'd eventually come to the rescue and relieve Mike from Pops' grip. She said, "I love you," often and hugged him always.

But when he looked at Bella, and he saw his wife as an artist first, and admired that she also kept their home and made the food and loved them all, he always wondered if his mother had wanted more, too. Had anyone ever encouraged her to have more? Or maybe this had been enough for her?

Was he doing enough to encourage Ana and Piper?

He let out a sigh as he got to the bedroom door. Maybe he could take the time now to get to know his mother outside the rink and encourage her to try something different, if that's what she wanted.

"Hey Mom," he said. He walked in and saw her going through Pops' things. Mostly his clothes and shoes. "Bella said you might need some help."

"Just his closet and dresser drawers." Marie folded a shirt and tucked it into a box as Mike walked over and gave her a hug.

"You're doin' great, Mom," he said quietly.

She nodded against his shoulder, and he held on for a second longer until she dried her eyes. She had her hair and make-up done and was wearing a pale, pink blouse and black capri pants with black sandals.

She's trying to move on.

"You look pretty, today, Mom. You dress up for me?"

She slapped his shoulder with a laugh as she pulled away. "No. I was just tired of…looking tired."

He smiled encouragingly at her as she grinned. He could see her eye make-up had been reapplied a couple times and the edges of her eyes were puffy.

"Is there anything you want?" she asked as she glanced around at the boxes.

"His hockey stuff," Mike said. "The Orr sweater."

Marie smiled and nodded to a box in the corner. "Already done."

"Thanks," he said. He started folding clothes into boxes and bags. The memories of his father came alive in the various shirts Mike touched. The

Hawaiian shirt he'd worn to the team dinner at Mike's house. Glaz had loved that damn thing. And the black pants Pops always wore to Mike's practices. "They're practical, son," Pops had said.

Mike held the Hawaiian shirt to his nose and shut his eyes as he smelled his father's cologne on it.

How long would it be until Mike forgot even the little things about these items? How long until all that was left of his father was the Bobby Orr sweater and the unfillable void of his absence?

"He wouldn't want you to keep this stuff," Marie said as if on cue. "He'd say it was junk. And to throw the damn stuff away."

Mike laughed and said, "Yeah, he would, wouldn't he?" He gave the red shirt with big green leaves a questioning glance, then folded it gently into the box in front of him.

"Your father is not his clothes, Mike," Marie said. She smiled at him. "He's you. And he's in you. Right here." Marie tapped her heart.

"Thanks, Mom," Mike said quietly. She nodded and kept folding.

He eyed her for a second, then asked, "Are you wanting to stay in the house?"

Marie was quiet for a moment as they continued packing. Surely, she knew that Pops would say the same thing about the house and farm as he did about that shirt.

Finally, she said, "I think it's a bit much, Mike."

Mike nodded as he glanced at her. "I'll help you go anywhere you want."

She huffed a laugh as she kept folding. "Where would I go?"

"A condo in Florida? Retirement village near us? You can even stay with us for a little bit until you figure it out."

"You're a good son, Mikey," she said as she gave him a tired smile. "Let me think about it, okay?"

He nodded. "Of course. We'll figure it out."

She stopped folding and looked at him. "I thought he'd always be here, you know? It's like…I don't know what to do."

She put her hands on her hips as her eyes glistened with emotion.

Mike stopped folding, too, and said, "You have friends, right? Church group? What about that couple you have dinner with?"

She shrugged at him. "I'm not part of a couple anymore."

Mike's heart panged as he looked at his mother's drooping shoulders. She seemed so small. *Childlike.*

"I just feel a little lost, Mikey. That's all," she said quietly. She went back to folding clothes.

"You've got time to figure it out, Mom." Mike walked over and pulled her into a hug. "You're still young. Take your time. Hey, why don't you come stay with us, tonight? I'll get Johnny to cook something delicious."

She nodded into his chest. "I'd really like that." She patted his arm.

"Good," he said. He kissed her head and rocked her. It was just like she used to do for him. "We got you, okay?"

She nodded quietly as she leaned into his shoulder
and cried.

55

If I Could Take It Back

Hendrix walked into his apartment after a night spent in the arms of a blonde whose name he couldn't remember now. He dropped his keys on the kitchen counter and grabbed a water from the fridge. He leaned against the counter and knew the time had come.

He couldn't bang his grief and anger out of him anymore, or play it away, or fight it off. He was going to have to face it head on.

He put the water down with a sigh and walked to his bedroom, grabbed his bag, and tossed it on his comforter. He opened it up and pulled out the envelope. He stared for a moment at the tiny handwriting, then took a deep breath, flipped it over, tore it open, and pulled the letter out.

He opened it up and then immediately closed his eyes. His nerves were firing like firecrackers on a dirt road. What was it going to say? How was he going to feel?

"Fuck it." *Like a band-aid.*

He opened his eyes as his heart pounded. He started to read.

Teddy, the judge told me I had to write to you and apologize, but I would have done it anyway.

Teddy closed his eyes and remembered the night it happened. Celebrating with his friends. The last text he ever got from his father. The cops coming into the bar. He opened his eyes again and continued reading.

There's no words, no excuses to explain what happened that night. No reasons why your dad died and I lived. It was the stupidest mistake I ever made in my whole fool life. It cost you someone you loved.

Hendrix closed his eyes against the tears that were brewing as he remembered being on his grandfather's farm with his dad. How they worked on cars together. Laughing with his dad and playing hockey.

"Oh fuck," Teddy squeaked out as the pain came hard and fast into his body. He inhaled through his nose, then roughly exhaled. Teddy opened his eyes and pushed through the grief.

If I could take it back I would. I'm sorry. Those words will never be enough, I know that.

But, I hope someday you can forgive me for what I've done. For the pain I caused you. It ain't who I am. And I'm sorry. Truly sorry. Sincerely, Carter Jenkins.

Hendrix folded the letter and shoved it back in his bag. He laced his fingers and rocked on the edge of bed.

Game five was tonight. And after that game six. If he didn't let this poison out of his body, it was going to bring them all down.

The tears welled up and spilled out as the pain of the last four years tumbled from his body.

56

I'm Good

PHL Cup Finals
Game Five

Columbus Thunder v. Winnipeg Ice
Series: Two-Two
Columbus, Ohio

Mike could see that Hendrix was trying to keep his wits about him. The whole team understood the ramifications of losing this game. Unfortunately, that knowledge hadn't put any points on the scoreboard. And in front of their home crowd, no less, who were fucking pissed.

"Boooo!" they hissed. He smirked at their ire. The team deserved it.

Winnipeg was simply better than them tonight as Hendrix fought his demons while trying to play hockey. It was an intimate dance Mike was all too familiar with.

Mike had tried to reach out to Hendrix several times over the last couple days, but the kid wasn't ready. He'd basically fled Ron's house on his motorcycle and then actively avoided Mike at every turn.

I wonder if he read that letter yet?

As the game returned to action with only ten seconds left, O'Reilly laid into Hendrix with a heavy body check that dropped him just as the buzzer sounded.

"O'Reilly, you mother fucker," Mike said as he turned to the guy. But he was too late, Tuck was already there, gloves on ice, fist in face. Within seconds, it was a line brawl. Everyone was on the ice. The crowd was happy for a brief second as bloody fists became the main attraction.

Mike searched for a dance partner as Hendrix jumped up and joined in. The way the kid tore into the Winnipeg defenseman in his hands showed much more frustration than just simply losing game five.

It's pain. Yeah, Mike knew that move, too.

As the refs broke it up, Mike shook his head at the boo-birds in the stands. A few of them tossed some shit on the ice.

"Fuck," he said as he glided off. They went from leading the series two to nothing, to being down three to two with Winnipeg headed home for what could be the end of the series. The Cup was probably already gearing up for its flight to the Canadian city.

This wasn't the way they wanted this game to go. Winnipeg had the momentum. And the Thunder were struggling.

Mike glanced behind him as Hendrix skated off the ice, exhausted and spent.

Mike hoped the kid could figure his shit out in time, or game six would be the last and Columbus would be bounced from glory to the golf course.

And they had all sacrificed too much to go out like that.

* * *

Teddy stood in the post office and stared at the mail slot. His body and mind were screaming with exhaustion as he breathed in and then out, slowly, and with no concept of time passing.

"Sir?" Teddy turned to see a concerned postal worker standing there. He had questioning dark eyes hidden under bushy silver eyebrows.

"You okay, buddy?" the older man asked.

Good question.

Teddy cracked a weak smile. "Oh, uh, yeah. Sorry," Teddy said. He shook his head like he was clearing it. "I'm good. Thank you."

"You sure about that? You been standin' there a few minutes," he said politely.

"No, I'm…yeah, man, I'm okay, thanks," Teddy said. He nodded this time and slapped the envelope against his hand. He knew how he probably looked. Like a fucking madman with his crazy playoff beard and drawn eyes, one of them black and blue after last night's brawl. Hell, he barely recognized himself this morning in the mirror.

"Okay," the man said. He smiled and walked away as Teddy looked down to the letter and ran his thumb over the name it was addressed to: Carter Jenkins.

Teddy winced as his thumb crossed over the letters slowly, one by one.

The press was riding their asses today with Dani fucking Ashton leading the fucking charge. She'd held to her word, though, and hadn't ratted him out to anyone. She at least had that going for her.

But the Vegas odds were stacked against them at the highest they'd ever been. Nobody believed they could pull this thing off.

But nobody really knew Teddy, either.

For the first time since his father died, he felt like he belonged somewhere. He belonged here. With this team. With these guys. And he wasn't about to let that go.

Fuck. He even liked Mike. That mother fucker had a way of getting under your skin and making you better against your own iron fucking will.

He sighed as he gave the letter a hard stare. There was only one way to win this thing.

Teddy opened the mail slot for outgoing mail and dropped the letter inside. He let out a slow exhale as he shut the slot.

He felt a new energy emerge inside of him. *I recognize that.* It was that high octane shit he used to feel every night he touched the ice before his dad died. But somehow, now, it felt stronger. Like a power booster in a video game.

A grin slowly spread across his face.

I'm back, mother fuckers.

Now, he was ready to kick some ass.

57

Brothers

PHL Cup Finals
Game Six

Columbus Thunder v. Winnipeg Ice
Series: Two-Three
Winnipeg, Manitoba, Canada

Hendrix shifted in his sweaty uniform as he sat next to Mike in the locker room before the start of the second period in a crucial game six. They were tied at zeroes through the first and neither team was backing the fuck down.

As it should be.

Hendrix glanced to the boys as he tapped his skate nervously. They just needed a little shot of something. And while Tuck was doing his best to inspire the room, Hendrix knew exactly what that little something was.

The boys needed an injection of pure, unadulterated Teddy.

"I wanna say somethin' Tuck," Hendrix said as he stood. His heart was banging against his rib cage. No one interrupted Tuck or Mike, but it had to be done. Hendrix had done a half-ass job at leading alongside Mike. He needed to change that right fucking now.

Tuck looked to Mike and Mike nodded. Tuck sat down as Hendrix took the floor.

"I suck at this shit, so. Whatever," Hendrix said. He ran his hand through his wet, sweaty hair. "I just wanted to say, I've fucked up a lot…since my dad died. Everywhere I go."

He glanced at Mike and shrugged.

"My dad used to say that a great team feels like your home. Your brothers." He wiped sweat from his brow as he scanned the room. "I never felt like that, anywhere, one hundred percent. Boston was the closest. My dad was always my family. Me and him. And then he was gone. And then…I don't know…you fuckers. I get what he means now."

"Damn right," Chary said. He banged his stick on the locker room floor.

"Fuck yeah," Cots said.

Hendrix smiled as he saw the quiet nods from the room, including Mike and Tuck. He felt the energy ignite in his gut as it poured through his body. He scanned the faces of his team. There was Frenchie and his commercial-ready hair. Glaz and his cocky smile. Even fuckin' Harvey had made it back to the room with some stellar play.

My brothers.

"I was just thinkin'," Hendrix said. He shrugged as he half-grinned at them. "In the name of family. How about we scrounge up a W right now and make those mother fuckers send the Cup back to Columbus where it fucking belongs."

The chorus of "Fuck yeah's," rang the ceiling of the locker room as Tuck stood and pulled a Braveheart yell, hollering, "Let's fucking stay in this boys!"

The team followed suit as Hendrix bumped the gloves of each of them as they funneled out. Mike was the last to stand. Teddy's skate tapped as the sweaty captain approached.

Mike stood for a moment then finally said, "Not fuckin' bad, kid."

Hendrix let out a loud sigh as he said, "Jesus, man, I thought you were gonna punch me."

"Not tonight," Mike said. He slapped Hendrix's arm. "Took you fuckin' long enough to get here, though, Christ." Mike headed out of the locker room as Hendrix quickly grabbed his gloves and stick.

"Sorry. Some asshole was takin' up all my time," Hendrix chirped behind him.

"Fuck off, kid," Mike said over his shoulder.

Hendrix grinned as he followed the captain to the ice.

Finally. He was home.

58

That Hurt a Little

Dani Ashton walked into the Winnipeg visiting team locker room following the game six win and was still gob smacked by the thrashing the Columbus Thunder had handed the Ice in a two to nothing win. Whatever had been said between the first and second periods of the game caused a drastic shift on the ice.

The Thunder had looked like a completely different team.

Now the series was tied at threes and there would be a game seven. It would be a memorable one, she was certain. Both teams were headstrong, storied with legacy, and battling for their right to hoist the Cup.

Dani moved into the busy locker room and could almost taste the thick, foul smell of grown men sweating from every crevice all over everything.

People thought locker rooms were glamorous.

Pfft. She would never get used to the stench.

Dani quickly spied Mike and her stomach knotted up as she walked over to him. Forgiveness was not given easily in these locker rooms, or, sometimes, at all. She hoped they could get back on solid footing.

"Mike." She gave him a nod as he turned to face her.

"Dani." This time he tolerated her presence.

"Look, I—"

"I thought what you wrote was fair," Mike said, cutting her to the punch. He took a deep breath and sighed. "I don't like it. But it was fair."

"Thanks," she said. She tapped her voice recorder against her thigh.

"I can't speak for anyone else in this locker room," he said. "You understand."

"Yeah," she said. "You don't need to. I can take what they give."

"I know you can," he said.

Her brow furrowed as he tossed his shit in the bin. *He's being awfully generous.*

"Why so amenable?" she asked. "I mean, I appreciate it. But I did expect a little more bite."

She searched his face as he glanced around the room then back to her.

"Would you believe me if I said therapy?"

"Not on your life," she said. She grinned as he laughed. He was different, she could see that. Lighter somehow. His eyes turned up at the corners the way it does on people who are truly happy.

"How about we let sleeping dogs lie, huh?" he asked quietly.

She nodded as he continued to strip down, the sweat pouring from him.

"You know, you pull this off, the Cup…it'll be the only thing people remember," Dani said.

Mike nodded. "I'm countin' on it."

"Dani." Tuck walked up and tossed a few things in the laundry.

"Tuck." She smirked at him.

"I'm ready if you want an interview," he asked.

356

"Nope." She slapped his arm. "Thanks, though."

Dani turned to interview Hendrix as Mike laughed.

"That's bullshit," Tuck said.

"She wants to talk to a winner," Hendrix jabbed.

"Why's she talkin' to you then?" Frenchie chirped.

The guys laughed as the room relaxed. Winning solved a lot of problems, but Dani knew she hadn't been fully relieved of the ire they felt toward her. The truth was, she never would be. Not fully.

But at least for now, there was hope, a win, and a game seven.

* * *

Mike sat in his seat near the back of the plane and exhaled a relieved breath as they readied for takeoff back to Columbus. He grinned at Bella's text.

Bella: *Proud of you, baby. I've got a great way to celebrate...*

His eyes shot open as he admired her naked body on his phone.

Mike: *Imma take care of that when I get home.*

Bella: *I'll be waiting.*

Mike: *I'll be ready. Love u.*

Bella: *Love u too.*

He leaned his head back against the seat. He and Bella weren't completely healed yet, but they were getting there. The first family counseling session was in two weeks and couples counseling started after that.

But first, there would be a game seven. It was all the team could ask for. It had been a true battle with Winnipeg, and both teams had earned this moment.

Mike lifted his head as Hendrix walked down the aisle and paused next to the open seat by Mike.

"Can I?" Hendrix asked.

Mike moved his stuff and Hendrix sat down with his Beats in hand. A silence fell between them as Mike waited.

"I don't have to say it, right?" Hendrix finally asked.

"We're good," Mike said. He glanced at Hendrix with a smile.

"Good," Hendrix said. He started to put his headphones on, then stopped. He glanced at Mike. "Captain."

Mike laughed. "Oh shit."

A laugh tumbled out of Hendrix's chest.

"That hurt a little comin' out o' your mouth?" Mike jested.

"Fuck you, man." Hendrix slid on his headphones, leaned his head back, and closed his eyes.

Mike grinned as he took out a piece of gum, started to unwrap it, then put it back in his pocket, leaned his head back, and closed his eyes.

59

Something Good

Carter Jenkins shifted uncomfortably in his orange jumpsuit as he swept the floor of the prison. The other inmates came and went, and he did his best to just ignore them. He kept to himself and did as he was told in the hopes of earning an early release on good behavior. His plan was to clean up his life and start over.

He swept the junk into the dustpan and tossed it in the trash as one of the prison guards walked past him.

"Carter," he said.

"Sir," Carter said. He nodded as he put his broom in the closet and finished up, then headed to the bathroom. He glanced nervously around him. Carter wasn't sure how he'd react to the letter he'd gotten in the mail this morning and he didn't want anyone seeing.

Carter walked into the bathroom and checked to make sure it was empty. He pulled the plain envelope from inside his jumpsuit and checked its front and back. There wasn't a return address, but it was stamped from Columbus, Ohio. Anxiety ratcheted up in his veins. He was near certain who the letter was from, and he hoped for the best. Not that he deserved anything from Teddy Hendrix.

He fiddled with the envelope for a second, then took a deep breath and opened it. Tears filled his eyes as he read.

Carter, we all make mistakes. Including me. I don't know why it happened, and it won't ever quit hurting, but I forgive you. And I know my father would, too. Do something good with your life when you get out. That's how you can make it right. Teddy.

Carter wiped the tears from his eyes and his face as the image of the accident scene flashed in his mind. He'd taken John Hendrix's life. And now John's son had given Carter forgiveness, something he didn't deserve but desperately needed.

He let out a held breath and folded the letter carefully before tucking it in his pocket and heading back out to the prison.

60

Front of the Net

PHL Cup Finals
Game Seven

Columbus Thunder v. Winnipeg Ice
Series: Three-Three
Columbus, Ohio

An uneasiness settled into Bella's bones as she glanced around the Columbus arena in a game seven that saw the Thunder down two in the second period with only thirty seconds left. She glanced at the kids and Marie as the crowd lost its buzz following a shot from Hendrix that rang off the post.

"Dad's gonna find a way," Ana said with confidence. She flicked a glance at Bella. "He will."

Bella nodded as she said, "I believe you."

The kids and Marie cheered for Columbus and tried to raise their spirits as Jaime patted her back. She turned to face him.

"So glad you're here," Bella said. She reached over and squeezed his arm.

"Me, too," he said.

"It's crazy, right?" she asked.

"I love it," Jaime said. He sipped his beer and grinned proudly as he watched Tuck on the ice.

Bella looked around the arena as she thumbed her wedding ring. This place had been her and Mike's

life for most of their marriage, their kids had
practically grown up here, and Pops had become a
constant figure in these seats. After all those years of
building, and one game had changed it all in a matter
of seconds.

It was hard to watch the game and know this was
the last time they'd be here in this way, with Mike as
a player.

On the other hand, a new excitement was building
for what was coming next. It was like they had a
fresh start to explore themselves as individuals as
well as them as a couple and family.

"One minute remaining in the period."

"Come on, baby," she whispered.

Mike was on the ice with Tuck and Hendrix, and it
was clear they were trying to make something
happen. It wasn't for a lack of throwing rubber at the
net. Simply put, Sampson was just that good and on a
hot streak they hadn't been able to break over forty
minutes. As the period ending buzzer sounded, the
kids look deflated.

"Anything can happen, guys," Bella said. "You
know that."

As the team left the ice down the tunnel after two
periods, all she could think was, *I hope*.

* * *

The team sat silent as each player dripped with
sweat; some had their faces plastered back together

with liquid adhesive where blood used to be, others were being held tight with tape. Mike was tapped into the frustrated undercurrent in the room.

No one had said anything yet. That was Mike's job. He knew it. They all did. They were all dressed now and waiting to go back for the final period, the third one, the one where everything counts. Win or lose, overtime or regulation, it was his last time doing battle as a player. He had to leave it all on the ice and he needed them to do the same.

Mike looked around the room slowly. He took it all in, absorbing the moment as Howie whizzed by.

"Howie, wait," Mike said as the communications phenom turned around.

"Yeah?"

"I need you to do me another favor."

Howie said, "Kirby and his daughter are here."

"Yeah, well," Mike said. He smiled. "Can you make sure they're in front of the net for the third?"

"Wait, what?" Howie's face broke into a grin.

"Just, promise me."

"Yeah, Mike, done. I'll make it happen."

"Good. Thank you."

As Howie rushed out, Mike turned to the team. It was time. He stood as they all glanced up at him.

"So, I've always been a man of few words...and clearly Hendrix should follow in my footsteps."

Hendrix smirked.

"Yeah, what the fuck was that?" Chary said.

"Some kind'a bullshit," Cots said.

Mike grinned as the room gave Hendrix shit.

"You fuckin' loved it, Cots," Hendrix quipped.

Mike turned as the Stache and his assistants walked into the room for the final word. Coach took one look at Mike and stepped aside with a nod.

Mike took a deep breath and looked at them.

"Ah, this game...gets under the skin. We all remember the first bone we broke, right? First tooth down the drain? First scar that got us a girlfriend?"

"This one right here, Cap," Chary said as he pointed at his cheek.

"You never had a girlfriend," Cots said.

"More than you," Glaz cracked.

Cots flipped off Glaz as the room grinned. They looked back to Mike. He scanned their faces.

Fuck. I'm gonna miss this.

"This is my last time on the ice with you boys."

Mike nodded as the momentum shifted.

"They keep telling me life gets even better after this...but...I can't imagine anything better than this, right? I've been nothing but proud to be your captain."

They glanced to each other then back to Mike as the realization that this was the last time their captain would speak to the room sunk in.

"Every game in life comes down to this. The third period. The last one. The one where all of it counts. Because when it's done, all you're left with is regret or glory. Pops used to say that. He would be so pissed right now if he was in the stands."

"He is in the stands," Hendrix said.

A nod passed between them.

"We're down two, boys. The worst lead in hockey. And I fucking love it. This is what we're built for.

The comeback. Tuck, that asshole in Juniors who told you that you were too small? Fuck that guy. Look at you now. Chary, that Coach who told you that you weren't smart enough to know the systems? Yeah, fuck him, too. Me and Hendrix...well, we're head cases, right? We've been coming back our whole lives. But we haven't done it alone. And we won't tonight, either. Tonight...it's not about us. It's about them. The people who got us here."

Mike knew his family was in the stands and that Dr. Rosten had loved the drawing of the race car he'd given him. The good doc's television was probably turned on right now.

Mike was certain the reporters were on pins and needles. And even though she wasn't supposed to do it, Dani Ashton was rooting for him—for them—on the inside.

And then there were the fans, Bones, the bars and restaurants, the city in general.

Mike grinned. Somewhere right now, Howie was finding Kirby and taking him to the ice. It would be an extra special gift on top of the fact his daughter was in remission. Mike and Bella had visited them at the hospital when they heard.

The captain held all of them in his heart and soul. Hockey had always been, and would always be, about more than just the players. Anyone who ever stood where he was standing now knew that much about the game.

He wiped the sweat from his forehead and said to the team, "Every time you touch the ice tonight, it's about your family. Dads. Moms. Significant others.

Children. It's about the people who help us heal, the ones in the locker room, and the ones outside of it. It's about this community and the fans who stand with us, even when we play like shit. It's about our city, and what a win does for it and the people who live in it. When we win, they win. When we bleed, they bleed."

Mike took in all their faces and knew what had to be said.

"I know you're hurting. And I know you're tired and that we've seen a lot of shit together over this run. But we've got a choice to make. And one period left to make it. What's it gonna be, fellas? Setback? Or comeback?"

61

Five-Hole

Ana glanced nervously across the subdued Columbus crowd as they lazily chanted, "Thunder." Some were eating hot dogs and drinking beer; others were rushing their families to get their coats together so they could miss the parking garage traffic. Bones was the only one left standing, except for her.

No one was convinced that her dad could help his team find a way to win at this point. She twisted her hair around her finger.

"Come on dad," she whispered. As if on cue, the loudspeaker went quiet, and everyone turned to the Jumbotron, which read. "Get on your feet!"

"What the…?" she said under her breath as she let go of her hair.

The familiar notes of the song her dad had promised would only be played if they were going to win came through the speakers.

She couldn't stop the corners of her lips from spreading into a smile as tears threatened to burst from her eyes. It was AC/DC's, "Thunderstruck." And everyone knew what it meant. She glanced to her mom, who was now on her feet.

"It's dad," Ana said. "It's dad!"

Bella turned to her with an excited grin as they grabbed each other's hands and started jumping. Bella let go and faced the glass.

"Fuck yeah, baby," Bella said as she pounded the glass. They looked around as the crowd recognized its significance one by one, flicking their stares to the tunnel like prairie dogs looking for their leader.

Now they knew what Ana had known all along.

Dad's back.

"Thunder!" the crowd chanted along with the song as the beat's bass line thumped through the arena. "Thunder!"

Now Bones was on the jumbotron with all his friends, every single one of them standing, and Bones shouting, "We're gonna win!"

Fans sitting by the ice enthusiastically banged the glass and shot their fists in the air. The excitement neared fever pitch as Ana glanced over to the tunnel and the Thunder emerged like warriors to the battlefield, bandaged and broken, but ready to win the war.

They skated around the ice purposefully, egging the crowd to its feet.

The energy of the arena pulsed through Ana as her father appeared from the tunnel, pausing at the cusp of the ice, and taking it all in.

Note to self: tell dad he's not your hero because he's a hockey player.

Her dad was her hero because he was still standing.

People could say whatever they wanted to about the player named Mike Olsky, but she knew the character of the man who was her father.

"Go dad!" Ana screamed. He snapped his head to them and grinned.

"We love you, baby!" Bella screamed.

"Kick some butt, Dad!" Johnny hollered, as Marie and Piper joined in. He nodded to them then skated onto the ice and to the face-off circle.

Hendrix, Tuck, Glaz, and Cots took the ice with him as the arena thumped with adrenaline and hope.

"We're gonna win," Ana whispered.

The game was back underway as her dad swept the puck out and the crowd went wild.

* * *

Mike glanced at the scoreboard and tried desperately to embrace every second that ticked away on the clock. It seemed the harder he tried to slow it down and savor it, the faster it went.

Focus.

He skated to the bench and absorbed the crowd's energy as they now sat down by one with only three minutes remaining. Winnipeg was not going to let up the gas, and neither were they. Tuck and the defense had done their job obliterating the Ice and wearing them down. Tuck getting rewarded with a goal ten minutes in was fucking priceless. Tuck had squared up on the blue line and drove the puck through the zone then into the net against Sampson's will.

"Yeah, baby," Mike had yelled and smacked Tuck's helmet. He had cherished the joy in his friend's eyes, not only because he had netted the team an important momentum-shifting goal, but because Jaime was in the stands to see it.

"Showin' off," Mike chirped. Tuck had laughed and nodded, then looked over to where Jaime was seated next to the Olsky clan. His friend deserved that moment.

But now it was time for the offense to solve Sampson.

"Cots!" Mike waved the phenom over to him and Hendrix. "Be ready. You're gonna take the next one. Right now."

"Fuckin' ready," Cots said.

The crowd was on its feet as the puck dropped. Mike kicked it out and over to Hendrix. They raced down the ice as Hendrix picked off an Ice player and passed the puck to Mike. They both rushed to the net as Mike passed to Hendrix, who drop passed to Cots.

Cots was a mother fucking sniper when he was hot, which is exactly what they needed as the final minute of play approached. Delivering the goods as promised, Cots was clutch as he banged it in against Sampson's iron will, glove-side, and tied the game.

Boom!

"Ah-ha, yeah baby!" Cots said as the Columbus cannon fired. As Mike skated to Cots to celebrate, one of the Ice's players tripped him up. He slid into the boards, knee first.

"Fuck," Mike hissed. He rolled over in anger, more annoyed than anything else only to find Hendrix's sweaty mug right in his face.

"Get your ass up, old man." Hendrix grinned.

"Let's fucking finish this," Mike said.

"One minute of play remaining in the period."

This was it. Guts and glory and all that shit.

As the puck dropped in the face-off circle, Mike swept it up and he and Hendrix were on a rush to the net as Tuck and Glaz took one last stand to keep the Ice at bay.

Hendrix and Mike passed back and forth down the long, icy plane, right to the wolf's den as Mike took a shot, and it rebounded. Winnipeg picked it up and headed down the ice the other way.

"Fuck," Mike shouted. They hauled ass to the other end and Mike could feel the burning in his thighs and ass as his body started screaming at him, his lungs ready to burst. Tuck was already in the defensive zone waiting on the Ice's two-on-one that was about to challenge Frenchie's nerves and body. Winnipeg's sniper took his shot. Just as it looked like the puck was going to slide in glove side, Glaz made a heroic dive and stopped the puck with his jaw.

The crowd expelled a collective gasp as Mike glanced to the clock: thirty seconds. Tuck caught the rebound and swept it out of the zone to Hendrix.

The only way to honor Glaz's sacrifice was to score. He joined Hendrix on the rush and now it would be a two-on-one in their favor.

Mike glanced at the scoreboard: twenty seconds remaining. The crowd was on its feet. He could hear their fevered howling.

Mike was on Hendrix's flank now as they approached Sampson. Time slowed for Mike, bending to his nostalgia for a split second.

The last time you'll do this.

Mike saw Hendrix pass it to him for the shot. The kid was gonna let him ride out with the game winner.

Mike took the pass, faked out Sampson, then drop passed to Hendrix.

It's his team now.

Hendrix snaked up the puck and beat Sampson five-hole, right between the pads, as the goal light flashed red, and the cannon sounded.

The world was silent as Mike peered over at Hendrix. A single nod and the torch was passed.

Confetti fell as the roar of the crowd brought him back. The Thunder jumped the bench and pulled Mike and Hendrix into a group celebration.

"We did it, boys!" Mike yelled. They gripped each other tightly, understanding what it took for them to be here. Tuck had a hold of him and banged his helmet.

"You did, it man," Tuck said.

"We all did it." Mike banged his friend's helmet and then turned to look for his family.

Bella.

He skated toward her as she moved toward the glass and placed her hand on it with a grin.

"I love you," he mouthed to her. As she mouthed it back, he realized how much of this win was hers. There would never be any way he could repay her for that. He glanced to his children and mom, giving them a grin.

"Love you, Dad," Piper yelled.

Mike nodded at his family then turned back to the ice, the crowd, and his team as the PHL Cup was carried out.

The ride was over.
He was done.

62

Seriously

Mike stood at Pops' grave and grinned. He bent down, swept the grass cuttings and dirt from the base of it with his hand and stood back up. It was Mike's day with the Cup and it wouldn't have been right not to bring it here first.

He glanced at the shiny, silver trophy sitting next to his father's headstone, nearly as big as the stone was. Soon he would have his ring and his name engraved into that metal forever.

"Not bad, huh?" Mike asked as he glanced at the headstone. He bent down again and ran his fingers over his father's name. "Love you, Pops."

Mike gave no shits what people said about his old man. Pops loved him. He hadn't always done it right, but who did? Love was complicated, at best. And this Cup was as much as his as anyone else's.

"I wish you were here." Mike could feel the thing inside him ebb and flow. He let out a frustrated sigh. He had hoped it would quiet down and go away, but it wasn't cooperating. And it wouldn't.

"Forever, Mike," Dr. Rosten had told him. "It's gonna come at you for the rest of your life in moments that are difficult."

Mike sighed as he touched his father's grave, then reached into his pocket for gum as something to his right caught his eye. "What?"

Mike turned and caught a glimpse of a familiar red suit. "Glaz?"

Mike stood and looked up at the small hill to his right and slightly behind him.

The boys had come.

"We brought the booze," Chary shouted across the quiet graveyard.

"Jesus, shut up, man," Hendrix scolded as he cracked Chary in the ribs with his fist followed by a quick slap to the head from Cots.

"Fuck, alright," Chary said as he ducked. Glaz tried to laugh but his jaw was wired shut, fractured from the puck to his face.

Tuck shook his head as they started down the hill toward Mike.

Mike felt the thing settle as he put back the gum and took in a deep breath. The expectation was that once the game was done, you started to move on and in your own direction. Things changed. People changed.

As the team moved toward him, he understood it was probably the last time it would be this way. Before life inevitably took them all on different paths. That's the way it was in pro sports. New teams, new partners, new games, new days. But always, new.

The only thing that stayed the same was how it felt to step on the ice. And these were the only people on the planet who understood what that meant.

"You good?" Tuck asked. He slapped Mike on the shoulder.

"Better than good," Mike said.

Pop! The champagne tumbled out of the green glass as Cots aimed it in the right direction of the Cup, pouring a generous amount in before putting the rest of the sweet flow directly to his lips and drinking.

"Hey, asshole, save me some, damn," Chary whined. He grabbed it from Cots and took his own pull.

"Yeah?" Hendrix asked as he put one hand on the bowl of the Cup and the other at its base.

"Absolutely." Mike grabbed the other side in the same way, and they lifted it together then poured it into the ground by Pops' headstone.

"R.I.P. Pops," Tuck said as he tapped the headstone.

"R.I.P.," the boys said in a cheer to Mike's old man.

Mike and Teddy put the Cup back on the ground and stood still for a moment.

"So," Hendrix said after a few seconds. "What'll you do now, Maverick? Since you're officially retired and all."

Mike looked at him, picked up the Cup, and grinned.

"What the fuck does that mean?" Hendrix asked as Tuck laughed.

Mike chuckled as he headed toward his car, followed by the rest of the team with Hendrix bringing up the back.

"Mike? Seriously," Hendrix questioned. "What the hell does it mean?"

Mike grinned to himself. Well, life wasn't going to separate all of them just yet.

63

To the Net

Three months later

Hendrix skated his ass off until the whistle blew, gassing himself as all the muscles in his legs exploded with fire.

"Fuck," he whispered. He shook his head as he glided down the ice, then tipped his face in the air gasping for oxygen. As he passed the glass, he caught a glimpse of his reflection and smiled. The "C" looked good on him. It felt good on him. It felt the same way it did when he was leading teams before his dad died. He was finally back to good; he knew that would make his father happy.

That and the fact that not only had Teddy bought a home for the first time in his life, but he had been dating the same girl, and only that girl, for the last few weeks, which was better than his usual few hours.

Progress.

"Hendrix! What are you waitin' for? Your goddamn grandma? Drive your ass to the net!"

Hendrix shook his head at the familiar voice as he harnessed his remaining stamina and drove one more time to the net.

"Holy shit," he hissed. That was it. There was no more left in the tank as he glided over to the new assistant coach.

"You could of told me three months ago you were gonna be the assistant coach," Hendrix smirked. "Instead, I have to read Dani's fuckin' story."

"What fun would it be to just tell you?" Mike asked. He grinned as he shifted on his skates.

"You take too much pleasure in this," Hendrix quipped as Tuck skated over.

"Gentlemen," he said as he shaved ice.

"We're headed out tonight," Hendrix said. He tapped the ice with his stick. "Comin'?"

"Love to," Mike said. "Can't."

"Hot date with the wife?" Tuck asked.

"Somethin' like that."

"Is Jaime comin'?" Hendrix asked.

Tuck nodded as he pushed his helmet up. "Yeah, he's off tonight."

"He check my shoulder for me?" Hendrix asked.

"Fuck no, ask Beau to look at it." Tuck smirked as he headed off the ice and down the tunnel.

"But Jaime fucking loves it, Bro," Hendrix joked.

"Fuck off," Tuck hollered.

Hendrix grinned. "He's so easy to fuck with."

"Ask him about Vegas and the lingerie," Mike said as he followed Tuck down the tunnel.

"The what?" Hendrix questioned. "Wait, lingerie?"

Hendrix smirked as the rest of the players finished up and followed suit, leaving the ice one by one.

Hendrix had a word for each of them before he finally went down the tunnel himself. He didn't have to do it, he wanted to.

After all, this was his team. And they had seven months to make the playoffs and defend their title.

Teddy was going to make damn fucking sure they were ready to win.

After all, that's what a good captain did; he gave a shit about his players and took care of them. Teddy whacked the tunnel wall with his stick and grinned.

And he would know.

He had learned from the best.

64

Hockey Heaven

Mike pulled up to the art center and parked near Bella's car at the entrance. The place was packed, as usual, so he felt lucky to get a prime spot. He hadn't felt this kind of nervousness and excitement since he played his first game of hockey.

He hopped out of his Suburban and headed into the center with all its quiet murmuring from the different classes. He made a sharp turn down a staircase to the lower level as his heart ticked up.

This wasn't the only change. Sure, he was taking a couple different art classes to figure out which medium he liked best, but he was also enrolled in an online college program to get a business degree.

"Dad, just do it," Ana had said to him. "Just don't go to my college."

"Too late," he had said.

Mike couldn't be prouder of Ana getting a full ride to play hockey at Buckeye State. He didn't want to harsh her vibe, but he was lucky to get in there himself and he wanted that degree.

The admission counselor had assured him she wouldn't put him in any classes with Ana, since she was in-person and he was online. Plus, she had said Mike could test out of some of the courses, and the rest would take him three to four years, depending on his schedule.

The way his kids had looked at him when he got in had made him want it more. It made him start thinking maybe the front office would be a good home for him eventually.

"Is this seat taken?" he asked smoothly as he walked up to Bella just before class started. Fuck, she was gorgeous, sitting there with her hair pulled into a cute ponytail wearing a plain white T-shirt and tight blue jeans.

"Yes. By my very large, very jealous husband," she said coyly.

"Oh, I'll be careful then."

He leaned down and gave her a kiss as she slid her hand up his neck. It made his skin tingle to feel her warmth. Therapy was doing its job. They had not only gotten back to where they were before but had somehow moved beyond it into something new.

"You look beautiful."

"Thanks," she said.

"You got my gear?" he asked.

"I do," she said.

"Thank you for that," he said as she handed him his sketch book and pencils.

"What?" he asked as she grinned at him. She pulled out two thermoses from the bag. "Oh damn."

He took the thermos from her and opened it, taking a sniff, then smiling at her.

"You brought the good stuff. Orange sports drink."

"I know my husband." She raised her thermos in a cheer.

"God, I'm glad I married you." He clinked her thermos with his.

"You really are a lucky man."

He laughed as he took a sip.

"Pops would be proud of you, Mike," Bella said. "I didn't always agree with him. But I think he'd love what you're doing now."

"I think so, too," Mike said quietly. He eyed her and felt a deep love pulsate in his gut. "I know you don't have to be here. You could teach this damn class."

"I know," she whispered. "I wanna be here."

"Thank you," he whispered back.

He kissed her lightly as the instructor said, "Alright, class, let's get started."

Bella turned and accidentally knocked her pencils off the desk. As she bent down to pick them up, Mike glanced out the window.

Pops was standing there with a smile and nodded.

Mike sucked in his breath as Bella sat up, blocking his view.

Bella looked behind her out the window. "What?"

But Pops was gone.

Bella looked back to Mike. "Mike? What? What is it?"

Mike smiled with a slight laugh and shook his head. "Nothing. It's all good. Everything's good."

He leaned over and kissed Bella again as she smiled at him.

"Let's draw, huh?"

Mike smiled as class began.

* * *

Pops quickly stepped back from the window and smiled as he stared at his son. He wished he would have told Mike how good of an artist he was when he was alive. But it was apparent Mike knew. Bella and the kids would make sure he did. *He picked a good one.*

Pops' smile faded slightly. He should have told Mike how much he loved him as a person and not just a player.

"Regrets won't get you anywhere."

Pops smirked as John Hendrix leaned against the wall. Teddy's father was a real pain in his ass from the first day Pops had gotten into heaven. Still was. But John was a hell of a nice guy. Nicer than Pops was.

"Our boys did good," John said.

Pops grinned as he looked back at Mike sketching the bowl of fruit at the front of the room. "They sure as hell did."

He glanced over to John. "Glad we could see it."

"Heaven wouldn't be heaven without hockey."

"Hockey heaven," Pops quipped.

"You know it," John said. He stood away from the brick wall and started to walk away.

"What do you think our chances are next season?" Pops asked as he took in one final look of his son then turned to follow.

"No idea," John said. He shrugged. "But it'll be damn fun to watch."

Pops fell in beside John. "We can watch my granddaughter, too," Pops said. "A Buckeye State girl now. She's a hell of a lot like her father."

"Women's hockey," John said. "That's the next big thing."

"Damn straight it is," Pops said. His chest swelled with pride. "My granddaughter's gonna lead the next generation."

"You better believe it," John said as the two of them started to walk down the street. He gave a side-eye to Pops.

"Teddy'll outscore Mike this season in points," John said with a grin.

"Don't start with me, John."

John laughed and said, "I'm just sayin'. Prepare yourself."

"Your son needs to not drag his ass on the ice," Pops jabbed.

"My son?" John questioned. "Maybe if your son wouldn't ride him so hard."

Pops shook his head as the two fathers bickered all the way down the street before disappearing into the night air.

The game was over.

But in all the right ways possible, Pops knew that his son's life had just begun.

THE END

Did you love *The Third Period*? Then let everyone know! Leave a review on Amazon by scanning below.